MIRANDA HURRIED ON.

And then she stumbled. Twisting to keep her balance, she caught a glimpse of the obstacle which had tripped her, a pair of down-at-heel top boots, as she fell full length into the nearest bush.

The landing was unexpectedly soft.

For a startled moment she looked into a startled pair of startlingly blue eyes in a sun-bronzed face. Then an arm clamped around her waist, a hand caught the back of her head, and the ruffian kissed her.

Taken by surprise, Miranda lay there for several seconds absorbed in the extraordinary sensations created by the touch of lips on lips. Suddenly she came to her senses. Rearing back, she slapped the sun-bronzed face. She scrambled to her feet and glared down at her assailant as he emerged on hands and knees from the greenery.

"Sir, you are no gentleman!" she cried crushingly, if a trifle breathlessly.

WATCH FOR THESE ZEBRA REGENCIES

LADY STEPHANIE   (0-8217-5341-X, $4.50)
by Jeanne Savery
Lady Stephanie Morris has only one true love: the family estate she
has managed ever since her mother died. But then Lord Anthony Rider
arrives on her estate, claiming he has plans for both the land and the
woman. Stephanie soon realizes she's fallen in love with a man whose
sensual caresses will plunge her into a world of peril and intrigue . . . a
man as dangerous as he is irresistible.

BRIGHTON BEAUTY   (0-8217-5340-1, $4.50)
by Marilyn Clay
Chelsea Grant, pretty and poor, naively takes school friend Alayna
Marchmont's place and spends a month in the country. The devastating
man had sailed from Honduras to claim his promised bride, Miss
Marchmont. An affair of the heart may lead to disaster . . . unless a
resourceful Brighton beauty finds a way to stop a masquerade and
keep a lord's love.

LORD DIABLO'S DEMISE   (0-8217-5338-X, $4.50)
by Meg-Lynn Roberts
The sinfully handsome Lord Harry Glendower was a gambler and the
black sheep of his family. About to be forced into a marriage of convenience, the devilish fellow engineered his own demise, never having
dreamed that faking his death would lead him to the heavenly refuge
of spirited heiress Gwyn Morgan, the daughter of a physician.

A PERILOUS ATTRACTION   (0-8217-5339-8, $4.50)
by Dawn Aldridge Poore
Alissa Morgan is stunned when a frantic passenger thrusts her baby
into Alissa's arms and flees, having heard rumors that a notorious
highwayman posed a threat to their coach. Handsome stranger Hugh
Sebastian secretly possesses the treasured necklace the highwayman
seeks and volunteers to pose as Alissa's husband to save her reputation.
With a lost baby and missing necklace in their care, the couple embarks
on a journey into peril—and passion.

*Available wherever paperbacks are sold, or order direct from the
Publisher. Send cover price plus 50¢ per copy for mailing and
handling to Penguin USA, P.O. Box 999, c/o Dept. 17109,
Bergenfield, NJ 07621. Residents of New York and Tennessee must
include sales tax. DO NOT SEND CASH.*

WATCH FOR THESE ZEBRA HERCULES

MAYHEM AND MIRANDA

MAYHEM
AND
MIRANDA
Carola Dunn

Zebra Books
Kensington Publishing Corp.
http://www.zebrabooks.com

ZEBRA BOOKS are published by

Kensington Publishing Corp.
850 Third Avenue
New York, NY 10022

First Printing: October, 1997
10 9 8 7 6 5 4 3 2 1

Printed in the United States of America

Chapter 1

"Mornin', Miss Carmichael."

"Good morning, Dilly." Miranda smiled down at the little maid on her knees scrubbing the front step. "What a beautiful morning!" She looked out over the lawns, shrubbery and trees in the centre of Portchester Square, gleaming in the early sun after a nighttime shower.

"Luverly, innit? Ouch!" Dilly jerked back.

"Mudge, you horror!" With a yank on the leash, Miranda hauled the pug away. "I'm so sorry, Dilly. I fear my attention wandered." Hanging onto the fat little dog's collar as he did his best to sink his teeth into her wrist, she stooped to examine the damage.

" 'T'sall right, miss, skin's not even broke, see?" The maid held up a red, rough-skinned hand. "Cook says his teeth've got blunted with age."

"He can still give a nasty nip when he puts his mind to it. You haven't been using the rosewater lotion I made up, Dilly. You really must remember. You know how it distresses her ladyship when your hands are chapped."

"Cor, miss, my last place no one wouldn't've cared if

your hands'd fell off. I wouldn't want to upset her la'ship, not nohow. I'll try not to fergit.''

"I shall tell Mrs. Lowenstein to remind you. Patience, Mudge, I'm coming!''

The pug had spotted a black-and-white cat strolling towards the gardens. His short legs scrabbled as he pulled against the leash. With a wheezy yip, he dragged Miranda, laughing, after the impertinent creature which had the infernal cheek to cross *his* street.

Kneeling on the step beside her bucket, scrubbing brush in hand, Dilly watched. Miss Carmichael was a nice lady, a proper lady. Not a bit like her la'ship's last companion who, Cook said, was so stuck up she couldn't hardly see over her own nose. Miss was pretty as she could stare, too—for all she was a bit of a Long Meg—what with them big brown eyes and dark curls under her plain straw bonnet, and the nicest smile. She oughta be out dancing at grand balls every night, flirting with the gentlemen, not running to do an old lady's bidding and humour her odd fancies.

It was a strange household, and no mistake, Dilly thought, turning back to her task. A foreigner for a house-keeper what wouldn't do no work of a Saturday like ord'n'ry Christian folk, and a butler with a wooden leg. And as for her la'ship . . . well, there was no knowing what her la'ship'd take into her head to do next.

Still 'n' all, Dilly wasn't complaining. Like Pa said, she'd fallen in clover and she wasn't going to do nothing as might get her turned off. She scrubbed away with a will.

Meanwhile Miranda, with considerable difficulty, per-suaded Mudge he was by far too stout to squeeze through the railings after the cat. A disgruntled snort expressing his displeasure, he consented to accompany her to the gate into the garden.

Although most of the square's grand houses were shut up for the summer, their owners dispersed to country estates, bright flowers bloomed gaily in the neat flower-

beds. Amidst pink, white and crimson phlox, yellow mari-
golds and tall blue delphiniums, a speckle-breasted thrush
battled in a mighty tug-of-war with a large earthworm.
Mudge darted at it with a venomous growl. It flew off to
perch in a tree, singing as gloriously as if it had swallowed
the worm for breakfast.

Turning to watch the bird, Miranda loosed her hold on
the leash. In a flash, Mudge was off.

As he scampered towards the laurel bushes, the leash
trailing between his bandy legs, Miranda saw the black-
and-white cat fleeing before him. They disappeared among
the laurels and she dashed after him. Unlikely as it was
that the elderly pug could catch his adversary, if she let
him commit mayhem Lady Wiston would be dreadfully
upset.

She pushed through the bushes, each large, shiny leaf
depositing its burden of raindrops on her periwinkle-blue
muslin gown. Ahead, a flurry of furious, if asthmatic barks
suggested the cat had escaped, but it might have turned
at bay and be about to attack Mudge in turn. Miranda
hurried on.

And then she stumbled. Twisting to keep her balance,
she caught a glimpse of the obstacle which had tripped
her, a pair of down-at-heel top boots, as she fell full length
into the nearest bush.

The landing was unexpectedly soft.

For a startled moment she looked into a startled pair of
startlingly blue eyes in a sun-bronzed face. Then an arm
clamped around her waist, a hand caught the back of her
head, and the ruffian kissed her.

Taken by surprise, Miranda lay there for several seconds
absorbed in the extraordinary sensations created by the
touch of lips on lips. Suddenly she came to her senses.
Rearing back, she slapped the sun-bronzed face. She scrambled to her feet and glared down at her assailant as he
emerged on hands and knees from the greenery.

"Sir, you are no gentleman!" she said crushingly, if a
trifle breathlessly.

"No," he agreed with a cheerful smile, uncrushed. He stood up, his lanky, rumpled form towering over her by several inches. "I'm an adventurer." He bowed. "Peter Daviot, at your service, ma'am."

"At my service?" Miranda queried, outraged. "Your assault upon my person cannot be described as service!"

"Sorry about that," Mr. Daviot apologized, abashed penitence belied by the gleam of amusement in his eye. "I've been living in America, where customs are somewhat different."

"Different indeed, if gentlemen customarily sleep on the ground in city squares."

Openly grinning, he pointed out, "You've just said I'm no gentleman."

But his voice was cultured, with just a faint hint of an odd inflection. Miranda studied him. He looked to be about five or six-and-twenty, not much older than she was. His clothes were of decent cut and fit, though inevitably stained and crumpled after a night in the open. As she had already observed, he was tall, loose-limbed, with a long, humorous face, presently unshaven, and those extraordinarily blue eyes. His light brown hair, flopping over his forehead, had more than one twig caught in it. She almost reached out to remove the nearest, but stopped herself in time.

"Why were you sleeping in the bushes?" she asked.

"Why were you running through them?"

"Oh lord, Mudge!"

"I've been called many things in my life," he began, but Miranda did not wait to hear what doubtless justified epithets had been applied to the self-confessed adventurer over the years. Somewhere not too far distant the pug was whining. If the cat had bloodied his nose it was no more than he deserved, but she had best go and rescue him.

She burst from the thicket. Mudge stood at the base of a plane tree, glowering up at where the cat hissed and spat at him from the security of a high branch. The horrid beast's whine was not a sign of pain, it was sheer frustrated blood-lust.

Seeing Miranda, he gave a perfunctory wag of his ridiculous curled tail, and a sharp bark as if to command, "Get it down so I can chew on it."

Behind her, Mr. Daviot burst from the thicket. "Don't run away," he called. "I shan't assault you again, I promise." He stopped beside her. "Oho, is that your cat? I'll hang onto that devilish little monster of a dog while you coax it down."

He started forward and, before Miranda could warn him, bent down to grab the end of the leash. With the lightning speed so at odds with his pudgy wheeziness, Mudge slashed at his ungloved hand.

"Yeow!"

"Meow!" the cat echoed.

"The dog is mine, not the cat," Miranda disclosed stiffly, joining him but keeping well beyond Mudge's reach. "Has he drawn blood?"

"Yes, he has drawn blood." Mr. Daviot took a none too clean handkerchief from his pocket and applied it to the wound. "The brute's yours? Dammit, have I gone and offended you again?"

"No, he *is* a horrid little monster."

"Then why do you keep him?"

"Actually, he's not mine, he's my employer's, so I have no say in the matter."

"Your employer?" He looked her up and down. "Let me guess. Lady's maid? Oh, oh, now I *have* offended you again. Governess?"

"Companion."

"Truly? I thought companions were all small, grey, mousy creatures. But of course no mouse would have a hope of managing yon ravening fiend."

"I have not managed him very well this morning," she admitted. "You had best come home with me to have your hand cleaned and bound up with basilicum."

"I wouldn't want to land you in hot water with your employer."

Miranda laughed. "No fear of that!"

"Does she not rise until noon? I'm out of touch with fashionable ways. How do you propose to regain control of the pug, or shall you abandon him?"

Taking an aniseed comfit from her pocket, Miranda tossed it just in front of Mudge's nose. He instantly lost interest in the cat. While he snuffled in the grass after the sweetmeat, she picked up the leash.

Mr. Daviot applauded. "Clever! Bribery is always to be preferred to violence. If you're sure it won't get you into trouble, I'll come with you at least to wash the gash."

"No trouble."

"I'll just fetch my bag, then."

He returned with a disreputable top hat on his head and a large, battered, leather valise. As they set off, Mudge pattering along with a hopeful eye on her pocket, Miranda wondered bemusedly what on earth had got into her. Not that Lady Wiston would object to an unexpected guest, but how had he wheedled her into disregarding his outrageous insult to her person?

She cast a sidelong glance at him, only to find him gazing down at her.

"Your profile is superb," he said. "I wish I were an artist. A bite to eat wouldn't come amiss if it's not too much to ask."

"I suppose you believe flattery will win the day when you have not the means for bribery!"

His heavy sigh did not take her in for a moment. "It is too much to ask. Very well, then, no breakfast. Perhaps you will be kind enough to tell me," he went on with deceptive meekness, "at what hour I may reasonably call upon a lady? You see, I climbed the rail and dossed in the shrubbery because I arrived in London very late last night and didn't wish to disturb my aunt."

"Your aunt? Does she live near here?"

"Number nine, Portchester Square."

Miranda stopped and stared at him. "Lady Wiston is your aunt?" she asked, incredulous. "I thought all her nephews were pillars of rectitude."

"No, no, that's Sir Bernard's nephews. Aunt Artemis has only me, and no one has ever described me as a pillar of rectitude. Nor do I aspire to such an honour."

"Fortunately, for I'm sure it would be beyond you. Oh, I beg your pardon! I don't in general let my tongue run away with me, I assure you."

"Out of the mouths of babes and companions . . ." Mr. Daviot said blithely. "I'll forgive your insult," he continued with an engaging smile, "if you'll forgive mine."

Forgiven or not, that kiss was best forgotten, Miranda decided, especially since Lady Wiston was his aunt. She took refuge in primness. "I daresay we had best begin again from the beginning," she said in a repressive tone. "As you will have guessed, sir, Lady Wiston is my employer. I am Miranda Carmichael."

"How do you do, Miss Carmichael." He bowed again. "Peter Daviot, very much at your service." His momentary solemnity failed to last. "Don't fret," he advised her, grinning, "I shan't tell Aunt Artemis I kissed you."

Chapter 2

Miss Miranda Carmichael stalked into the house. Following behind, Peter admired her willowy figure in the plain, high-waisted gown. Her carriage was graceful despite its affronted stiffness. Sorry to have offended her, he vowed to himself to avoid any future reminder of the stolen kiss.

Not that he regretted the kiss itself, since Miss Carmichael showed no signs of considering herself compromised and obliged to wed to save her reputation. She was a pretty young woman, and spirited, but nothing could be further from Peter's plans than stepping into parson's mousetrap. In fact, had he not been jolted out of a delightful dream when she fell over his feet, he'd not have risked the embrace.

Though a fellow did deserve some recompense, dammit, when a female landed on him out of the blue like a hawk on a rabbit.

She turned as he closed the front door behind him. "You mentioned Sir Bernard," she said hesitantly. "Are you unaware of the admiral's demise?"

"Dead is he? I'm sorry to hear it. He was a splendid chap and deuced good to Aunt Artemis. She's in mourning?"

"No, it was several years ago, three or four. I've only been with her a few months. But she was sadly cut up, I collect, and still misses him. A few words of sympathy would not come amiss."

"I do know my manners, Miss Carmichael," he said severely, then relented as she bit her lip. "Not that I've given you much cause to credit it." He set his bag on the floor and dropped his shabby hat on the half-moon hall table, an incongruous blot on its polished marquetry surface.

Equally incongruous was the small figure now descending the airily elegant circular staircase, designed by Adam. Chubby and apple-cheeked, Aunt Artemis was clad in beige and green striped Cossack trousers, the fullness between drawstrings at waist and ankles billowing about her short legs. On top she wore a loose garment cut like a countryman's smock, of beige muslin sprigged with green leaves.

"Miranda, dear, what do you think?" she called anxiously. "Is the combination of stripes and sprigs too . . . ? Peter!" With that joyful squeal—at least, her nephew hoped it was joyful—the old lady hastened her steps.

As Peter moved forward to greet her, another squeal of joy sounded. The pug dashed between his legs and galloped up the stairs to fawn at her feet. She narrowly contrived to avoid tripping over him, but then she stepped on the trailing leash. Down she tumbled.

Peter caught her in a big hug and kissed her on both cheeks. Swinging her around, he saw Miss Carmichael's horrified face.

"Are you all right, Lady Wiston?" she cried.

"Quite all right, dear. Do put me down now, Peter, there's a good boy." Set on her feet, she patted her white curls, cut short and unadorned by a cap. "No, no, I have no need of smelling salts, Miranda. You know I abominate the stuff."

"You might have been hurt," Miss Carmichael said remorsefully. "How could I have been so careless as to let Mudge get away again?"

"It was not at all your fault, dear child. I should not have fallen had I not foolishly hurried. Wearing Inexpressibles gives one such a delightful freedom of movement, you see. Are you sure you do not care to have a pair made up?"

"I fear I am not quite brave enough, ma'am."

"A pity. Well, Peter, so you are come home at last." Aunt Artemis spoke as if he had returned a few hours later than expected after an absence of a day or two. "I daresay you would like some breakfast. Gentlemen always have such an appetite for breakfast."

"I had best wash first, Aunt Artemis."

"Yes, indeed!" said Miss Carmichael. "And I must see to your hand."

"It's nothing but a scratch."

"You are injured, dear boy?" his aunt asked in alarm.

"Mudge bit him, Lady Wiston."

"That dreadful dog!" She scowled down at the pug, who was planted directly in front of her, scowling up. "I have a good mind not to give him any comfits today. He is growing by far too fat in any case."

"If you stop spoiling him," Miss Carmichael warned, "he will start to treat you just like the rest of the household, and you know what that means."

"Nipped ankles." With a sigh, Aunt Artemis delved into the pocket of the smock and produced a pink sugared comfit. Mudge actually sat up and begged, slavering. "But all my clothes smell permanently of aniseed."

"Why on earth don't you get rid of him?" Peter asked.

"How I wish I could, but he belonged to a dear friend, the late Lady Egbert, whose dying wish was that I should take care of him. I must say he always seemed perfectly amiable before. I believe losing her soured his temper. Fortunately he spends most of the day asleep or I should have no servants and no friends left." Dropping another comfit, snapped up before it reached the floor, she went on, "Do go and wash, Peter. I am quite ready for my breakfast."

"Don't wait for me, Aunt. Perhaps I ought to change my clothes. I spent the night in the square so as not to disturb you, and one gets rather rumpled sleeping in the open, though I rather doubt the rest of my wardrobe is in much better case."

"It does not signify in the least. Was it pleasant? I have often thought it must be excessively pleasant lying out under the stars. Indeed, I cannot imagine why I have not tried it. The back garden is quite private." With a slightly mischievous look, she turned to her companion. "Miranda, if it is fine this evening, pray have Eustace and Ethan carry out the chaise-longue to the terrace, and a blanket or two."

"And a large umbrella, Lady Wiston," Miss Carmichael suggested calmly. "It rained last night."

Aunt Artemis seemed disappointed, but undeterred. "Yes, an umbrella is an excellent idea. My dear, I see now that your dress is quite damp, and you must be damp too, Peter. Do both of you go up and change at once, before you take an inflammation of the lungs! Or should one say, two inflammations of the lungs, I wonder?"

Leaving her pondering this weighty question, Peter retrieved his valise and obediently followed Miss Carmichael up the winding stairs. She untied the ribbons of her bonnet as she went, and took it off, revealing a mass of dark, glossy hair woven in an intricate knot pinned up on the crown of her head. Peter resisted the temptation to reach up and pull out the pins.

At the top, she swung round, held out her bonnet, and hissed accusingly, "You squashed my hat!"

There was indeed a dent in the back of the crown. "My humble apologies," he said, "but I expect it will steam out. Besides, I saved your gown from ruination in the dirt."

"I would not have fallen if your feet had not been in the way."

"You would not have fallen over my feet if you had stayed on the path. Let us not quarrel, when we can easily blame the whole incident on Mudge."

Her lips twitched. "He is a handy scapegoat," she agreed reluctantly, turning to the next flight of stairs, "though you can scarcely hold him responsible for . . . but no matter! Come, you shall have the blue chamber. Just ring for hot water. I expect Lady Wiston will invite you to stay for a few days. Shall you accept? If so, I must tell Mrs. Lowenstein to have the maids make up the bed."

"Yes, I cannot rush away after being reunited at last with my only relative."

On the tip of his tongue was a rueful admission that he had nowhere to rush to, nor any funds to procure lodging. He bit it back. That was a subject best saved for his aunt's ears, not for the companion who already disapproved of him.

Miranda went back down to her chamber on the first floor, next to Lady Wiston's. Swiftly she changed into a rose-pink mull muslin—her employer refused to let her wear the browns and greys generally considered suitable for a hired companion.

"Those dull colours are dreadfully depressing to the spirits," she had said adamantly when she offered Miranda the position. "Naturally I shall pay for new gowns. You cannot be expected to change your wardrobe at your own expense just to cater to an old lady's whim."

At first, her ladyship's odd whims had surprised and dismayed Miranda. She soon grew so accustomed to eccentricity that her previous life, even the alarms and starts of life with her happy-go-lucky, debt-ridden father, seemed woefully dull in comparison. The future no longer stretched ahead as a bleak desert of fetching shawls, sorting embroidery silks, and retiring to her room when there was company unless needed to make up numbers.

Moreover, Lady Wiston's kindness and generosity quickly won her affectionate regard. If such a lovable lady chose to wear unconventional clothes, hold unconventional views, and entertain unconventional acquaintances, her behaviour harmed no one. Not even herself, for she was as shrewd as any barrow-woman, by no means easy prey for leeches hoping to take advantage of her liberality.

Even Mudge was bearable, Miranda felt, since her employer, far from doting on him, loathed the little beast quite as much as she did.

She wished, though, that the pug's escapade had not caused her to fall into Peter Daviot's arms. All too aware of the dangerous charm allied with his frivolous manner, she was going to find it difficult to remain properly aloof after such an introduction. To have him staying in the house for several days as a welcome guest promised to be awkward, to say the least.

The less she saw of him the better. Nonetheless, she felt obliged to minister to his bitten hand. His teasing had confused her as to whether Mudge had actually inflicted a gash or a mere graze.

Pushing a hairpin more firmly into her topknot, she tidied the curls on her forehead and donned a lace-trimmed cap—when she insisted on wearing caps, as was only proper to her age and position, Lady Wiston had insisted on buying her pretty ones. With a final glance in the looking-glass, she went back up to the blue chamber.

She knocked.

"Come in," called Mr. Daviot.

Miranda opened the door. He was standing by the wash-stand in his shirtsleeves, rolled up to the elbows, and stockinged feet, his face buried in a towel.

"Good gracious," she exclaimed, hastily shutting the door again. How dare he ask her in when he was not decently clad! Was the wretched man quite determined to put her to the blush? From her brief acquaintance with him, she would not put it past him.

Before she could turn away, the door re-opened and he appeared before her, waistcoatless, his shirt open at the neck to display a triangle of tanned chest. Instantly dropping her gaze, she found herself staring at a big toe poking out through a hole in his hose. She covered her eyes.

"I thought you were the footman bringing back my boots."

"I just came to look at your hand," she said crossly.

"You can't see it with your hands over your eyes."

"You are not dressed!"

"The important bits are covered." He sounded as if he was grinning. "I didn't mean to shock you, though. You didn't blink at Aunt Artemis's costume."

"That is different. Is your hand mangled or not?"

"I'm badly injured," he said in a failing voice. "I claimed it was only a scratch so as not to distress my aunt."

Not for a second did she believe him. "Wash it well," she advised, "and come down to Sir Bernard's study."

She went down to the small room at the back of the house, its window opening onto a garden full of roses. The walls were sea-green, the coffered ceiling blue. Over the mantel hung a large painting of Nelson's *Victory* at the Battle of Trafalgar, and on one wall a map of the world with Admiral Sir Bernard Wiston's voyages traced upon it.

Furnished with a large roll-top desk, two comfortable chairs, and several bookshelves, the late admiral's study now served a multitude of purposes.

Beside each chair stood a workbasket, seldom used as neither Miranda nor Lady Wiston enjoyed needlework. Her ladyship justified her aversion by saying that stitchery, if one could afford to pay someone to sew for one, was taking bread from the mouths of the poor. She and Miranda were far more likely to pass a cosy evening with the backgammon set or a novel from Hookham's Circulating Library. Both were to be found on a card table by the fireside.

One shelf held a small chest with a variety of common medicaments, court-plasters, and bandages. Lady Wiston required her companion rather than her housekeeper, as was more usual, to treat her servants' minor ailments. On learning her duties, Miranda had sorted out the muddled contents of the chest, neatly relabelling the porcelain pots and coloured glass bottles and ranging them alphabetically.

She lifted down the chest, unlocked and opened it, pleased with the orderly array of jars and vials. There was the basilicum, in its place next to the Balm of Gilead.

Spreading a clean white napkin over an occasional table, she set the pot of basilicum on it. From their separate compartments in the chest she took a pair of scissors, a roll of pale pink silk impregnated with isinglass, and a small notebook.

As she fetched the ladderback, cane-seated chair from the desk, Mr. Daviot came in, shaven and respectably if not fashionably dressed.

"Let me do that," he said, taking the chair from her. "Good gad, you're all set up for a major operation. You're not going to amputate, are you, Doctor?"

"I like to do things properly in the first place, to avert the need for amputation. Did you wash the wound well, or shall I send for water?"

"Clean as a whistle," he said meekly, placing a second chair opposite the first. As Miranda sat down, he glanced about the room. "By Jove, this is perfect!"

"It is a pleasant room," she responded, surprised and a trifle suspicious of his enthusiasm. "The admiral preferred to sit here in the evenings when they had no guests, and Lady Wiston has kept up the habit. Do take your seat, sir. I daresay you are as ready for your breakfast as I am for mine."

"More so, I expect. I didn't dine last night."

He sat down and held out his hand, like himself long and lean but strong-looking, as sun-browned as his face. Across the back Mudge's eyetooth had slashed a groove, less than a gash though more than a scratch. Miranda applied basilicum.

"Would you like a court-plaster?" she asked, picking up the pink silk and the scissors. "On the whole minor wounds heal as well without if they are kept clean. It should be covered if you decide to sleep in the garden again."

"Not me! No, I'll do without a plaster, thank you. Plaguey things, always falling off. What are you writing?"

She looked up from her notebook. "I keep a record of every medicine I dispense to see which are effective. I have already discarded James's Powders and Hervey-Ward's Pills from my pharmacopoeia, and Daffy's Elixir is on the way out. I find the more varied ills they claim to cure, the less efficacious they prove for any."

"Jove!" He took the book from her and studied it. "You ought to be a physician, bedamned if you oughtn't. More sense than half the quacks with their favourite nostrums, I shouldn't wonder."

Miranda was torn between annoyance at his improper language and gratification at his compliment. "More sense, perhaps, but little learning," she said. "I have not even such ladylike accomplishments as French and music and the use of the globes, or I should have sought employment as a governess, not a companion. All I can do is read and write and figure a little."

"Damned . . ." Glancing up with a considering look, he caught her frown and changed the offending word. "Dashed neat hand you write, every letter clear as day. That's a more useful accomplishment than any number of globes."

Though she smiled, Miranda had a distinct feeling that he was buttering her up for his own purposes. His helpfulness in lifting the chest back onto its shelf did not alter by one whit her resolve to reserve judgement on Mr. Peter Daviot.

She led the way to the dining parlour.

Lady Wiston was spreading a hot muffin with strawberry jam. "I simply could not wait, my dears," she said, waving them to the laden sideboard.

Miranda saw that cold meats, ale and coffee had joined the usual eggs, muffins, tea and chocolate. Mr. Daviot piled high his plate.

As they took their places at the table, Lady Wiston said, "Now, Peter, while you eat, I trust you will tell us what you have been doing all these years since you left to seek your fortune."

"Not making my fortune, alas," he said ruefully, cutting into a thick slice of York ham.

Miranda had guessed as much. He had slept in the open after going without his dinner, though the inns of the greatest city in the world never closed their doors. His pockets were undoubtedly to let. She suspected he hoped to hang on his aunt's sleeve.

He would find Lady Wiston less easy to impose upon than he expected. And if a sentimental attachment to her sister's son, her only living relative, overbore her capacity to resist undeserving spongers, she had Miranda to protect her.

"What a pity," said her ladyship, her sympathy all too obvious. "I daresay it was impossible for an Englishman to grow rich in America while we were fighting the colonists again."

"I certainly chose the wrong moment to cross the Atlantic!" he agreed. "Within a month of my arrival, the Yankees declared war. I thought it wisest to make for Canada. Canada, Miss Carmichael, is a name for British North America, which lies to the north of the United States."

"I know!" Miranda said indignantly. "I am not absolutely ignorant of geography, in spite of never being taught the use of the globes."

"Nor was I," said Lady Wiston, "and when Sir Bernard tried to explain to me I must confess I utterly failed to comprehend the connection between the celestial and terrestrial globes. I gather they keep moving in relation to each other in the most confusing fashion. As for lines of longitude and latitude—my dear, it seems they are quite imaginary! How they can have assisted him in navigation I cannot think. So you went to Canada, Peter?"

"Not quite. Before I came to the frontier, I fell in with a band of Iroquois Indians."

"Gracious heavens!" his aunt gasped. "My dear boy, how did you escape?"

"Oh, they didn't take me prisoner. Most of them fought with the British in the American Revolution, you know. Many fled to Canada, and those who remain in the United States are in general still favourably disposed towards us. They welcomed me and took me to their village, and there I stayed until I heard a few months since that peace was made at last."

"That must have been interesting," said Miranda. In a severe tone, she added, "But when the peace freed you to make your fortune, why did you rush back to England?"

"I decided my new scheme had a better chance of reaping rich rewards here, because of the larger population, a greater choice of publishers, and any number of wealthy patrons of the arts. You see, if I can only find a patron, I mean to write a thrilling popular account of my life among the Iroquois."

"What a splendid notion, dear," Lady Wiston exclaimed, surrendering without a fight. "You will live here, of course, while you are writing."

With a quizzical glance at Miranda which told her he was well aware of her dismayed disapproval, Mr. Daviot smiled and said, "Thank you, Aunt Artemis, I shall be delighted."

Chapter 3

"That is all settled, then," said Lady Wiston, beaming.

"I shall move out of my chamber as quickly as I can," Miranda said resignedly.

"Good gracious, dear, whatever for?"

"It is the second best chamber, ma'am. Your nephew. . . ."

"I shouldn't dream of dispossessing you, Miss Carmichael," Mr. Daviot protested. "The blue chamber is perfectly comfortable."

"Quite right," his aunt agreed. "You are all settled, Miranda, and there is not the least occasion to uproot yourself. The admiral's study will be perfect for your work, Peter. Miranda, pray order plenty of paper and pens and ink."

"I shall go by the stationer's this morning on my way to do the marketing." Miranda was determined to make sure he had no excuse not to keep his nose to the grindstone. "How much paper do you suppose you will require, Mr. Daviot?"

"Oh, a ream I suppose will do the trick. Or do I mean a quire?"

"I have not the least notion."

"Perhaps I had best go with you. I'll be glad to carry your basket."

"Thank you, sir, but that is not necessary." *She* was not going to succumb to his blandishments. "I take one of the footmen, and in any case all the tradesmen deliver to the house."

Lady Wiston's mind had moved on to the marketing. "Miranda, if the greengrocer has good red and black currants, pray order plenty. Cook shall bake tarts for my at-home this afternoon and put up the rest for the winter."

"You expect callers this afternoon, Aunt?" Mr. Daviot enquired. "As I recall, London is generally rather thin of company at this season."

"The *ton* may go off to their country houses, but they are a very small proportion of the population. London still abounds in interesting people. Only last week, when we visited St. Bartholomew's Hospital, we met a Lascar seaman, a charming gentleman."

"A Lascar seaman a gentleman!"

"I find," said Lady Wiston with some severity, "that if one treats common men and women as ladies and gentlemen, they almost invariably strive to live up to one's expectations. I gave Sagaranu my card. I hope he will come today. The name was Sagaranu, was it not, Miranda?"

"Something of the sort, Lady Wiston. I wrote it down in my notebook. I shall check before he arrives."

"What an excellent secretary you are, my dear."

Miranda smiled at her affectionately. "If I am to be a good marketer also, I must be on my way, or all the best currants will be sold." She finished off her cup of tea and folded her napkin.

"Don't forget to go by the bookseller's and tell them we did not receive the latest *Examiner*. I shall be sadly disappointed if the Hunts close down the paper and cease to bedevil the government now they are out of prison at last."

"Yes, indeed! What should we discuss over our Sunday breakfast?"

Miranda went upstairs to put on her bonnet and shawl. When she came downstairs a few minutes later, she was surprised to find Mr. Daviot waiting for her in the hall, gloves and well-brushed top-hat in hand.

"I told Ethan I shall accompany you in his place, Miss Carmichael," he said.

"I am quite capable of ordering paper and pens for you, sir."

"Of that I have no doubt. You strike me as a singularly capable female. That is why I wish to consult you."

"Oh?" said Miranda coldly, sure he thought to win her over by flattery and enlist her aid in fleecing Lady Wiston. Only a fear of being overheard in the house could explain his choosing to consult her in the street.

He said no more until they were outside. The square was quiet, devoid of its usual bustling traffic. Most of the houses were shut up, only caretakers in residence, the knockers removed from front doors for the summer. Miranda and her unwanted escort turned south towards Oxford Street.

"I am a little concerned about Aunt Artemis," said Mr. Daviot, a supportive hand beneath her elbow as they crossed the cobbled street. "As you know, I have been absent for several years. I don't recall her being so freakish when I left."

"Freakish! Lady Wiston is an original, perhaps even a trifle eccentric, but I would not call her freakish."

"What, when she reads seditious newspapers, invites ramshackle sailors to her at-home, visits hospitals. . . ."

"And orphanages," said Miranda, not without relish, "and prisons."

"Prisons!"

"We were at Newgate recently with Mrs. Elizabeth Fry, the prison reformer—we met her a fortnight ago, when we attended a Quaker meeting."

"Aunt Artemis doesn't go to Church?"

"The Church of England? Sometimes, but she likes to try a different place of worship every Sunday. She says each sect is quite convinced it possesses the only truth, and since they cannot all be right, it behooves every individual. . . ."

"Yes, yes, I see her point. But what's all this about visiting prisons?"

"Lady Wiston believes one ought to see conditions for oneself so as best to direct how one's alms are employed. Besides, she thoroughly enjoys delivering little comforts to the unfortunates confined in such places, and we make the acquaintance, as she told you, of the most fascinating people."

"But to invite them to call upon her!" Mr. Daviot said feebly.

Miranda stopped and turned to face him. "Your aunt happens to be remarkably lively and interested in the world about her," she asserted, "unlike all too many old ladies whose only concern is their ailments. She gives many people a good deal of harmless pleasure, and injures no one."

"Not even you? I'd have thought a well-brought-up young lady must find it trying to be obliged by her position to assist in such activities."

"Not even me."

"You don't find shopping for household necessities demeaning? Is that not commonly regarded as part of a housekeeper's duties?"

"Yes, but Mrs. Lowenstein speaks very little English. She is a refugee from Poland, you see, where Jews are much persecuted."

"I suppose you met her when you attended a synagogue!"

"As a matter of fact, yes." Miranda regarded his stunned face with amusement. "Though she communicates very well with the maids—indeed, no one could complain of their slacking at their work—dealing with shopkeepers is beyond her at present, while I don't mind in the least."

"You are an exceptional woman, Miss Carmichael."

"Not I. Did you not say yourself that you conceived all

hired companions to be grey, mousy creatures? I was well on the way to becoming just another such until Lady Wiston engaged me. I can never be sufficiently grateful."

"You grey and mousy?" He shook his head with a smile. "Inconceivable. Well, you defend Aunt Artemis so ably that I have not another word to say on the subject. In fact, I confess I begin to look forward to this afternoon's outlandish at-home."

Chuckling, Miranda pointed out, "After living among Iroquois Indians for several years, you are unlikely to find the occasion excessively outlandish."

"Touché! Say rather that I anticipate no little amusement from meeting my aunt's acquaintance."

His smile really was alarmingly attractive, Miranda reflected as they continued on their way. She was going to have to make an effort to remain on her guard.

As hostess, Aunt Artemis wore a gown, in a dazzling vermilion sarcenet which made her look, Peter thought, like a plump, cheerful robin redbreast. He wondered whether her companion had had to persuade her to abandon her comfortable trousers for the nonce.

"Is Mudge safely shut up?" she asked.

"Yes, Lady Wiston, at a large cost in comfits for bribery."

"He does enjoy them so, as I trust our visitors will enjoy this spread." Aunt Artemis regarded the laden table with a contented sigh. "Plum cake, seed cake, bread-and-butter, currant tarts and Bakewell tarts, Shrewsbury biscuits, macaroons—excellent. I'm sure you are right, dear, about the bowl of cherries. So difficult even in the best company to deal politely with the stones."

"Very wise, Miss Carmichael," Peter agreed gravely. "One cannot wish to force one's guests to choose between swallowing the stones and spitting them into the fireplace."

Miss Carmichael appeared to be trying not to smile at his bald statement of the possible alternatives. "It seems sensible not to face people with that quandary," she said.

As Lady Wiston trotted through to the drawing room to take her place behind the tea-table, Peter continued in a low voice, "I must say I'm surprised my aunt doesn't provide more substantial victuals, hams and barons of beef and such. Surely some of those she invites seldom eat well?"

"True," she said, favouring him with an almost approving look. "Lady Wiston regards these at-homes as purely social affairs, like those to which she invites her fashionable acquaintance during the Season. She finds plenty of other opportunities for charity, and you may be sure none of her friends goes hungry. Ah, there goes the door knocker. You are about to make the acquaintance of Daylight Danny—he is always the first to arrive."

"*Daylight* Danny?" he asked, bemused, following her through to the other room.

She threw a mischievous glance over her shoulder. "Do ask him how he came by his name. Lady Wiston," she addressed her employer severely, "I wish you will let me pour. Last week your wrist ached for two days from lifting heavy teapots."

"I shall call for help before it grows tired," Aunt Artemis promised. "Ah, here they come."

The tap-tap of the butler's peg-leg was heard in the hall. Twitchell was an ex-Chief Petty Officer who had sailed with the admiral and lost his leg at the Battle of the Nile. He had been with the Wistons ever since, an excellent if unique butler. Eccentricity was nothing new in this household, Peter reflected.

The door opened. His leathery face impassive, Twitchell announced, "Mr. and Mrs. Potts, my lady."

Behind him loomed a hulking, villainous fellow with a low brow, a squashed nose, two cauliflower ears, and a broken-toothed grin. Peter sprang forward, his immediate reaction that the butler must have run mad to admit a prize-fighter to his mistress's drawing room. Then, recalling the Lascar seaman, he hesitated.

Twitchell stepped aside, revealing a neat little woman

at the bruiser's side. Perfectly self-possessed, she advanced into the room. "How do, my lady, miss?" she said with a curtsy.

Her mountainous husband bowed awkwardly. "Here I be, m'lady," he said, his slow country voice overlaid with a touch of Cockney, "but it do seem today there's another forrarder nor I." The glare he turned on Peter was a fearsome sight.

"Good day to you both," said Aunt Artemis. "This is my nephew, Mr. Daviot, come home from America to live with me for a while. Peter, Daylight Danny and Mrs. Potts."

Daylight Danny apologized to Peter for taking his presence amiss. "I likes to be here first, you see, sir," he said in a confidential whisper. "There bain't no knowing what sort o' rum custermers her la'ship'll take into her noddle to arst into her house, bless her heart. She needs summun to look out for her at these here at-homes, she do."

"I must be grateful to you for taking on the task," Peter assured him, somehow contriving not to smile. His own coat, he had to acknowledge, was quite shabby enough to mislead the man into doubting his respectability.

"Lor' bless you, sir, 'tis nowt. My Mary and me, we'd do a mortal sight more'n that for your auntie arter what she done for us."

"What was that?"

"Why, she set us up in business, didn't she. In the hospital I were, being took mortal bad arter me last bout in the ring. You'll have mebbe guessed as I were a boxer?"

"You do have the look of a pugilist."

"Pugilist! Ay, 'tis a grand word for a nasty business. Well, I arst you, sir, is it a decent trade for a cove to go bashing another cove wi' his fives, all for a few quid?"

"You have a point," Peter admitted.

"My Mary, she didn't never like it, but the Fancy were the only trade I knowed to keep body and soul together. Not that I were ever one o' the best, neither, not like Mendoza or Gentleman Jackson. Daylight Danny they call me, acos there weren't never a fight where I didn't come out wi' both me daylights darkened.''

"So you wanted to leave the Fancy?"

"Aye, but there's not many'll hire a cove as looks like me, not for honest work. Even on the markets and down the docks, they've only to set their glims on me to think I must be too quick wi' me fives. The which I bain't, being a peaceable cove.''

"You met my aunt in the hospital?"

"She come visiting, her and the long-faced gentry mort she had afore this un.'' Danny cast an appraising glance from Peter to Miss Carmichael, which seemed to afford him some obscure satisfaction. "This un's a prime article, sir, mark my word.''

"Now, Danny." The diminutive Mrs. Potts appeared at their elbows. "Don't you go talking the ear off the gent. There's others come he'll be wanting a word with and you haven't barely spoke to my lady.''

"Yes, Mary," said the giant obediently.

"I'm happy to make your aquaintance, Mr. Potts.'' Peter offered his hand rather gingerly, but it was engulfed in an almost delicate clasp. "I'll see you again later, no doubt.''

"Right, sir.'' The bruiser beamed. "Call me Danny, do.''

He went off to the tea-table, now surrounded by a motley crew. Miss Carmichael was talking to a dark-skinned man in a turban who must be the Lascar seaman. Peter turned to Mrs. Potts.

"I like your husband, ma'am.''

"He's a good fellow at heart, sir, and no mistake.''

"He told me my aunt helped you set up in business. I didn't get around to asking what business you are in?''

"Hot pies, sir. I bake 'em, he takes 'em, selling out in the streets, like. My Danny's not fast like the Flying Pieman you've maybe seen, but he can carry four times the load and we do well enough. *And* we've paid back every penny to my lady, not that she asked, but someone else needs it more nor we do now.''

"I'm glad she was able to help you," Peter said sincerely,

feeling a trifle less guilty about his intention of sponging off Aunt Artemis. It wasn't as if he meant to do so for ever, only until his book made his fortune, and besides, he was truly fond of the old dear.

"I've brought you a cup of tea, Mr. Daviot." Miss Carmichael arrived, accompanied by the Lascar. "May I present Mr. Sagaranathu? He comes from the East Indies."

Sagaranathu spoke surprisingly good English. In fact, he was an educated man by his country's standards, and had visited Bart's Hospital not as a patient but to study Western notions of medicine.

He had become a sailor, he explained, because it was the only way open to him to see the world. Living frugally on his pay, he was able to spend several months in each port he visited. Peter had an interesting discussion with him about the Hindoo and Iroquois mythologies.

In the meantime, Miss Carmichael had gone to take his aunt's place at the tea-table. As he talked, he watched her dealing in the friendliest manner with all the disparate guests. Aunt Artemis had been lucky to find her, he thought. From various snippets, he gathered the previous companion was far less satisfactory, easily overset by her employer's oddities.

Aunt Artemis came over. "Go and meet some of the others," she ordered, and whisked Sagaranathu away to a corner for a private cose.

Peter obeyed. Among others, he met a market-woman, a Chinese pedlar, a barrel-organ grinder with his monkey on his shoulder, and the seamstress who created her lady-ship's unusual costumes. He found it was easy to tell which were regular visitors and which had never come before. The latter gazed wide-eyed at their surroundings, hardly believing they had been invited to call upon a real lady.

The drawing room was an elegant apartment in Robert Adam's unmistakable style. White walls and ceiling with plaster mouldings picked out in gilt and blue were comple-mented by blue brocade curtains and chairs upholstered in blue and white striped satin. No speck of dust marred the gleaming woodwork. A whatnot and shelved niches on either side of the fireplace displayed curios collected by Sir Bernard in every corner of the world.

The visitors seemed particularly awestruck by a striking full-length portrait of the bewhiskered, ruddy-faced admiral in his dress uniform, liberally adorned with gold braid. Peter wondered what he would have made of his widow's choice of company.

At last Twitchell ushered out the last guest. Every currant tart, every crumb of cake had vanished from the dining-room table.

"Well, Peter," said Aunt Artemis, sinking onto a sofa and patting the seat beside her, "what do you think?"

He joined her. "Interesting people, Aunt, those I spoke to, and some of them charming. I must say I particularly liked the Pottses."

"They are dears, are they not?" said Miss Carmichael, sipping a last cup of tea.

"Do you never have a failure?" he asked. "I mean, find you have invited someone who turns out to be not quite as unexceptionable as you had supposed?"

"Oh yes," her ladyship admitted with a sigh. "Miranda, pray do not send the captain a card next week. He utterly refuses to change his ways."

"Which was the captain?" Peter queried. "I don't believe I met him."

"Captain by virtue of his own imagination, I fear," Miss Carmichael said dryly. "A Captain Sharp, and by no means willing to reform."

"A card-sharp?"

"I am afraid so." Aunt Artemis looked positively guilty. "He is quite amusing, and he has taught me several of his naughty tricks, but he will not stop fleecing pigeons and take up some more respectable line of work."

"Fleecing pigeons!" Miss Carmichael laughed.

"You know what I mean, dear."

"Of course, and I know that you are tired. Do take a nap before you dress for dinner, Lady Wiston. If you have no need of me, I shall go and thank the servants for their usual splendid efforts, and then finish the letter to my brother which I began yesterday." She went out.

"Miss Carmichael has a brother, does she?" said Peter. "I assumed she was alone in the world, I don't know why."

"She might as well be," his aunt snorted. "Her mother died when she was quite small, and her father four or five years ago. Her brother is a sanctimonious country clergyman with a feckless wife, five children, and an inadequate benefice."

"Then I quite understand why she prefers the life of a companion, however dismal, to residing with her relatives."

Inexplicably, Aunt Artemis brightened. "Miranda told you it is a dismal life?"

"She told me she was well on the way to becoming a little grey mouse before she came to you, dear ma'am. She appears to positively enjoy your . . . er . . . interesting ways."

Her face fell. "She has me quite at my wits' end!"

"At your wits' end? What the dev . . . deuce do you mean? Miss Carmichael seems to me an ideal companion for you."

"She is, she is. Oh dear, I suppose I had best explain, then perhaps you will be able to advise me. You remember, I expect, that I was a lady's companion, a little grey mouse, just as you describe, before dear Sir Bernard married me."

"A perspicacious gentleman, I have always considered him, to see past the twitching nose and long whiskers to the. . . ."

"Really, Peter, this is serious! I was utterly miserable, and he was a gallant gentleman who could not bear to see my unhappiness."

"Gammon, Aunt, he adored you. That was plain even to a heedless youth like me."

She beamed. "Well, I do think we were happy together. Which is what made me think, after I lost him, that every girl in such a situation deserves a chance of such happiness.

But it was not until Frederick offered for Aurelia that I actually came up with a *plan.*"

"Tell me," urged Peter, wondering with misgivings what sort of plan the original little lady had devised.

Chapter 4

Twitchell tapped through from the dining parlour. "Shall we clear away in here, my lady?" he asked.

"Another cup of tea, Peter? No? Yes, you may clear, Twitchell. But you are looking rather tired, dear man. You are not sickening for a summer cold, are you?"

"Thank you, my lady, I believe not."

"Well, do go and sit down and rest your leg. The boys are quite capable of taking away the tea-things without your eagle eye upon them."

The butler was not about to allow himself such a dereliction of duty. At his signal the youthful footmen, Eustace and Ethan, came in, smart in their blue and grey livery and powdered wigs. Swiftly, carefully, unobtrusively, they cleared the tea table and circled the room picking up stray cups and saucers.

As they vanished through the door into the hall, Aunt Artemis sighed. "I am afraid they will have to go," she said.

"I fear so, my lady." Twitchell echoed her sigh. "I shall advise them to look out for positions elsewhere." Bowing himself out, he closed the door.

"But why?" Peter asked. "They seem particularly competent footmen."

"They are, dear. Twitchell has trained them up, and now they are fit to serve the dear Prince Regent himself, we must start again with another pair rescued from the streets. I believe it was the one thing which most distressed Julia, my third companion. I must admit life is always a little difficult for a few weeks while they find their sea legs, as Twitchell puts it."

Envisaging months of cold shaving water and soup spilled in his lap, Peter suggested, "Why not take one new lad at a time? Then the earlier-comer can help to train the later, thus lessening the burden for Twitchell."

"True," she said dubiously. "He is not as young as he was, which is the silliest phrase, is it not, for it applies even to a baby in the cradle! The first pair were brothers, you see, who could not be split up, and since then it has always seemed sadly unfair to make one leave before the other. I shall consult Twitchell."

"Do that, Aunt. But now I am all agog to hear your scheme for marrying off your companions."

"You must swear not to breathe a word to a soul."

"I swear." He glanced round as an imperious yap sounded at the door.

"Let Mudge in, will you, dear? He will scratch the paint dreadfully else."

Peter went to open the door. The pug cast a longing glance at his ankles but apparently recognized the impervious nature of his boots. Scampering past, the brute plumped down in front of Aunt Artemis and fixed her with a beady eye. Automatically she felt for a comfit.

Reseating himself on a chair at a safe distance, Peter said, "Aurelia and Frederick gave you the notion, you said?"

"Do you recall Frederick Fenimore, the admiral's nephew? A most respectable young man, a solicitor at Ipswich, in Suffolk, with excellent expectations from his papa even without what he might hope for from his uncle."

Peter nodded. "Yes, I recall Fenimore." As a dry, pomp-ous stick who snubbed the youth without prospects or profession Peter had been at their last encounter.

"Frederick came to visit—all Sir Bernard's nephews have been most kind and attentive—and found Aurelia in tears. Every little thing overset her. She was afraid of Mudge, and she could not bear to look at Twitchell because of his missing leg. I had asked her to read aloud to me a French novel which she thought not quite proper, I seem to remember. Aurelia was sadly straitlaced, besides being such a prodigious watering-pot, though she did cry beautifully, I will say that for her. Well, Frederick took one look at her and proposed marriage."

"Good lord, she must have cried exceptionally beauti-fully!"

"Oh, she did. Not a trace of red in her eyes, only tear-drops hanging like pearls in her lashes. She never even sniffed!"

"So Fenimore wed the fair Aurelia."

"Yes, and it did make me think, I promise you, even though the novel turned out to be shockingly tedious, after all."

"What a shame," Peter said, laughing.

"Yes, I quite gave up French novels after that. I did not see why I should be bored to tears just to drive my companions to tears, so I had to find something else. That was when I started to visit orphanages and hospitals, and to invite interesting people to call. Marjory, my next, was convinced she was going to catch some dreadful disease in those horrid places, but she married James instead."

"Another of the admiral's nephews? Ah yes, I have it, James Redpath, Squire of Redpath Manor." A red-faced, loud-voiced booby contemptuous of any man who did not live for the pursuit of the fox.

"Redpath Manor, near Brighton," said Aunt Artemis complacently. "A very pretty property, though not large, and in such a healthful situation on the Downs, quite perfect for Marjory. So much fresh country air." She waved her hands vaguely.

"And then came Julia, who objected to untrained footmen?"

"Yes, though now I come to think of it, that was not the worst. She felt marketing was beneath her, but what really gave her the vapours was attending a different service every Sunday. She feared her soul would be damned for lack of fidelity to the Anglican church, but how is one to discover the truth if one only ever hears one side of it?"

"Very true, Aunt." Peter had no desire to find himself involved in theological debate. "I suppose she married Sir Bernard's clergyman nephew?" he asked hastily.

"Yes, dear; Edward Jeffries, Canon at Winchester Cathedral. Edward will be a bishop one day, I am sure."

And quite as sanctimonious as Miranda Carmichael's brother could possibly be. Jeffries wouldn't have suited that lively young lady at all, even worse than Redpath or Fenimore. So who did Aunt Artemis destine for her?

"Miss Carmichael . . . ?" he said.

"I am still searching for some way to throw her into high fidgets. Do you know, I even took her to a series of lectures on Natural Philosophy—electricity and fire-damp and such things. I understood not one word in ten but she found them fascinating and even volunteered to be electrified! She simply never takes exception to anything I do."

"She is actually grateful to you for rescuing her from her previous dull existence. Perhaps you should limit your acquaintance to the most respectable members of the Polite World, your charity to knitting for the poor-basket, and your reading to sermons. Anglican sermons, of course."

"Good gracious," cried Aunt Artemis, aghast, "I should very soon expire from sheer boredom!"

"Then you must gird up your loins to be actively unkind."

"Oh, I could not possibly be deliberately unkind, dear.

No, no, I shall think of something. In fact, I have a new scheme in hand at present." In a conspiratorial tone she added, "Do not be surprised if you see Mr. Sagaranathu calling frequently."

"Miss Carmichael seemed to enjoy his company," Peter pointed out.

"Yes, but I am not inviting him for his company. Just wait and see if this does not shake Miranda's composure!"

"And if it does, who is to be the lucky. . . . Ye gods, Aunt Artemis, you aren't expecting *me* to marry the girl?"

It was Peter's turn to be aghast, his composure very thoroughly shaken by alarm lest his aunt regard him as a rescuer of forlorn maidens. Not that Miss Carmichael was not a devilish attractive maiden, at least when she smiled instead of frowning. He had enjoyed their brief stolen kiss and had no aversion to repeating the experience. In fact, he liked her very well—but he liked his freedom better.

Besides, he was in no position to support a wife, he recalled thankfully. He was about to draw this indisputable fact to his aunt's attention when she got there first.

"Heavens no!" she exclaimed in horror. "Miranda's father was a care-for-nobody just like you. I could not wish to shackle her to another such penniless rapscallion."

Peter found himself stunned into wordlessness at this home truth from his hitherto amiable, obliging relative. She continued:

"Even if she would have you, which I cannot credit. She is not so lacking in common sense! No, Miranda shall have Godfrey. She is by far the nicest of my companions and she deserves him. How I shall go on without her I cannot imagine, but I daresay she will like to be a baroness."

"Baroness?" Peter said blankly.

"Did you never meet Godfrey Snell? His mama was Sir Bernard's eldest sister. Perhaps you did not know his papa was a baron, for he succeeded to the title quite recently, while you were in America."

"Godfrey, Lord Snell?"

"And Miranda, Lady Snell." Aunt Artemis beamed.

Though Peter failed to recollect having met a Snell in any shape or form, he conceived an instant and utterly irrational dislike for the man. No cousin of the abominable Fenimore, Redpath, and Jeffries, however blue-blooded, could possibly be worthy to win the hand of Miss Miranda Carmichael.

Seated at the bureau, Miranda glanced round as Mr. Daviot entered the study. He appeared oddly uneasy for one who had so blithely obtruded himself into the household with not the least sign of any qualms.

"Has Lady Wiston gone up to rest?" Miranda asked. "She does find her at-homes tiring, much as she enjoys them."

"Yes, she said she'd lie down for an hour. I don't mean to disturb you."

"No matter. It is merely a duty letter to my brother. He frets if he does not hear from me once a month, but I confess I often find it difficult to fill a page."

Leaning against the desk, he looked at the half-blank sheet and observed, "You must write larger. Aunt Artemis told me he's a churchman? I daresay he'd be shocked if you described what is involved in your present employment."

"Yes, indeed! Apropos, have you recovered from your shock at the company Lady Wiston keeps?"

"Quite recovered. I believe I shall enjoy residing here as much as you do."

"Even more, I imagine," Miranda said dryly, "since you are not obliged to earn your living. Oh dear!" She bit her lip, perturbed at her own impertinence. "You seem to have a disastrous effect on my ability to hold my tongue! I beg your pardon, sir."

"Unnecessary." Mr. Daviot was unwontedly serious. "I am aware of your doubts, your discomfort with my aunt's offering a home, however temporary, to one who has announced himself an adventurer. I can only be glad she has someone sincerely concerned for her welfare. I'm truly fond of her, you know, and I have every intention of working hard at my book.''

Fine words, Miranda thought. She, for one, would wait and see.

His momentary gravity vanished and he grinned at her. ''Fine words—you are saying to yourself—butter no parsnips. You're quite right, of course, but then I never did care much for parsnips.''

She sighed. ''As long as you don't run off with the silver, no doubt we shall contrive to live in tolerable harmony. Lady Wiston would be sadly distressed if there were dissension in her house.''

''It's a bargain, ma'am. I shall endeavour not to plague you, and you must endeavour not to scold me for minor misdeeds.''

He offered his hand and she laid hers in it, all too conscious of the warm firmness of his clasp. Quickly she turned her attention to the damage done by Mudge that morning.

''Your scratch is already beginning to heal nicely,'' she remarked with satisfaction.

''I was fortunate in having expert medical care.'' Mr. Daviot gave her his most engaging smile. ''Well, I shan't keep you from your letter any longer. I just came in to make sure all the stuff from the stationer's was delivered. I promised Aunt Artemis to set to work bright and early tomorrow morning.''

''Everything is here. I checked.'' Miranda waved at the table in the corner. Beside several brown paper packages of various shapes and sizes stood a huge bottle of black fluid.

''Perhaps a gallon of ink was rather overdoing it,'' he said with a look half rueful, half laughing. ''It didn't look so vast in the shop.''

''Better too much than to run out in the middle of a fit of inspiration. Shall you use this desk? If so, I must clear away a few odds and ends.''

''No, I believe that table will suit me better. I daresay

Aunt Artemis will not mind if I have it placed under the window to take advantage of the daylight?"

"I doubt it." Miranda doubted her ladyship would deny any reasonable request of her nephew's. She had to admit that none had been unreasonable. So far.

"Which reminds me," he said, crossing to the door, "do you really mean to allow her to sleep out on the terrace tonight?"

"Mr. Daviot, I do not allow or disallow Lady Wiston's actions. She is her own mistress—and mine also."

"True, but I suspect you are quite capable of effective discouragement, or encouragement, where you consider it appropriate."

"As a matter of fact," she said, disconcerted, "I was going to insist on Baxter, her abigail, and a footman standing guard to help her move indoors should it rain. I doubt she will choose to subject them to the discomfort."

"I knew it!" he exclaimed, laughing.

To Miranda's annoyance, she felt herself blushing. "I prefer not to interfere," she defended herself, "but even if the night remains fine there is bound to be a heavy dew. I cannot think it advisable for a lady of your aunt's years to subject herself to the damp."

"Oh, I quite agree. As I have said before, she is extremely lucky to have found so determined a protector."

With that, the infuriating man whisked from the room, leaving Miranda with her cheeks hotter than ever.

Chapter 5

"And then," said Mr. Daviot, helping himself to a third slice of steak and kidney pie and a spoonful of spinach, "the sea-serpent opened a mouth as wide as a barn door. With a single gulp he swallowed the pirate captain, treasure map and all, leaving our attackers in disarray and permitting our escape. Unfortunately, his tail swept the sheep pens and fowl cages from our deck, so that we were forced to subsist on hard tack the rest of the way home."

"Have another potato, dear boy," urged Lady Wiston. "Your ship was some thirty yards distant from the pirate ship, you said? Gracious me, what a very large sea-serpent."

Miranda laughed. "And what very sharp eyes, to make out the treasure map in the pirate's hand!"

"You forget, Miss Carmichael," he said, his tone injured but his eyes agleam with amusement, "our captain had lent me his glass so that I could observe the monster with scientifical thoroughness."

"Ah yes. How fortunate that irreplaceable instrument was not struck by one of the scores of cannonballs bouncing around you. Tell me, sir, is your proposed book to be fact or fiction?"

"A good point." He regarded her with an arrested look. "I intended a true tale of my sojourn among the Iroquois, but perhaps a fiction would sell better. Or fact spiced with fiction? What, after all, is truth?"

The question was rhetorical, but Miranda found herself wondering whether Peter Daviot was actually capable of distinguishing fact from fiction. If only she could be certain when he was serious, when he was teasing, and when he was shamming, or simply giving free rein to his undoubtedly lively imagination!

She was never quite sure how to react to him. The uncertainty perplexed her, adding to her reluctance as she approached the study door towards the middle of the next morning.

The origins of her reluctance were twofold. In the first place, the errand driving her thither was to bring up to date the household accounts, her least favourite task. Second, she did not wish to disturb the author at his labours—always supposing he had actually set pen to paper. In the end, her eagerness to find out drove her to march in without a preparatory knock.

His tilted chair wavered wildly. Grabbing the edge of the table, he contrived to save himself from going over backwards. Hastily he removed his feet from the table and swung round to face Miranda.

"You might give a chap a bit of a warning," he said reproachfully. "Or are you so wild for the practice of medicine you actually wish me to break my head?"

"I assumed you would be so absorbed in writing you would not hear me if I crept in to fetch the account books. I ought to have taken them with me yesterday but. . . ." She hesitated.

"No, no, don't spare me. *But* you were by no means convinced I should actually start work today?" Heaving a sigh, he turned and waved at the table-top. "It seems to be rather more difficult than I reckoned on."

Miranda went over to stand beside him. The top sheet of the small pile of paper, shoved aside to make room for his feet, had the beginnings of three paragraphs, all heavily scratched out. On either side lay a score or so of sharpened quills, their nibs innocent of ink. Another stood in the inkwell.

"I see you have prepared enough pens to last quite some time," she observed, trying not to sound critical.

"At this rate, they will last the rest of my lifetime. We purchased a gross, you may recall."

"What is stopping you? You were fluent enough last night."

"It's easy enough to talk." He ran a distracted hand through his hair. "When one writes it down, for a start one has to decide where to begin."

"Need you decide now?" she queried doubtfully. "That is, can you not go back and add a proper introduction later?"

"It might work," he said, equally doubtfully.

"After all, you are not carving your adventures in stone, with no chance to make changes."

"Thank heaven. I'll try it your way. If I just put down a description of my meeting with the Iroquois braves, I shall get into the way of this writing business, and later it will be easy to do the dull stuff about how I came there."

Drawing the pile of paper towards him, he took the top sheet, crumpled it, and tossed it through the open window. His pen poised over the blank sheet.

Tactfully, Miranda withdrew to the bureau. She rolled up the top as quietly as she could and took the account books and tradesmen's bills from their pigeonholes. Her hands full, she turned.

The pen was still poised. Mr. Daviot stared blankly at the blank top sheet.

"Damn . . . dash it, I still don't know where to start," he groaned. "Should I describe the forest? It is like nothing that has been seen in England for centuries. Or shall I dive straight in with that eerie feeling of being watched?"

Miranda set down her papers, turned her chair to face

him, and sat down. "Tell me the story," she invited. "Then at least you will have it straight in your head."

"You don't mind?"

"I will do practically anything to postpone the bookkeeping. What was it like in the primeval forest? You were on horseback? Were you afraid of the Americans pursuing you?"

"In reverse order: not really, being far too insignificant for them to take the trouble; yes; and awe-inspiring."

As he talked about the vast tracts of ancient trees, undisturbed by man, Miranda listened on two levels. She was interested in what he said, and also in how he said it. He had a knack for interspersing description with increasingly dramatic incidents.

First came the spine-tingling feeling of being watched, which turned out to be a pair of chipmunks, "creatures like miniature squirrels with stripes," he explained. Then there was the morning he awoke in his camp by a stream to see a mother bear teaching her two cubs to fish not five yards from the ashes of his fire. After a nerve-racking half hour, they had wandered on, leaving half a salmon for his breakfast.

And then came the day his horse stepped into an open glade and halted nose to nose with an Indian brave.

"My heart stopped," said Mr. Daviot, his animated face expressing the terror of the moment. "I had heard all the settlers' tales of massacres, of course. He stood there motionless, his arms folded, his tomahawk at his belt. Reaching back for my rifle, which I carried slung over my back, I glanced around. I found myself surrounded by a band of braves sprung up out of nowhere, a dozen or a score, I did not take the time to count! All I cared for was that enough arrows and muskets were trained on me to kill me several times over."

"End of chapter," said Miranda. "If you leave your hero in such a predicament, who will be able to resist reading on?"

"No hero, only me. A hero would doubtless have leapt

from his horse, seized the leader, whipped the tomahawk from his belt, and held it at his throat until the others disarmed. I am an arrant coward, I assure you. I spread my empty hands and said, 'Good afternoon, gentlemen.'"

Miranda burst out laughing. "Did you really?"

"I did. The other would make a better story, though, would it not?"

"I don't believe so," she said, reflecting. "Stay with the facts. Suppose you present the fictitious hero's actions as a plan which flashed through your mind. Then when your readers find out what actually happened, they will laugh as I did. Some may not like it so well as pure adventure, but others will like it a great deal better."

"You think so?"

"I am sure of it. Besides, the anticlimax seems to be your natural style and will therefore very likely prove easier to write. And when you have them laughing, you may explain to your new Indian friends why you are travelling through the forest, thus averting any need for a dull introduction," Miranda added triumphantly.

"A splendid notion!"

"But that is for the next chapter."

"Yes, ma'am. And I know just where to start now." He turned to dip his pen. "Thank you, Miss Carmichael. Are you sure you're not Thalia in disguise?"

He was already scribbling away, so Miranda did not feel called upon to answer. She slipped out silently and went to the housekeeper's room to go over the domestic accounts with Mrs. Lowenstein, who fortunately had a better grasp of numbers than of the English language.

Miranda's hatred of accounts stemmed from the years of keeping house for her father, who had never paid a bill until he was dunned. In fact, they had had the bailiffs in the house twice, and Mr. Carmichael had narrowly escaped debtor's prison. Now, with plenty of funds available to settle accounts as soon as they were presented, she took pride in her neat columns of figures. Yet at the sight of a stack of bills the old anxieties still shook her.

Mr. Daviot's insouciant attitude towards his empty pockets reminded her all too strongly of her late papa. If he actually completed his book and made his fortune, no doubt he would squander it in two shakes of a lamb's tail.

At least it now seemed possible that he intended to make a serious effort to write down his adventures and observations. Miranda was glad to have been able to help him get started.

But what had he meant by asking whether she was Thalia in disguise?

Finished with the housekeeper, Miranda went in search of Lady Wiston. "Her ladyship's upstairs in the green sitting room," the footman on duty in the hall told her mournfully.

"Thank you. I am sorry you have to leave, Eustace."

"So'm I, miss, right sorry, but it's not like we wasn't warned when we came. And her ladyship says we'll always be welcome at her at-homes when we can get away."

"Good. Well, I hope you find an excellent position."

"Ta, miss. Mr. Twitchell says we won't have no trouble after he's had the training of us. Mr. Sagaranathu's with her ladyship, miss," he added as she nodded and turned away.

On her way up the circular stair, Miranda pondered the sad fate of the footmen. Arbitrary as it seemed, it made sense, as most of Lady Wiston's actions did when considered in the right light. The young men had been taught a respectable trade and it was time for two others to be given the same chance. They were not expected to depart until they had found good posts elsewhere.

All the same Miranda was relieved that her ladyship did not treat her companions thus. Impossible to imagine ever finding another position equally enjoyable!

In spite of which, she could not help wishing for a home of her own, a husband and children. She knew her three predecessors had all left to be married, by odd coincidence to three of the late admiral's nephews. However, the only nephew left was Lord Snell. It was too much to hope for that a member of the nobility should stoop to marry a mere gentlewoman forced by straitened circumstances to work for her living.

Indeed, whenever he called upon his aunt-by-marriage during the spring Season, Lord Snell had scarce noticed Miranda's existence. She bore him no ill will. She might not feel like a grey mouse any longer, but in the eyes of most of the Upper Crust, that was what a lady's companion was, almost by definition.

Sighing, she pushed open the door of the sitting room.

It was a charming apartment, hung with apple-green silk and decorated in dark green, white, and buttercup yellow. But Miranda had no eyes for the furnishings. Sagaranathu stood with his back to the fireplace, gazing down. In the middle of the floor Lady Wiston lay, flat on her back with one leg in the air.

Decently clad in Cossack trousers, a red and grey pair, Miranda had time to note as she started forward. "Good gracious, ma'am, are you all right?"

"A little stiff, dear." Her ladyship lowered the waving leg and foot shod in a beaded moccasin—a gift from her nephew—though she made no move to rise. "But Mr. Sagaranathu assures me that will pass if I practise faithfully every day. Indeed, it is one of the purposes of the exercises."

"The benefits of *yoga* are physical as well as spiritual," the Javanese agreed gravely.

"I have hired Mr. Sagaranathu to give me a daily lesson while he is in London. Will you not join me, dear?"

"I believe not, Lady Wiston," Miranda said hastily, quailing at the thought of thus exposing her limbs. "Walking Mudge and shopping twice a week give me all the exercise I desire. I beg your pardon for interrupting."

"No matter, dear. You were looking for me?"

"I just wanted to check these accounts with you, the milliner's and the haberdasher's, but they can wait. In fact, I shall take Mudge to the park now, while the sun is shining. Is he in here?"

"Asleep on his cushion in the corner, as usual. Perhaps Peter would like to go with you. He must be accustomed to an active life."

"I would not for the world distract him, Lady Wiston. He is busy writing."

"He is?" In her excitement, Lady Wiston struggled to sit up. Sagaranathu gave her a hand. "I confess, I had serious doubts. I have wronged the dear boy, I fear. What splendid news!"

"Is it not? But one morning does not make a book," Miranda warned. "It is to be hoped his diligence matches his good intentions."

"Pray don't be so fierce, Miranda! Give the boy the benefit of the doubt."

"Yes, ma'am." Not without difficulty, she succeeded in stopping herself pointing out that Mr. Daviot was no longer a boy. He was a man, and the time for making allowances was surely past. Still, he had made a good beginning, with her assistance. "Do you know who Thalia is, Lady Wiston?" she asked.

"Thalia?" said her ladyship with a dubious frown. "No. Why?"

"Mr. Daviot mentioned her."

"He has a sweetheart? How delightful! Does she live in the country? I must invite her to stay."

"From the way he spoke of her, I fancy she is not a sweetheart." Or was that wishful thinking? No, of course not, she had no reason to hope he had not left behind a beloved when he went to America. "A figure from poetry, or mythology, perhaps?"

"Alack, my education was sadly lacking in the study of mythology as well as the use of the globes."

"Mine also," Miranda admitted. "The only female I recall is Venus, goddess of love, who was Cupid's mama, I believe."

"There was my namesake Artemis, of course, and Medusa, who turned people into snakes, or something of the sort. *Not* a desirable acquaintance. We shall have to ask Peter for an explanation.''

"Oh no, ma'am, pray do not trouble him.'' She would prefer not to learn from his own lips that he had compared her to someone vaguely disreputable, like Venus, or downright unpleasant, like Medusa. Not that he had any cause for the latter, but she considered him quite capable of the former, however unjustifiable. ''I daresay he has forgotten all about it.''

''Well, I believe Sir Bernard had a dictionary of Classical mythology. A number of Navy ships are named after obscure gods and goddesses and heroes, and he always liked to know who they were. No doubt the book is on a shelf in the study.''

''I shall consult it later, then, when Mr. Daviot is finished for the day. Now I'll be off and leave you to your lesson. Can you spare me a comfit to lure Mudge from the room?''

Lady Wiston produced the necessary sweetmeat. Apologizing again to Sagaranathu for the interruption, Miranda bribed the pug from his repose and set off for Hyde Park.

Her first chance to search for the dictionary was just before dinner that evening. After changing her gown, she slipped down to the study. The writing table was strewn with sheets of paper, some written all over, some with no more than a line or a paragraph. Sternly repressing the temptation to pry, Miranda crossed to the bookshelves.

The dictionary of mythology was tucked away among the volumes on navigation and naval regulations. No wonder she had never noticed it. She took it down and found the entry for Thalia.

Confusingly, there were three Thalias. Surely Mr. Daviot had not meant to compare her to a Nereid, attendant on the god of the sea? One of the Graces, perhaps. Beautiful, modest, decorous—very good so far—but oh dear, they were attendants on Aphrodite, who was the Greek version of Venus and no doubt equally immodest. Surely he did not equate his aunt with Aphrodite.

Before hunting down the third Thalia, Miranda looked

up Artemis. Goddess of the hunt, of chaste maidens, and of the changeable moon—so Lady Wiston had an excuse for her whimsical nature! Miranda chuckled.

She turned back to Thalia: one of the nine muses, who danced and sang to entertain the gods on Olympus. And Thalia was the patron of comedy. That must be it. When Peter Daviot made the comment, had she not just advised him to make his readers laugh?

She found she rather liked being compared to the merry muse.

Chapter 6

Lady Wiston looked up from her breakfast muffin as Miranda entered the dining room.

"I shall buy a horse," she announced. "A saddle horse. A hack, as I believe they are called. Yes, dear, another cup of chocolate if you please. A hunter will hardly be required."

Miranda, pouring chocolate, was glad to hear it. "You are going to take up riding?" she enquired.

"Alas, I cannot think it would be quite seemly at my age. No, for Peter. He is working far too hard."

"Mr. Daviot has certainly kept his nose to the grindstone for several days now," Miranda agreed, helping herself to eggs, a muffin, and a cup of tea. "Though he does join us every evening after dinner. Only last night you beat him handily at piquet."

"I find the captain's tricks amazingly simple," said her ladyship proudly, adding with a guilty look, "Not that I should employ them were I to play for money! But Peter takes no air or exercise. He must go to Tattersall's and buy a horse."

"Would it not be more practical to hire a mount for him when he wishes to ride?"

"He might hesitate to ask. If it is waiting for him in the mews, he can simply go off whenever he chooses. Miranda, dear, do you think he would be affronted if I were to offer him a small allowance? There must be any number of odds and ends he would like to purchase, and a gentleman ought to be able to drop into a coffee house now and then, to meet other gentlemen."

Since wheedling his way into the household, Mr. Daviot had been singularly slow to request further benefits of his fond aunt, Miranda had to admit. Only yesterday, the washerwoman had requested an interview with her to disclaim all responsibility if the gentleman's shirts entrusted to her should disintegrate into rags. Mrs. Lowenstein had told her the obliging Dilly, though it was no duty of hers, washed one of his two neckcloths every night so that he always had a clean one. Even his two coats were both worn at the elbows and beginning to fray at the cuffs.

He made no complaint. Possibly he had insufficient effrontery . . . or perhaps he was biding his time.

Miranda had thought of drawing the parlous state of his wardrobe to Lady Wiston's attention. She had decided it was hardly her place. However, now she was asked for her opinion on an allowance, the subject naturally followed.

"Doubtless Mr. Daviot would be very glad of a little money in his pocket," she said. "He is not touchy, not at all quick to take offence, but to salve his pride you might suggest he may reimburse you once his fortune is made."

"An excellent notion," her ladyship approved.

"There is another matter." Miranda hesitated. With any less amiable mistress, her suggestion would be rightly treated as a gross impertinence.

"Yes, dear?"

She ventured onward. "I daresay you have not noticed, but it has been drawn to my attention. . . . The laundry-woman, when she brought back the linen, mentioned. . . . The fact is, ma'am, Mr. Daviot's wardrobe is sadly in need of replenishment. But perhaps you mean to make him an allowance sufficient to cover such expenses?'' she added hastily.

"Dear me, no, I had not noticed any deficiency. Do you suppose I need spectacles, Miranda?'' Lady Wiston anxiously enquired.

"I doubt it, ma'am,'' Miranda reassured her. "I expect it is just that you are unaccustomed to judging people by the state of their clothes and so failed to pay any particular attention to Mr. Daviot's shabbiness.''

"Shockingly remiss of me! But how kind in you, my dear, to concern yourself for his welfare. My nephew must not go about in rags, but I fancy it would be unwise simply to hand over sufficient funds, do not you?''

"I'm sure I cannot say, Lady Wiston!''

"A young man unused to such comparative wealth,'' she mused, "might well fritter it away on trifles and be no better dressed at the end. No, he must have the tailor and hatter and haberdasher and glover and boot-maker send their bills directly to me. Pray tell him so.''

"Me! I mean, I?'' Miranda cried in dismay.

"If you please,'' her ladyship said firmly. "I shall find it difficult enough to offer him an allowance, without criticizing his clothes into the bargain.''

So that was the penalty for meddling in what was none of her affair! Mr. Daviot would be quite justified in resenting her interference. Even so easygoing a gentleman must find it humiliating for a mere companion to be involved in his financial arrangements with his aunt. Very likely he would never speak to her again, at least not in the friendly, informal fashion to which she had already become accustomed.

She would be sorry to lose his esteem and goodwill, Miranda thought unhappily, buttering her muffin.

Mr. Daviot came in a few minutes later. "Good morning, ladies,'' he said cheerfully, dropping a kiss on his aunt's cheek on his way to the sideboard. "I'm a bit late after burning the midnight oil last night. I'm glad I've caught you, Miss Carmichael. I should like your advice, if you have a moment to spare this morning."

"Have you come to a standstill already, Mr. Daviot?"

"On the contrary, it's all going along swimmingly since you set me on the right track. At least . . . but I'll have to show you."

"I must go and have a word with Cook and Mrs. Lowenstein now. After that, I am at your disposal, sir. Unless you have need of me, Lady Wiston?"

"Not until we go to the hospital, dear. The vicar threatened to call this morning, but I daresay I can hold up my end in our dispute without your presence. I hope to be able to make Mr. Sagaranathu known to him."

"Do you think it wise, ma'am?" Miranda asked.

Lady Wiston gave her a mischievous smile. "If not wise, at least interesting."

Mr. Daviot grinned. "I wouldn't miss it for the world! Never fear, Miss Carmichael, I shall make sure we finish our business in time to attend."

"Then I had best be on my way," Miranda said tartly.

Domestic concerns dealt with, she repaired to the study. Mr. Daviot was already there. He stood by his desk under the window, staring not down at the higgledy-piggledy muddle of papers but out at the rain-drenched garden.

Hearing Miranda's entrance, he swung round, a frown clearing from his brow.

"I am in some perplexity, ma'am, and sorely in need of your counsel," he said. "Do sit down."

Miranda took one of the easy chairs. Mr. Daviot perched on the edge of the writing table, his back to the window so that she could make out little of his expression. His voice, however, was unwontedly serious.

"You looked not quite happy, Miss Carmichael, when I entered the dining parlour just now. Would I be wrong in supposing my aunt had just proposed to you certain expenditures on my behalf?"

"It cannot have been for this you requested my advice!"

"Oh, that can wait," he said with an impatient gesture. "Is my conjecture correct?"

"Yes, sir, but it is not my place to approve or disapprove her ladyship's char . . . expenditures."

"Charities? I am, after all, Aunt Artemis's nearest relative."

"I do beg your pardon, Mr. Daviot," Miranda said contritely. "That was an unfortunate slip of the tongue. Of course her support of her nephew cannot be regarded as charity. May we wipe clean the slate and begin again?"

"Certainly." He smiled. "It won't be the first time."

Recalling her first request of that nature, and the kiss which preceded it, Miranda was annoyed to feel her face grow warm. As a result, it was with some asperity that she said, "Lady Wiston announced her intention of purchasing a horse for your use. She also desired my opinion as to whether the offer of an allowance would affront you. I daresay it was not quite proper to discuss the matter with a hired companion, but. . . ."

"But my aunt cannot be relied upon to do what is proper, bless her!"

"I was going to say: but I had no choice in the matter. I am heartily sorry if you are offended."

"Not in the least. She is wise to rely upon your judgement, Miss Carmichael. How can I think otherwise when I mean to do the same? Did you tell her I should be affronted?" he asked with apparent real interest.

"Hardly! As a matter of fact, I suggested her insisting on your paying back any outlay on your behalf."

"I might have guessed!" he said, laughing. "I could not credit Aunt Artemis coming up with that notion, though it was less of a demand than a hint. But all this is beside the point. You were right, I was far too grateful to feel insulted, but before I accept. . . ."

"You have not accepted?" she exclaimed in astonishment.

"Provisionally. I wish to be certain that my aunt can stand

the nonsense without discomfort to herself or a lessening of her charity to more worthy objects than myself. Short of applying to her lawyer, who would doubtless kick me down-stairs, you are the person most likely to be able to tell me just how well to pass the admiral left her."

"I see." Impressed by his consideration, a moment later Miranda found herself doubting. Was he cozening her, whether to make her think well of him, or to discover the extent of Lady Wiston's wealth for his own purposes? "I am not fully acquainted with her ladyship's affairs," she said hesitantly.

"And not sure you ought to tell me what you know. But if you fail to warn me off, you will be as responsible as I for any subsequent hardship."

"I don't know how much she proposes to give you."

"Nor I, but she spoke of a *small* allowance." Mr. Daviot grinned. "If that will not break the bank, then at least advise me whether I am to look at Tatt's for a handsome bit of blood and bone or a broken-winded nag."

"Tattersall's does not deal in broken-winded nags." She smiled. "So long as you don't spring for a race horse, I daresay there is no need to go to the opposite extreme and purchase a slug."

"That's a relief! The admiral cut up warm, I collect?"

"He added a good deal of prize money to various family inheritances, I believe. He left his entire fortune to his wife, with full use of the income. As to the capital, it is held in trust but she may bequeath it where she will. For all her charities, Lady Wiston is not purse-pinched, nor like to be."

"Then, much as I regret adding to your poor opinion of me, I shall accept her largesse."

"You mistake me, sir," Miranda cried in some agitation. The truth was, she still found herself quite unable to make up her mind about him.

The indecorous circumstances of their original meeting, together with his willingness to sponge on his aunt, had created an unfortunate first impression. Since then, he had indulged Lady Wiston's peculiarities with every appearance of sympathy; he was an amiable and amusing companion; and he had made a serious start on his book. On the other hand, his perseverance and his sincerity remained to be proved.

Miranda could not help liking him, but she was far from ready to trust him. Unwilling to tell him so, she said lamely, "It would be muttonheaded to refuse an allowance your aunt can well afford. Besides, it would distress her."

"And the last thing the admirable Miss Carmichael will permit is that anyone should distress Lady Wiston."

Mr. Daviot's jaunty tone made Miranda suspect he was quizzing her. She wished his face were better illuminated.

She took refuge in primness. "That is surely my chief duty in this household. It is only to spare her embarrassment that I allowed her to prevail upon me to . . . to mention to you. . . ." She simply could not think of a tactful way to find fault with his apparel.

"Yes, Miss Carmichael? What is the distasteful matter you are to mention to me?" There was light enough to see his teasing smile. The wretch was enjoying her discomfort!

"Your rags," she said, abandoning tact. "Her ladyship wishes you to fig yourself out decently and have the bills sent to her."

"Most willingly," he consented with a rueful laugh. "It will be a pleasure not to have Twitchell wince every time he cannot avoid setting eyes on me. There, that was not so difficult, was it? Did you fear a high dudgeon?"

"Well, it was scarcely courteous to notice your . . . disarray."

"Rags, Miss Carmichael, rags. It's too late to mince words! No dudgeon. I cannot afford to be at outs with you when I'm so desperately in need of your help."

Miranda was glad to change the subject. "With your book?" She crossed to the desk. "What is the trouble?"

Before he answered, Mr. Daviot pulled out the desk chair for her. She sat down, scanning the scattered sheets.

"Just look," he said plaintively. *"Primo,* I write fast

because the ideas are bubbling over in my head. Therefore my scrawl is illegible."

"Oh no, I can make out the odd word here and there," Miranda teased, then consoled him, "Doubtless publishers are used to deciphering a poor hand."

"I daresay, but there's worse. *Secundo,* I write a page or two, and then I think of something I left out, so I write it on a new page with asterisks and daggers and numbers to indicate where it belongs. And then I reread what I have written, and I cross out a bit here, write in a word there, until no printer in his right mind could make head or tail of it. Even I myself am confused when I attempt to put the pages in their correct order."

"Yes, I see. But all you have to do is make a fair copy before you approach a bookseller."

"I've tried it, with the beginning." He reached across for a fan of a half dozen sheets and spread them before her. "It's just the same all over again. New ideas come, I start rearranging, and in no time the muddle is as bad as ever."

"But sooner or later you must be satisfied."

"Perhaps, but when? I've no desire to hang on my aunt's sleeve for the next several years, I assure you!"

"No." Glancing up at him, Miranda had to believe him. His bright blue eyes shone with an eager sincerity impossible to mistake. Their glow made her feel quite peculiar inside. Reminded of his shocking conduct in the gardens, she hastily looked down.

"What am I to do, Miss Carmichael?"

"What you need," she said reluctantly, "is someone to copy it for you. Someone you trust to correct obvious errors, or at least to draw them to your attention before proceeding, yet someone firm enough not to allow you to make further major alterations."

"And someone with a neat, clear hand." Mr. Daviot sighed. "I know only one person who meets every criterion, but Aunt Artemis keeps her far too busy for me to ask her to undertake such a monumental task."

Miranda echoed his sigh. "If Lady Wiston is willing to grant me the time, I am willing to undertake it."

She had anticipated this, so how had he succeeded in wheedling her into it without even trying?

The incumbent of St. Mary le Bone Church had departed tight-lipped.

"The poor man finds it difficult to castigate me as he feels he ought," said Lady Wiston blithely, "because I always give a donation to the Parish poor even when I don't attend his service."

Her ladyship and the unruffled Sagaranathu retired to the green sitting room for the *yoga* lesson. Notwithstanding the rain, Mr. Daviot went off to Tattersall's on a preliminary scouting expedition.

Even if Miranda had cared to brave the drizzle, Mudge refused absolutely to set foot out of doors in such weather. Having prepared a basket of comforts for the patients of St. Bartholomew's Hospital, for once she found herself at leisure.

Returning to the study, she sat down at the writing table. When she concentrated, Mr. Daviot's handwriting was quite legible, but his system—if it could be called a system—of changes and additions took more effort to puzzle out. A bookseller might well not choose to take the trouble, she realized, especially with an unknown author.

She read through the first few pages, the attempted fair copy. He had decided after all to begin with his landing in the city of New York. The arrival within the month of the news from the capital, Washington, of the declaration of war against Britain made a fine dramatic incident.

His lively style reminded Miranda of the way he spoke. She enjoyed reading the tale. Yet something was missing.

Chin in hand, she gazed out at the dripping rose-bushes, musing. What was it the written story lacked?

She pictured Peter Daviot in this chair, herself seated at the bureau, listening as he related his adventures, watching him. Watching, that was the difference. The animation of his features had added an inexpressible sparkle to the story which the written word was unable to convey.

Finding herself smiling at the memory, Miranda called herself sternly to attention. What mattered was that readers who did not know him could not know what they were missing.

Despite her suspicion that she had been manoeuvred into offering, she rather thought she would enjoy working with him.

Unsurprisingly, Lady Wiston was perfectly willing to donate her companion's services to her nephew. Mr. Daviot made the request when they gathered at luncheon.

"Of course, dear," she said. "Mrs. Lowenstein's English is much improved, quite enough to take over the marketing. Take her with you to the shops tomorrow, Miranda, and introduce her to the shopkeepers. Only think, today I mastered the Candle!"

Mr. Daviot exchanged a glance with Miranda. "The Candle?" he enquired cautiously.

"I shall show you later. Mr. Sagaranathu says one must wait two or three hours after a light meal."

"Oh, the Candle is one of your *yoga* exercises!"

"Congratulations, Lady Wiston," said Miranda. "I look forward to a demonstration. Had you equal success this morning, Mr. Daviot, at Tattersall's?"

"Nothing quite right, but I talked to a couple of fellows and got the name of a reputable tailor. I don't aspire to Weston or Stultz! Aunt Artemis, will your sewing woman make up some shirts for me?"

He was not at all embarrassed to discuss his new wardrobe. Miranda agreed to go with him to Grafton House on the morrow to help him choose lengths of linen for shirts and muslin for cravats, as he knew nothing of the subject.

After luncheon, he went off to find the recommended tailor, while Miranda and Lady Wiston set out for St. Bartholomew's.

Lady Wiston's carriage was a vehicle of her own devising. The double-hooded landau body was slung far above the ground on great springs between four enormous wheels. More comfortable and more stable, if less dashing, than a high-perch phaeton, it gave an amazingly smooth ride and provided its passengers with an excellent view. The chief disadvantage, the need to clamber up three steps into it, made it unlikely ever to become widely popular but naturally failed to daunt Lady Wiston.

As the landau rumbled over the cobbles, her ladyship leaned back against the blue velvet squabs and turned to Miranda.

"When we return home, dear," she said, "write a note to my lawyer, if you please. Ask him to call at his earliest convenience as I wish to alter my will."

"Yes, ma'am. You are not feeling unwell, are you?"

"Not at all. I have never felt better since Mr. Sagaranathu taught me to breathe properly. You really ought to learn. But as the admiral always said, life is uncertain and one must not postpone these matters."

"Very wise." She smiled, relieved.

"I am going to make better provision for Peter. He is more in need than Sir Bernard's nephews, though of course I should not dream of cutting them out, when every penny was their uncle's to start with. They shall still have the greater share, only I wish Peter to have enough to make a fresh start."

"That seems fair enough."

"But I cannot wish the dear boy to suppose I have no faith in his making a fortune with his book, so pray don't tell him, Miranda."

"My lips are sealed, Lady Wiston," Miranda vowed.

If Peter Daviot, self-confessed adventurer, learnt that his future was secured, no doubt he would give up his authorial efforts and go off adventuring again. While Miranda would naturally be indifferent to his departure, she told herself, his aunt would be sadly grieved. And it was Miranda's business to see that nothing distressed her ladyship.

Chapter 7

Peter met his new acquaintance from Tattersall's at the tailor's shop. A first lieutenant in the Royal Navy, James Bassett was in London on half pay, awaiting a commission as commander and appointment to a ship of his own.

Under Bassett's tutelage, Peter was measured for new clothes and came to a satisfactory agreement with the snyder. The two young men repaired to a coffee house to swap stories of their adventures in distant parts of the globe.

Over a pot of ale, the time passed so pleasantly, Peter was dismayed to realize it was nearly six o'clock.

"I must be on my way," he exclaimed. "My aunt dines at seven."

"Staying with an aunt, are you?" said Bassett. Such trivial domestic details had not hitherto interrupted their conversation. "Thought we might take a bite together, but I daresay she's expecting you."

"Yes, I'd better turn up."

The lieutenant looked so wistful, Peter was about to invite him to dine in Portchester Square. He doubted Aunt Artemis would object to an unexpected guest. But then he remembered she was going to demonstrate her Candle pose, an event perhaps best kept in the family.

"See you at Tatt's tomorrow?" Bassett asked hopefully. "Not that I'm on the lookout for a horse—stands to reason, not much use on board—but it's as good a place as any to fiddle away the hours while the Admiralty's mills grind on."

"I shan't have time." Grafton House with Miss Carmichael in the morning, a bit of writing if he could fit it in, and . . . "My aunt is 'at home,' as they say, in the afternoon. If you've nothing better to do, why don't you call in?"

"I say, my dear fellow, not quite the thing. I'm not acquainted with the lady, she don't know me from Adam."

"She won't take snuff, I promise you. Aunt Artemis is anything but toplofty."

"Truth is, I ain't much in the petticoat line."

"Oh, it's not a matter of doing the pretty to a set of genteel tabbies. You'll meet some interesting characters. The fact is, my aunt's a bit of an eccentric and invites all sorts of rum people. Not that I mean to say there's anything rum about you, old chap!"

"And you're quite sure she won't take a miff?"

"Devil a bit. Lady Wiston, Nine Portchester Square, half past three to half past five."

"Lady Wiston? Not the admiral's widow? My first year as a midshipman, I sailed under Admiral Sir Bernard Wiston."

"Then dammitall, Bassett, you owe it to the old lady to come and pay your respects. She'll be delighted to see you."

They shook hands, and Peter hurried home.

" 'Er lidyship's hupstairs, guv'ner," the new footman informed him. Alfred, a weedy youth who had hitherto eked out a living as a crossing-sweeper, had run after Lady Wiston in the street to return the guinea she handed him in mistake for a smaller coin. Now profiting by his honesty, he carried out his new duties in a state of beatitude and a suit of livery two sizes too large. He would grow into it after a few good meals, according to her ladyship. At least his wig fitted, more or less.

"Dressing for dinner?" Peter asked.

"Oi 'asn't took 'ot water up yet."

Taking the stairs two at a time, Peter opened the sitting-room door, an apology for his lateness on the tip of his tongue. The words died as he saw his aunt stretched out flat on her back on the carpet, her eyes closed.

He sprang forward. Miss Carmichael stopped him, a warning hand raised. Shaking her head, she came to him.

"Hush," she whispered. "Your aunt is breathing."

"I'm glad to hear it!" he choked out.

"That is, she is practising *yoga* breathing, which is, I collect, considerably more complicated than the ordinary kind. You are just in time to witness the Candle."

"Good." Peter gave her a shaky smile. "I feared she was dead, or at least in a fit. Mutton-headed, when her cheeks are as rosy as ever."

As he spoke, Aunt Artemis's Cossack-clad legs rose slowly from the floor until they pointed straight at the ceiling. He held his breath. Her short, plump body uncurled until she was standing on her shoulders, supported by her hands on her hips. And there she stayed.

A glance at Miss Carmichael showed her spellbound, but then her brown eyes met his and he saw the mirth brimming there. If Aunt Artemis had hoped to shock and dishearten her companion, the plot was an utter failure.

His aunt's descent began equally slowly but ended with less grace when her buttocks thudded to the floor. Her legs followed suit.

"Bother!" she said crossly. "That is just what one must strive to avoid."

Miss Carmichael took a step towards her. "Have you hurt yourself, Lady Wiston?"

"No, not at all. I am well padded." She turned her head to cast a covert glance at Miss Carmichael, and looked disappointed. "Hello, Peter. I must just do the Fish to straighten out my neck. It is nothing to gape at so you may both take yourselves off. Miranda, ring for Baxter to my chamber, pray. I shall be there in a trice."

Peter followed Miss Carmichael out into the passage. Closing the door, he said, "I fear Aunt Artemis was disappointed not to show us a perfect Candle."

"She only failed at the very end. I hope I am half so vigorous at her age. Is she not amazing?"

"I wouldn't have missed it for the world," he vowed with a grin.

Seated behind her tea-table, Aunt Artemis was once again the gracious hostess. Peter devoutly prayed she would not take it into her head to demonstrate the Candle for her guests for the sake of disconcerting Miss Carmichael. Surely now she was wearing a gown such a display was too shocking even for her.

"Mr. Potts, my lady."

Daylight Danny tramped in, made his clumsy bow. "Arternoon, m'lady. My Mary sent her . . . her . . ."

"Regrets?" Miss Carmichael suggested.

"Ta, miss, them's her very words. Her sister's took poorly, see. Got a bun in the oven, she has, her seventh." He turned to Peter as the ladies absorbed this information without a blink. "What cheer, mate? Ow!" He winced.

"What is the matter, Danny?" Aunt Artemis asked. "You have not been fighting, I trust."

"Not me, m'lady. Blow me if I didn't feel my Mary's elbow in me ribs, and her a mile orf. What I oughter've said's 'Howjer do, sir.' "

"Mate will do very well," Peter assured him.

He shook his head mournfully. "She'd have me liver and lights, she would, sir. Well now, who's yon flash cove?"

Peter followed his suspicious gaze towards the door, as Twitchell announced, "Lieutenant Bassett, my lady."

Bassett, smart in his dress uniform, recoiled before the

combined assault of Daylight Danny's ferocious scowl and
the ladies' questioning looks.

"A friend of mine," Peter hastened to inform Danny,
going to meet him. "Aunt Artemis, as I told you last night,
Bassett sailed with Sir Bernard."

"Only briefly, ma'am," the sailor stammered bashfully,
"and I was only a midshipman at the time."

Aunt Artemis gave him a warm welcome and a cup of
tea. Several more people came in just then. Peter lost sight
of Bassett for a while, and when he next saw him he was
chatting quite happily with Miss Carmichael and Daylight
Danny.

In fact, Miss Carmichael, who was looking particularly
delightful in yellow-spotted muslin, appeared to hang on
his words. He must be impressing her with tales of his
exploits at sea, grossly exaggerated, no doubt. Peter
frowned.

At that moment, his aunt signalled to Miss Carmichael
to relieve her at the tea table. Whatever her interest in
Bassett's boasts, she had never ceased to observe her ladyship, and at once she excused herself. Her way took her
close to Peter.

Pausing beside him, she said with a smile, "Mr. Bassett
is charming. I am glad you invited him. One may turn up
one's nose at girls who run after any man in uniform, but
I must confess there is something prodigious dashing about
it, all the same."

She moved on. Peter wished he at least had his new coat,
since he could not aspire to the glory of a uniform.

Devil take it, what did he care? As long as she was willing
to help with his book, Miss Carmichael might admire a
thousand sailors with his good will! He went to talk to a
comely young actress whose wages his aunt supplemented
in an effort—probably doomed—to dissuade her from
taking a lover.

When the girl discovered Peter was Lady Wiston's
nephew, she hung on his words almost as keenly as Miss
Carmichael had hung on the lieutenant's. However, notic-

ing a tendency for her eyes to stray to that damned dashing uniform, he soon moved on. He happened to be quite close to Aunt Artemis when Bassett came to take his leave and thank her for her hospitality.

"Why, Mr. Bassett," she said, "I have had no chance to talk to you. If you are not engaged elsewhere, do pray stay to dinner."

Blushing, he accepted. Someone else came up to speak to her, and he turned to Peter.

"Lucky dog!" he said. "You told me Lady Wiston is eccentric, but not that she is so kind, nor that she has a companion just as kind, and pretty to boot."

"You said you are not in the petticoat line," Peter pointed out indignantly.

"No more I am. In general, I'd rather face a battery of French guns than a room full of ladies, so maybe it's just as well it'll be years before I'm able to support a wife. But Miss Carmichael made me feel at home. And what a character that Daylight Danny is!"

"He's quite a fellow, isn't he?" said Peter, mollified. "If you could but see him with 'his Mary' as he calls his wife. The top of her head scarce reaches his armpit yet her word is law."

Bassett laughed. "So I gathered. He had orders to consult Miss Carmichael about the health of his sister-in-law, who suffers from some female complaint he was too embarrassed to describe. She set the poor chap quite at his ease, said she'd talk to him privately later." He glanced around the room, now thin of company. "I expect that's where she's gone. Oh well, thanks to Lady Wiston's invitation I shall see her at dinner."

There was absolutely nothing in this speech for Peter to take exception to. Clearly the man admired Miss Carmichael as much as she admired him, but it was none of Peter's business. He'd just drop a word in Aunt Artemis's ear, a mention of Bassett's inability to support a wife. It would never do for his aunt to attempt to promote a match in that quarter.

* * *

Miranda donned her best gown for dinner, in honour
of Lieutenant Bassett's splendid uniform. Amidst Lady Wiston's unfashionable guests—not to mention her still
threadbare nephew!—the poor fellow had felt horridly
conspicuous in his gold braid, a peacock among sparrows.
Daylight Danny's all too audible comment about a "flash
cove" did not help. Danny had explained to her that the
phrase signified "a buck what's dressed up all dandified
like."

Mr. Bassett had shyly apologized to Miranda for his *faux
pas*. She assured him her ladyship could only take his smart-
ness as a compliment. Presenting Danny to him, she
encouraged the young officer to talk about his voyages
and he soon felt quite comfortable.

She had not been able to resist quizzing Mr. Daviot about
his friend's magnificence, though she would never have
said a word had not his own shabbiness been well on the
way to relief.

Her evening dress was as fine as Lady Wiston could
persuade her to accept. The white sarcenet slip had amber
silk roses set on around the hem; the shorter frock of
amber net was caught up at the side with a posy of white
roses, and another rose adorned the brief bodice. It went
perfectly with Miranda's sole ornament, a necklace of
amber beads, a gift from her father which he had never
pawned only because she kept it well hidden from him.

Altogether she felt very fine, much too fine for a hired
companion. She thought of leaving off the necklace, but
without it the neckline looked far too low and even less
suitable for a companion.

Lady Wiston did not think so. "Charming, dear," she
said with approval when she and Miranda met at the top
of the stairs. She too was dressed to the nines. In forest
green silk festooned with white lace, a collar of pearls, and
white curls topped with a green toque, she looked rather
like an evergreen tree bedecked with snow.

A pang of guilt struck Miranda. "I fear Mr. Daviot, in his aged attire, will be sadly piqued."

"Fiddlesticks! We have donned our finery in honour of his friend, have we not? It will be very pleasant to have a naval gentleman at table, I vow. Quite like the old days. I am very glad Peter has made Mr. Bassett's acquaintance. A young man ought not to be tied to an old lady's apron strings."

Descending the stairs, they heard an uproar from the drawing room below. A volley of high, sharp barks vied with a string of distinctly seafaring oaths.

"Oh heavens!" cried Miranda, picking up her skirts. "Mudge has taken exception to Mr. Bassett."

She ran down, bursting into the room from the hall just as Alfred dashed in from the dining room next door. With great presence of mind, the new footman flung a napkin over the pug's head. Startled by his unexpected blindness, Mudge stopped yapping and started whining. A moment later Lady Wiston puffed in with a handful of comfits.

The dog was bribed into temporary complaisance; Alfred was congratulated, Mr. Bassett apologized to, and they all went in to dinner.

Lady Wiston asked the lieutenant about his voyage with the Admiral, and then about his travels since. "And what brings you to London?" she enquired at last.

"I'm waiting on a promotion and a posting, ma'am. Lord Derwent has recommended me to a command— Captain Hurst as was ; I sailed under him—but the Admiralty moves slowly, especially since the peace. One must keep reminding them."

"I remember very well! So you are tied to Town for the present. Where do you stay?"

"I have taken a room in a lodging-house in Westminster, ma'am."

"Is it comfortable? Do they take good care of you?"

"Not very," admitted Mr. Bassett, his expression saying *not at all,* "but I don't care much for that. I should be very happy with such quarters in Portsmouth or Plymouth, or anywhere where there are plenty of our fellows about. The worst of it is, I have small acquaintance in London and most of them gone down to the country for the summer. I count it mighty good fortune to have fallen in with Daviot, and dev . . . dashed kind in him to present me to you, ma'am, and Miss Carmichael.''

Her ladyship gave Miranda an odd, considering look. What was she up to now? She glanced at Mr. Daviot, then turned back to Mr. Bassett.

"I have a splendid notion," she said briskly. "Why do you not come and stay here?"

"Oh but, ma'am, I couldn't dream of imposing. . . ."

"Fiddlesticks. When Sir Bernard was alive, we often had young officers to stay." She overruled Mr. Bassett's admittedly half-hearted protests. "Miranda, after dinner, pray tell Mrs. Lowenstein to have a bed made up in one of the spare chambers."

"Yes, ma'am," Miranda assented, hiding her qualms. After all, what did they know of Mr. Bassett? He seemed a charming, shy, ingenuous young man, but Mr. Daviot had scraped up an acquaintance with him only yesterday— and in any case, Mr. Daviot's approval could scarce be regarded as evidence of trustworthiness. Inviting him to the at-home, even to dinner, was one thing. Having him stay in the house was quite another.

When she and Lady Wiston retired to the drawing room, leaving the gentlemen to the Admiral's port, Miranda ventured a mild remonstrance.

"A naval commission is no guarantee of respectability," she pointed out.

Lady Wiston's eyes twinkled. "No, indeed, dear. I have known some far from respectable officers in my time! But Mr. Bassett is an amiable young man and, besides, he sailed with Sir Bernard. I have no fear of our being murdered in our beds. Should he decamp with the silver, well, I daresay his need is greater than mine."

With that Miranda was forced to content herself. She had no opportunity to broach the subject with Mr. Daviot that evening, for he and Mr. Bassett went off to fetch the latter's things from his lodging.

Not being murdered in her bed, Miranda was down early next morning as usual to take Mudge out into the square, a task which could not be delegated as he refused to go with anyone else. Twitchell did not report the silver vanished. Her misgivings had been for nothing.

When she and the pug returned to the house, she found Mr. Daviot alone in the dining parlour.

"I'm sorry about Bassett," he said. "I saw last night you weren't quite happy about his removing hither."

"Oh dear, was it so obvious?"

"You hid it well. I very much doubt the others noticed, but I made a point of observing your reaction. I trust you don't hold me responsible? When I asked him to call, I never for a moment expected Aunt Artemis to add him to the household."

"With Lady Wiston, it is as well to expect the unexpected. Still, I cannot hold you to blame. Mr. Bassett is a great deal more presentable than many of those she invites to the house on a moment's whim! I daresay he will make a pleasant addition to our company."

Mr. Daviot looked as if that was not quite what he wished to hear, but all he said was, "He's a good enough fellow. We must hope he is not shocked by my aunt's whims, or not so much as to show disrespect."

Miranda laughed. "That is highly unlikely. He held the admiral very much in awe, I believe. I doubt he is capable of seeing any fault in Sir Bernard's widow, even had he no cause for gratitude. He plainly considers himself very much obliged."

"His garret was certainly far from a desirable residence," Mr. Daviot admitted. "I'd a thousand times rather live in an Iroquois long-house. Are you at liberty to assist me this morning?"

"Certainly. You know Lady Wiston has released me from other duties for that purpose."

"I don't wish you regard it as a duty," he said roughly,

to Miranda's surprise. "If you prefer not to, I shall make all right with my aunt."

"That is not what I meant. I am perfectly content to help you, and certain it will be interesting. I did offer my services, did I not?"

"Yes." He grinned ruefully. "After I backed you into a corner. Promise you will tell me if you begin to find it tedious? Today, at least, will not be all transcribing my scrawl. I want to consult you as to the best way to combine information about the customs of the Iroquois with lively incidents, so as not to send my readers to sleep."

Lady Wiston and Mr. Bassett came in together just then. Miriam soon found it was indeed pleasant to have a bashfully admiring gentleman about the house. He went off to the Admiralty while she was working with Mr. Daviot, but he made a point of returning to escort her when she took Mudge to the Park. Mudge resigned himself to the lieutenant's presence, and attacked his ankles no more often than those of the rest of the household.

Life settled into a new pattern. Mr. Daviot bought a horse, and thereafter devoted somewhat less of his time to his *magnum opus*. Also, he and Bassett went out on the town now and then, as the state of their thin purses allowed. Nonetheless, the piles of papers in the study continued to grow in a most satisfactory fashion.

Late one morning, a fortnight after Mr. Bassett's advent in Portchester Square, he was at the Admiralty as usual. Lady Wiston, above stairs at her lesson with Mr. Sagaranathu, was "not at home" to callers. Mr. Daviot and Miranda were in the study, laughing over one of the misunderstandings which had dogged his early days among the Iroquois when someone knocked on the door.

Orders had been given that they were not to be disturbed short of an emergency. Miranda jumped up, convinced Lady Wiston must have injured herself attempting some exotic pose.

"Come in," she cried, starting for the door.

It opened to reveal Twitchell. "Beg pardon for interrupting, miss, but. . . ." He stopped and glanced back as impatient footsteps sounded in the passage behind him.

"She will not deny *me!*" said an imperious voice.

Twitchell turned back to Miranda, his shoulders rising a fraction of an inch in an almost imperceptible shrug. "Lord Snell," he announced.

Chapter 8

Godfrey Aloysius Snell, Baron, of Northwaite Hall in Derbyshire, was a tall, fair, well-built gentleman something above thirty years of age. His superbly fitted blue morning coat, snowy linen, buff pantaloons, and glossy Hessians became him to perfection. In general a haughty expression somewhat marred his otherwise handsome features, but as he entered the study that July morning, he was smiling.

"How do you do, Miss Carmichael."

"My lord." Miranda curtsied, flattered by the smile and by his recalling her name. "I regret that Lady Wiston is unable to receive you just now. May I present her nephew, Mr. Daviot?"

Bowing, the gentlemen eyed each other assessingly. Peter Daviot was the taller by an inch or two, but his lanky frame was unimpressive next to Lord Snell's powerful figure. Though new, his clothes could not match those of Weston's make. His fingers were ink-stained, his brown hair rumpled where he had clutched his head in the throes of composition.

"I fear I have interrupted your labours, Daviot," said Lord Snell, gracious yet dismissive.

"A *brief* respite is seldom unwelcome, Snell."

His lordship's lips tightened, whether because of the pointed "brief" or because he had expected to be addressed by his title.

Miranda hurried into the breach. "Mr. Daviot is recently come from America, sir. He is writing about his experiences."

"Admirable." The sarcastic inflection was unmistakable.

"Lady Wiston will be down in half an hour or so for luncheon, my lord. Do you wish to wait? May I offer you some refreshment in the meantime?"

"Thank you, ma'am, a glass of my late uncle's excellent Madeira would not come amiss." Again he smiled at her. "And I was hoping to speak to you privately before I see my aunt."

"Shall we go to the drawing room? Pray excuse me, Mr. Daviot. I shall catch up with the work this afternoon, I promise you."

"Pray do not feel obliged, Miss Carmichael," said Mr. Daviot ironically. "I see you have other fish to fry."

She gave him a hurt glance. Surely he must understand that her first duty was to attend to her employer's noble relative? "I shall catch up," she repeated and preceded Lord Snell to the drawing room.

Eustace brought the Madeira. Miranda, perched slightly nervously on the edge of her seat, was glad the competent footman had not yet left, for the ramshackle Alfred would have given the baron a lamentable shock. His lordship sniffed the wine, tasted it.

"Aah." He breathed a sigh of satisfaction and sipped again. "Sir Bernard knew how to choose his wines. I've nothing better in my cellars."

Miranda uttered a polite murmur.

"Miss Carmichael," he continued, "I must tell you that I am just this instant arrived in Town. I wish to enquire of you as to whether it would inconvenience my aunt Wiston to accommodate me for a few days. I know her hospitable notions! She will never admit to any impediment once she discovers that my alternative is a hotel. My town house is all shut up for the summer, you see."

Miranda would have found it impossible to deny him even if every chamber in the house were occupied, but how considerate of him to ask! Why had she ever thought him more than a trifle top-lofty?

"Lady Wiston will certainly not allow you to go to a hotel, my lord," she said. "Even with Mr. Daviot and Mr. Bassett, we have a chamber available for you."

"Mr. Bassett? Another relative?"

"Lieutenant Bassett is a naval officer."

"Ah, an old friend, no doubt."

"He did sail under the admiral, sir, but Lady Wiston never met him, nor heard of him that she recalls. He is a recent acquaintance of Mr. Daviot."

Lord Snell's eyebrows rose. "Indeed!" he said with displeasure.

"Her ladyship, not Mr. Daviot, invited Mr. Bassett to stay while he is in London," Miranda hastened to assure him.

"Indeed," his lordship repeated more reflectively. "I fear report has understated matters."

"Report?" she asked uneasily.

"Miss Carmichael, I find I must take you into my confidence. Perhaps you are aware that Lady Wiston's solicitor, Bradshaw, called upon her recently, at her request?"

"Yes, I wrote the note summoning him. But I was not present at the interview."

"Then you cannot know that my aunt harangued—yes, I believe harangued is the proper term—harangued Bradshaw on the shocking conditions inside Newgate, of which she claimed personal experience."

"Not experience exactly, my lord. We visited the prison in company with Elizabeth Fry, the Quaker reformer, and found conditions to be truly shocking." Miranda had tried to drive from her mind the memories of ragged, half-starved women and children crammed pell-mell into dark, filthy, overcrowded cells. Debtors and prisoners on remand, not yet convicted of any crime, rubbed shoulders with prostitutes, thieves and murderers.

"It is certainly not a fit place for a gentlewoman to visit!"

"It was dreadful. I believe her ladyship gave Mrs. Fry a large donation."

"So Bradshaw informed me. He felt, and I must agree, that criminals are no fitting objects of charity. You must understand that I am joint trustee with him of the funds left by my late uncle. Bradshaw is alarmed lest Lady Wiston find herself outrunning the constable, as the phrase goes, and in need of broaching her capital, an expedient both of us should be loath to permit. Diminished capital means diminished income. I should hate to see my uncle's widow struggling in straitened circumstances."

The sentiment did him credit, Miranda thought. "You need have no fear of that, sir. Lady Wiston is prodigious careful never to overspend her income. She entrusts me with the keeping of her accounts, so I am in a position to reassure you."

"Splendid," said Lord Snell, but then he frowned. "However, this prison business, together with her inviting a complete stranger to reside with her, makes one wonder whether one may rely upon her to continue in her sensible course."

"Her ladyship is perfectly sensible, sir, in spite of her little quirks."

"You are admirably loyal, Miss Carmichael. We all of us want only what is best for Lady Wiston. At least, I daresay Mr. Daviot's chief concern is that she should remain able to support him."

"I believe Mr. Daviot to be sincerely fond of his aunt, my lord," Miranda said, jumping to his defence although she acknowledged to herself some truth in Lord Snell's surmise. But whatever his other motives, Mr. Daviot *did* hold Lady Wiston in great affection, of that she was convinced.

His lordship appeared unconvinced, but forebore to press the point.

The drawing-room door opened and Lady Wiston trotted in. "My dear Godfrey," she cried. "Twitchell told me you were come."

Mudge scuttled past her and with a bellicose yip assaulted Lord Snell's gleaming boots. Jumping to his feet, his lordship yelled. Miranda sprang up and lunged at the pug. Lady Wiston scattered comfits across the carpet with liberal abandon.

Alfred appeared in the doorway, struggling out of his coat. "Oi'll get 'im, miss," he shouted, as Miranda seized Mudge's collar. Distracted by the blissful aroma of aniseed, the pug failed to maim her.

"I have him under control, thank you, Alfred. Pray take him away and shut him up for the present."

Gingerly accepting custody, the footman-in-training addressed Lord Snell. "Slobbered on them boots, 'as 'e, your lordship? Hoby's make Oi'd say by the look on 'em, and Oi knows boots, Oi does, watching 'em day in, day out like Oi used to. Whip 'em off and Oi'll clean 'em up nice."

"I never permit anyone but my man to touch my boots," said Lord Snell icily.

"Oi'll tell 'im to come and get 'em, then. Oi'd better come back meself and pick up them comfits, my lady, afore they gets trod in. Just you leave 'em to me, ducky." With a cheery wave he departed, Mudge under one arm.

"What an obliging boy he is, Miranda," said Lady Wiston, "and so willing to learn, Twitchell tells me. I am sorry about Mudge, Godfrey. The naughty creature must have forgotten you. He generally only attacks strangers with quite such gusto. He has not done any permanent damage to your boots, has he?"

Lord Snell glared down at his Hessians. "I believe not, Aunt. I wonder that you don't dispose of the beast."

"I only wish I might, but poor dear Lady Egbert entrusted him to my care. Do sit down again, dear boy, and tell me what brings you to Town."

As she seated herself, Lord Snell looked at her properly

for the first time. With a stunned expression, he blinked at the Cossack trousers and smock. Then he caught sight of something beyond her and his mouth dropped open. Miranda glanced round. Unnoticed, Sagaranathu had followed Lady Wiston into the drawing room.

After the pug, the footman, and her ladyship's costume, the shabby, dark-skinned Lascar might well discompose even so urbane a gentleman as the baron! Sagaranathu appeared quite at his ease, his face as bland as ever though Miranda guessed he had witnessed the preceding chaos. Mr. Daviot would have laughed till he cried, she was sure. Unlike him, the seaman had a proper sense of decorum.

"Good morning, sir," she said.

He bowed to her as Lady Wiston swung round. "My dear Mr. Sagaranathu, my wits have gone a-begging, I do declare. Godfrey, let me present my teacher, Mr. Sagaranathu." Disregarding Lord Snell's infinitesimal nod in response to the Lascar's polite bow, she went on happily, "He is taking luncheon with us today. Miranda, you did remind Cook that Mr. Sagaranathu does not eat meat?"

"First thing this morning, ma'am."

"You will stay to luncheon, will you not, Godfrey?"

Lord Snell appeared to be in two minds. He could not very well refuse to sit down with his aunt's beggarly guest and then request accommodation.

Miranda was confident good manners would win the struggle, as proved the case. "Thank you, ma'am," he said smoothly, "I shall be delighted to join you. In fact, I was hoping you might be able to put me up for a few days. Any garret will do."

"Garret! That will not be necessary. Of course you must stay here."

"I shall go and start removing my things at once, Lady Wiston," said Miranda.

"No, no, dear, you are not to put yourself out. But do go and tell Mrs. Lowenstein to have the bed made up in the—let me see, Peter is in the blue chamber, and Mr.

Bassett in the rose. You shall have the gold chamber, God-frey. How pleasant it will be to have a houseful of gen-tlemen!"

Despite its impressive name, the gold chamber was small and inconvenient and up two pair of stairs. On her way to the housekeeper's room, Miriam wondered if she ought to remove from her spacious chamber on the first floor in spite of Lady Wiston's instructions. The blue chamber might do very well for Mr. Daviot, who was not averse to sleeping under a bush, but a peer of the realm was entitled to better.

However, Lady Wiston quite often popped in, clad in nothing but her bedgown and a shawl, to see Miranda. It would not do to have her wandering about the house in such garb in search of her companion. Best to arrange matters as she wished. After all, Lord Snell meant to stay only a few days, and he could use the fourth spare chamber as a dressing room.

What a fine, upstanding gentleman he was, so flatteringly courteous to a mere companion, so concerned for his uncle's widow. And how noble of him to condescend to sit down to a meal with Sagaranathu, who, however estima-ble, was scarcely the sort of person his lordship was accus-tomed to consort with.

It was a shame Mr. Daviot had so obviously taken the baron in instant dislike. Perhaps it was inevitable. Lord Snell was everything he was not, titled, wealthy, fashion-able, polished, not to mention settled and dependable. If Lady Wiston did ever run into difficulties, his lordship could be relied upon to rush to the rescue, as he had now at the least hint of trouble. Mr. Daviot might wish her well, but an irresponsible adventurer was not to be depended on in adversity.

Miranda sighed. She liked Mr. Daviot, and she was far more comfortable in his company than Lord Snell's, but his lordship's character was undeniably infinitely more admirable.

* * *

That afternoon the gentlemen all went out about their own business or pleasure. Lady Wiston proposed to visit two or three of her charity families, and to drive on to Bond Street to the shops and Hookham's Library. Miranda begged leave to stay at home to finish transcribing Mr. Daviot's latest efforts.

Miranda saw her ladyship off. She was escorted by her abigail, a tall, grizzled woman silently and rather grimly devoted to her mistress, and by both footmen. Her stalwart coachman, Ted, was up on the box of the high-perch landau.

Undaunted by the climb into her carriage, Lady Wiston was no more cowed by the whistles and catcalls her vehicle invariably evoked from the vulgar in the less salubrious parts of town. However, before they set off, Miranda made a point of sternly forbidding Alfred to respond with his fists to such inevitable discourtesies.

Miranda retreated to the study, mended a pen, and set to work. As she wrote, now and then a smile flitted across her face when she came to a phrase or an anecdote she had discussed with Mr. Daviot.

Because of their debates, for the most part she puzzled out the complex insertions and changes without great difficulty, feeling almost as if she could read his mind. She had nearly finished when she came to a passage with so many arrows and asterisks she found herself at a loss.

Frowning over the tangle, she was beginning to make sense of it when the door opened and Lord Snell came in.

"Miss Carmichael, I. . . ."

Miranda held up her hand. "Pray excuse me just a moment, sir." Yes, that bit belonged there, which meant this word squeezed in must be canoe, not tattoo. She must write it all out while it was fresh in her mind.

She turned back to Lord Snell. To her dismay he looked offended. "I do beg your pardon, my lord, but I fear I must beg your indulgence for ten minutes or so. I *promised* Mr. Daviot to complete this transcription today. Afterwards I shall be entirely at your disposal.''

"By all means continue, ma'am," he said with somewhat forced graciousness. "Your diligence and your fidelity to your word are estimable."

He went over to the world map on the wall and stood there studying it. Miranda returned to her work. The temptation to hurry was near irresistible, but Lord Snell admired her trustworthiness and Mr. Daviot trusted her to write with her usual neatness.

At least, she supposed he did, though he had seemed to believe she meant to ignore his claims in favour of Lord Snell. With a sigh, she blotted the final line.

"I am sorry to have kept you waiting, my lord. You wished to speak to me?"

"I find myself perplexed, Miss Carmichael. Rather than risk perturbing my Aunt Wiston, I turn to you for answers."

"I will answer what I can, sir."

"Thank you." He sat down. "Lady Wiston gave what I must endeavour to regard as an adequate reason for keeping her vicious animal. Perhaps you can explain why she employs as footman a guttersnipe who appears to have been recently dragged in off the street? Surely, especially in the summer, well-trained servants are not difficult to come by?"

"Alfred *was* recently rescued from the street, sir. All servants must begin their training somewhere, and Lady Wiston chooses to give unfortunates a chance to find a decent place."

"I see. A pity the household must be inconvenienced by her charitable impulses. The Lascar is another charity case, no doubt, though there was some mention of his being my aunt's teacher. What does he presume to . . . ?"

The door burst open. Alfred appeared, breathless and wigless, on the threshold.

"Oi'm to warn you, miss," he panted, " 'er la'ship's

nabbed a bung-nipper and tapped 'is claret somefing cruel.''

Miranda jumped up in alarm. "Lady Wiston is badly hurt?" she demanded, trying to make sense of the extraordinary message. She hurried to take down her medicine chest, though it was sadly inadequate in the face of a serious injury. "Is a surgeon sent for?"

"Ain't no call for a sawbones, miss, nor it ain't 'er la'ship what's in queer stirrups." Alfred took the chest from her and dropped it with a thump on the table on top of Mr. Daviot's papers. "It's the file what got 'is nob scuttled."

"Speak plain English, boy!" snapped Lord Snell as Miranda felt in her pocket for the key to the chest.

"The cove's bleeding like blood was water," said the footman succinctly.

"Then tell them to bring him to me in the scullery," Miranda said calmly, opening the chest and taking out basilicum and bandages.

Alfred darted out, but from the passage was heard tramping feet and a tirade of which Miranda understood not one word in ten. The words she understood made her glad the rest was incomprehensible. Lady Wiston pattered in, followed by a grimy, unshaven man of indeterminate years with blood pouring down his foxy face and Eustace's hand on his collar.

"I am afraid I hit him rather hard, Miranda," said Lady Wiston guiltily. "He tried to steal my reticule as I descended from the carriage and, having my new umbrella in my hand, I struck out without thinking. Eustace believes no serious damage is done. Pray bind up his head."

"Not here!" expostulated Lord Snell.

"No, take him to the scullery, please, Eustace," said Miranda.

Lord Snell protested, "I meant the villain should be turned over to a constable, who will doubtless provide any necessary care."

"He has been punished enough. I did not intend to hit so hard."

Miranda left them arguing and followed the footmen and the pickpocket down the back stairs. His lordship was probably right, she reflected, but his aunt would undoubtedly win the argument. Never a dull moment!

"I am beginning to give up hope, Peter," said Aunt Artemis gloomily. "There she was actually closeted with Godfrey in the study, when I marched in and insisted on her physicking the rascal. A dirty fellow, with the rattiest face you have ever set eyes on and blood pouring down, and did she burst into tears? My dear, she did not so much as blink! What am I to do?"

Peter dropped into the chair beside her dressing-table. "Dashed if I know, Aunt," he said with equal gloom.

His blue devils arose from a different cause. He was afraid his aunt's plotting might succeed. Miss Carmichael deserved better than that starchy, pompous oaf, even if she did show signs of being impressed by his title and taken in by his handsome face and unctuous manner. At the very least, his presence disrupted a pleasant friendship.

"Perhaps I should have made her move out of the second best chamber," Aunt Artemis sighed, "but I know how unsettling it is to have no space one can truly call one's own."

"She offered to remove," Peter reminded her, "so she'd not have been overset if you had agreed. Shall you give up the *yoga,* since that too has failed?"

"Oh no, dear, the health benefits are already evident. I did hope Miranda would not like my standing on my head, but her composure remained quite unshaken."

"Your trouble is, she's just too even-tempered." He fingered his cheek, recalling the slap Miss Carmichael had delivered when he kissed her. Yet five minutes later she had offered to bind up his bitten hand.

"She is such a delightful girl," said his aunt. "Had I been blessed with children, I should have liked a daughter just like Miranda. I do want to see her happily settled. I

shall have to think of something else. Or perhaps Godfrey
will offer for her in spite of her cheerfulness. He is paying
her far more attention than he ever did in the Spring. Do
you think he is trying to fix his interest?''

"Who can guess?" Peter grunted sourly.

"I shall send Baxter to dress her hair," Lady Wiston
decided.

"Don't do that, ma'am! Er . . . Lord Snell might suppose
her to be making a dead set at him."

"You are right, that would never do. She is quite pretty
enough to catch him without artifice, is she not?''

"No doubt," he reluctantly agreed.

Maybe Godfrey Snell had been suddenly struck by Miss
Carmichael's unquestionable charms. But Peter, proceeding to his own chamber to change for dinner, had an
uneasy feeling that his lordship was involved in a darker,
deeper, more devious plot than ever his amiable aunt had
contemplated.

Chapter 9

"And close with 'your affectionate aunt,' dear," Lady Wiston dictated. "It is such a shame Frederick and Aurelia are so rarely able to come up to Town."

Seated at the small writing table in the green sitting room, Miranda blotted the letter and presented it to her ladyship to be signed. "Do you wish to write to Lady Garston now, ma'am?" she asked. "If so, I must first make a new pen."

"I'll make it for you," offered Mr. Daviot, turning from the window where he stood in conversation with Mr. Bassett.

"Not before dinner, Miranda dear. I fear your hand will grow cramped from so much writing. Besides, I have just time enough for my exercises before I change, and you know how I have to concentrate. I cannot dictate at the same time."

Lady Wiston lowered herself to the carpet as Miranda returned to the desk to fold, seal and direct the letter. Mr. Daviot was already sharpening a new quill for her future use.

"Do you get cramps in your hand?" he asked in a low voice. "I've no wish to cause any such discomfort."

"No, I cannot claim to suffer. Mr. Sagaranathu suggested some exercises for the hand which I daresay have helped."

"You must show me. And you must tell me if I work you too hard!"

Miranda smiled at him. "I shall, but you know I enjoy it. Now watch. It is quite simple."

Intrigued, Mr. Bassett came to join them, and soon they were all three stretching and clenching their hands, circling their wrists, pretending to play upon an imaginary piano. They were inured by now to Lady Wiston's *yoga,* only speaking softly so as not to distract her.

"Good Lord, ma'am!" Lord Snell's voice rang out in the quiet room. "What *are* you about?"

Miranda and Mr. Daviot exchanged a brief glance of dismay. His lordship would never understand, Miranda thought, turning towards him, her finger to her lips. Lady Wiston, upside down in a perfect Candle, smiled an upside-down smile but said nothing.

"Her ladyship is concentrating on her breathing," Miranda explained, crossing swiftly to Lord Snell. "Pray do not interrupt, sir, or she may lose her balance and hurt herself."

She ventured to put a hand on his arm and urge him over towards the others. Looking grave, he complied.

"My aunt is an enterprising lady, is she not, Snell?" said Mr. Daviot. "Never fear, she knows what she is about."

"Is she not amazing?" Mr. Bassett put in eagerly. "Elderly ladies in general don't have much opportunity to benefit from vigorous exercise, but Lady Wiston makes her own."

"Her ladyship already feels the benefit," Miranda assured Lord Snell, "though she has been practising *yoga* only a fortnight or three weeks."

He continued to look grave. "I am sure she has convinced you, Miss Carmichael, of the benefit, or else you would have made every effort to dissuade her from such

extraordinary and undignified behaviour. What can have
put the notion into her head?"

"This is what Mr. Sagaranathu teaches her. You recall
asking me the other day? I had no chance at the time to
explain."

"Ah. I was certain the fellow was taking advantage of
her in some fashion. No doubt he pockets exorbitant fees
for teaching this nonsense. The charlatan has bamboozled
her."

Miranda was again impressed by his readiness to protect
Lady Wiston, though in this case she believed him incor-
rect. As she hesitated, wondering how to contradict without
offending him, Mr. Daviot took up the challenge.

"You're quite out in your reckoning there, old chap,"
he jeered. "Sagaranathu is an excellent fellow, a natural
gentleman and learned to boot. You're too quick to value
a man by his looks. We can't all patronize Weston and
Hoby."

Lord Snell loftily ignored the imputations of error and
overhasty judgement. "Learned, is he? Cambridge?
Oxford? Paris, perhaps, or Bologna?"

"He's learned in the ways of his own people, and has
increased his learning by wide travel and acute observation.
Bassett will join me in attesting to the broadening effects
of travel on the mind."

Mr. Bassett nodded with an air which suggested he would
have much preferred to be left out of their dispute.

"Indeed, my lord," said Miranda, "Mr. Sagaranathu is
most gentlemanlike and knowledgeable. He spoke little
when he took luncheon with us the other day, but his
manners were perfectly unexceptionable, were they not?"

"A charlatan must needs adapt his manners to his company." Lord Snell glanced thoughtfully at Lady Wiston,
now sitting on the carpet with her forehead approaching
her knees. Turning back to Miranda, he smiled at her with
a slight bow. "But I should not dream of contradicting a
lady. I will concede that he appeared inoffensive."

She returned his smile. The baron was a most gallant

gentleman. Mr. Daviot would do well to emulate his good breeding instead of seizing every opening to gibe at him.

On the whole, the cousins-by-marriage contrived to conceal their mutual antipathy from their aunt. Nonetheless, Miranda was astonished when, at dinner that evening, Lord Snell addressed Mr. Daviot with an affability which was almost jovial.

"You must have had a great many interesting experiences in America, Daviot. How goes the book?"

Mr. Daviot raised his eyebrows. "Quite well," he said tersely.

"I suppose you are a member of the Explorers' Club? Or has the name been changed to the Travellers' Club? There was some talk of it, I believe."

"I don't know. I wasn't aware of its existence."

"You must join, Peter," said Lady Wiston at once. "Only think what fascinating people you are bound to meet at a club with such a name."

"I daresay, Aunt, and I confess I should like to, but I imagine one must know some of them before one can become a member."

Lord Snell nodded. "I am acquainted with several members, two or three of whom are quite likely in Town at present. If you wish, I shall introduce you and vouch for your being qualified. The chief prerequisite, I understand, is having travelled at least five hundred miles in a straight line from London."

Mr. Daviot gave him a curious, mistrustful look. "That I have done," he said guardedly.

"Five hundred miles," Mr. Bassett guffawed. " 'Tis little enough, by my faith!"

"Nothing to you seafaring men," his lordship agreed. "You must find life ashore tedious. Would you like me to put in a good word for you at the Admiralty?"

"Thank you, my lord," the young lieutenant stammered. "I have recommendations from Lord Derwent and Lady Wiston, but another just might speed them up. It's deuced obliging of you."

"Not at all. The nation cannot afford to waste a good officer's time. The peace with France makes little difference, considering England's interests all over the world."

Lady Wiston beamed at him. "I did not realize you had such an excellent grasp of naval matters, Godfrey. Sir Bernard was used to say that the Army could go hang, for it is the Navy keeps England strong."

"Sacrilege, Aunt Artemis," Mr. Daviot teased, "since Wellington's great victory at Waterloo."

"Not at all! The Duke could not have fought and won that battle if the Navy had failed to keep Buonaparte from invading our shores for so many years."

"Nor had they failed to let him escape from Elba!"

Her ladyship continued her lively defence of the vital importance of the Royal Navy. Miranda noticed that Lord Snell watched and listened with a slight frown. She hoped he did not disapprove of females expressing opinions on serious subjects—and with such vigour. Though it might be considered forward, even indecorous, conduct in a young woman, surely a certain license must be granted at Lady Wiston's age.

No doubt his lordship simply disagreed with her ideas. Unlike Mr. Daviot, he was far too polite to argue with his aunt, though she was thoroughly enjoying the debate. She had a supporter in Mr. Bassett who seconded her with enthusiasm whenever called upon.

At last Mr. Daviot appealed to Miranda. "Come, Miss Carmichael, don't let me be outnumbered. Will you not uphold the supremacy of the Army? Only think of their dashing scarlet coats!"

"If a scarlet coat were infallible proof of superior excellence, sir," she retorted, laughing, "you might buy one for yourself."

"And how am I to take that, ma'am?" he asked with a grin. "Are you saying a scarlet coat is not infallible, and if I donned one I should remain my imperfect self? Or do you mean that I am perfection's self and only want a scarlet coat to prove it?"

"You may take it as you please, Mr. Daviot, but do not expect me to uphold the Army in the admiral's house."

"Bravo, ma'am!" cried Mr. Bassett.

"Alas, I am outgunned, I fear. The admiral's shade cannot be denied. Aunt, I concede."

"Very good, dear. Have another veal cutlet to console you."

Lord Snell passed the dish of cutlets. "If you are not otherwise engaged tomorrow afternoon, Daviot," he said, "shall we approach those Explorers' Club members I spoke of?"

Miranda rather wondered at his persisting when his first offer had received so ungracious a response. His motive could only be to give his aunt pleasure, for he had no possible reason to conciliate her nephew.

Indeed, Mr. Daviot seemed surprised. The gaze he turned on his would-be benefactor was momentarily penetrating. Somehow it reminded Miranda that he had survived among the fierce Iroquois for several years.

Then he smiled and was his usual irreverent self. "You are too kind," he said. "Yes, I am free tomorrow."

"Then name the hour, and I am at your disposal." Their outing arranged, Lord Snell turned to Miranda. "That will leave me time to try out the new curricle I am disposed to purchase. Will you do me the honour, Miss Carmichael, of joining me for a turn in the Park?"

"M-me?"

"It will be job-horses, I fear, as I left my team in Derbyshire, but I hope that will not deter you. I am accounted a tolerable whip, ma'am, and will engage not to overturn you."

"Of course not, but. . . ." Overwhelmed by the honour, all on her side, Miranda turned a gaze of entreaty on Lady Wiston.

"You must certainly go, dear. You have been getting too little fresh air recently. We cannot allow the roses to fade from your cheeks."

Miranda blushed, the heat in her face intensifying as all

three gentlemen looked at her. Lord Snell's expression was enigmatic, Mr. Daviot's ironical, Mr. Bassett's frankly admiring. She hastily lowered her eyes.

"Thank you, my lord, I shall look forward to it."

Was it possible his lordship did not consider a hired companion beneath him? Her father had been a gentleman, after all, though a happy-go-lucky and improvident one.

She called herself severely to task. A drive in Hyde Park was not a proposal of marriage. During the Season, when London was full of elegant, accomplished, and well-dowered young ladies, Lord Snell had scarcely noticed her existence, she reminded herself. No doubt he simply liked female company when taking the air, perhaps just to admire his handling of the ribbons. A touch of vanity was an endearing crack in the shell of his superiority.

It was excessively generous in him to offer his assistance to Mr. Daviot and Mr. Bassett, especially since Mr. Daviot had been anything but cordial. He ought to be ashamed of himself, but Miranda knew him too well to imagine him in the least abashed.

He would enjoy belonging to the Explorers' Club, no doubt. Miranda only hoped it would not keep him too much from home. She . . . Lady Wiston would miss him.

"What the devil does the fellow mean by it?" Peter fumed, pushing away the port decanter as the dining-room door clicked shut behind Lord Snell. "He has something up his sleeve, I'm convinced of it."

"You won't catch me looking a gift horse in the mouth." Bassett refilled his glass. "Another titled gentleman putting my name forward can't hurt. I'd say his lordship's devilish obliging."

"And I'd say the devil's in it somewhere all right. He barely knows you. How can he puff off your competence as an officer?"

Bassett laughed. "Promotion has less to do with competence than with one's friends. Come now, Daviot, how can you quarrel with his offer to introduce you to the Explorers' Club?''

"It's not the offer I quarrel with, it's his motive in making it. Lord knows, I've not been conciliating to his high-and-mighty lordship, let alone toad-eating him.''

"I hope you don't think I've toad-eaten him!''

"Gad no, old fellow, but at least you have treated him with a proper, dignified respect.''

"In my position I can't afford not to,'' Bassett said candidly, finishing his port. "Shall we join the ladies? It's my belief Lord Snell's generosity is in compliment to Lady Wiston.''

Or to Miranda Carmichael? No, Peter's and Bassett's welfare was no concern of hers, whereas Snell might hope to please his aunt by attentions to her nephew and the naval guest in whom she took such an amiable interest.

And by attentions to her companion. A drive in the Park, forsooth! Peter returned to the two equally disturbing alternatives: either Aunt Artemis was right and Lord Snell strove to fix Miss Carmichael's affections, or he was buttering her up for unguessable and probably blackguardly reasons.

Buttering them all up, come to that. Perhaps tomorrow Peter would find out why.

The first part of the next afternoon's outing went exactly as proposed. Lord Snell presented Peter to Thomas Legh, M.P., of Lyme Park in Cheshire, a young man who was writing a book about his travels in Egypt and Ethiopia; and to the Honourable Mountstuart Elphinstone, first British envoy to Kabul and author of a work on Afghanistan shortly to appear. Mr. Elphinstone, eager to return to India, talked fretfully of the iniquities of publishers and printers, but he added his approval of Peter to that of Mr. Legh.

Though Peter could not be elected to the Explorers' Club until a quorum was assembled—unlikely at this sea-

son—by the agreement of the two he was granted a temporary membership. With a note from each of his sponsors,
the club's premises, in North Audley Street, were at his
disposal.

"Most convenient to Portchester Square," said Lord
Snell with satisfaction as they left Mr. Elphinstone to his
misprint filled galley-proofs and strolled up the sunny
street. "I daresay it will not take you more than five or ten
minutes to walk thither. Shall we go that way now?"

"Yes, I'd like to take a look."

"You will find it a peaceful place to write, free of the
disturbances of my aunt Wiston's house."

Was his purpose, then, to separate Peter from Miss Carmichael, the better to pursue his own suit?

"I'm quite happy writing at home," Peter demurred,
"and Miss Carmichael's assistance is invaluable to me. But
I am grateful for your introductions," he added reluctantly.
"It will be agreeable to have somewhere to meet gentlemen
of similar interests, especially once Bassett has his ship."

"Ah yes, the worthy Bassett. I called at the Admiralty
this morning and was informed of the sloop *Adder*'s being
near ready to leave Deptford dock yard after refitting. I
have some hopes of Mr. Bassett being appointed into her.
A small, antiquated vessel, I believe, but he will not expect
more for his first command."

"No doubt he'll be glad to put to sea in anything larger
than a wherry," Peter observed, wondering if his lordship
regarded Bassett as another rival for Miss Carmichael's
heart.

"Yes, I am sure he will be happy to be off." Lord Snell
hesitated, then continued, "He must find it embarrassing
to be Lady Wiston's guest."

"Not at all. He accepts her hospitality in the friendly
spirit in which it was offered."

"That is not quite what I meant. Look here, Daviot, I'm
going to be frank with you."

"I only wish you would!"

"It can scarcely have escaped your notice that Lady Wiston has been behaving extremely oddly. Do you not think it has passed mere idiosyncrasy and entered upon . . . lunacy?"

"Lunacy!" Peter stared at him with narrowed eyes.

Snell shrugged. "Call it senility, or what you will."

"I cannot consider anyone senile who could so ably defend the Navy."

"I cannot consider anyone sane who would stand on her head at the behest of a ragtag Oriental!"

Peter was in a quandary. He knew a good part of his aunt's eccentricity was deliberately assumed for her own purpose. Yet he had been sworn to secrecy and Godfrey Snell was the last person, besides Miranda Carmichael, to whom she would want her plot revealed. Not to mention that the plot itself could at a pinch be taken as further evidence of derangement.

He suspected Snell's motive in fearing for her sanity was not pure solicitude. Yet his only reason for distrust was the antagonism he had felt for the baron from the instant of making his acquaintance.

If he was too violent in defence of Aunt Artemis, Snell would not confide whatever he had in mind. Yet if he failed to defend her, his silence might be taken as agreement.

His silence had already lasted long enough to be taken as implied interest, at least. Snell went on.

"You must admit her conduct is strange enough to warrant concern. If nothing is done, her mind may degenerate until she commits some dreadful act we should regret not having foreseen and forestalled. I propose to call in a physician to observe her, to diagnose her condition and inform us as to whether further measures are advisable. Ah, here we are."

They stopped, having reached 29, North Audley Street, where a brass plate announced the Explorers' Club. Lord Snell, a member of White's, eyed the narrow, unimpressive house with disdain.

"They are looking for new premises, I believe. I daresay

they will change the name when they remove. Do you wish to go in now?"

"Yes, I think I will."

"I must walk on to Portchester Square to keep my appointment with Miss Carmichael."

"Let us finish our discussion first, if you don't mind standing for a moment. You mentioned a physician?" Peter said neutrally.

"Two physicians, as a matter of fact. I understand two opinions are required for committal."

"Committal!" He could not hide his outrage.

"Not to a common asylum!" Snell hastily assured him. "Naturally Lady Wiston would be privately cared for. You need not fear for your own situation, Daviot. When she is confined—purely for her own sake, as I need hardly say— I shall have control of her funds, at least with Bradshaw's concurrence, which he will scarce withhold from *me.*"

So that was it. Lord Snell's hidden motive was nothing but plain, common-or-garden greed.

Oblivious of Peter's disgust, the baron continued, "Her fortune is very large. I shall make sure an income is settled upon you sufficient to live on in reasonable comfort. All I ask is that you support my petition to the court."

"I'll see you damned first!" Peter cried, prudence overwhelmed by fury. "If you imagine I'd sell my aunt into captivity, she is saner than you, my lord, and you may go to hell!"

Chapter 10

Miranda gazed at herself in the cheval glass. The walking dress of canary jaconet, with its single modest flounce of chestnut-brown mull, became her. She was tolerably pretty, she thought, trying to be objective, but besides being too tall she had not the sort of beauty which might tempt a peer to forget what was due to his rank.

She *must* not refine upon Lord Snell's kindness. That could only lead to his disgust and her disappointment.

Donning her chestnut lustring spencer, she tidied her hair. Her chipstraw bonnet, gloves, and reticule she carried downstairs to the drawing room and set in an inconspicuous corner. If his lordship had forgotten the promised outing, he must not suppose her waiting for him.

She picked up the new *Examiner*. Lady Wiston declared the radical paper sadly tamed since the end of the Hunt brothers' imprisonment for libelling the Prince Regent, but Miranda found its views interesting. Not that she could concentrate while straining her ears for the sound of a curricle drawing up in front of the house, or Lord Snell's footsteps in the hall.

Lord Snell strongly disapproved of the *Examiner*, she

recalled. Hurriedly she folded it and laid it aside. Then a flash of defiance took her by surprise. What did it matter if he caught her reading it?

If all he wanted was her company for an hour, her political opinions could not affect him. If his regard for her was deeper, but could not survive seeing her reading the *Examiner,* then better it should die. Miranda took up the paper again and tried hard to pay attention to an article on the Duke of Wellington.

She succeeded to the extent of noticing neither the arrival of the curricle nor the opening of the front door. She glanced up as the drawing-room door opened.

Lord Snell looked preoccupied, even annoyed, a frown engraving lines between his eyebrows. Knowing he had just been with Mr. Daviot, Miranda wondered what that gentleman had said or done to discompose the baron.

In her view Mr. Daviot had by no means shown adequate gratitude for the offer to aid his application to join the Explorers' Club. Sometimes he seemed positively determined to offend Lord Snell. It was odd in an otherwise friendly, easy-going gentleman who had happily fraternized with, among others, both Sagaranathu and Daylight Danny.

Whatever Mr. Daviot's misdeeds, his lordship was sufficiently distracted to pay not the slightest heed to her newspaper. "Ah, there you are, ma'am. Are you ready?" he said impatiently.

"Yes, my lord." Miranda quickly retrieved her bonnet, gloves and reticule. It was a pity she did not possess a parasol.

"Where is my aunt?"

"At her lesson, sir, above stairs."

"The Lascar always comes at this hour?" He stood aside to let her precede him out to the hall.

"Yes, except on Sundays."

"And she practises before changing for dinner every day?"

"Faithfully," said Miranda, rather surprised at his interest.

Out in the street the new curricle awaited them, a smart vehicle painted black with the wheels picked out in crimson and a crimson leather seat. Hitched to the pole stood a team of four matched blacks, held by a groom from the coach-builder. Lord Snell handed Miranda up, took the reins, and joined her.

"Wait here," he said curtly to the groom.

They set off towards Hyde Park. Lord Snell negotiated with ease the traffic of Oxford Street, busy despite the absence from Town of most of the Polite World. The blacks trotted through the Cumberland Gate. Turning southward, his lordship urged them to a canter.

Despite the fine day, there were few people about. Miranda rather wished the Ton was out in force to observe her bowling along at the side of her handsome escort. She saw a few strollers and nursemaids with children, half a dozen riders, a platoon of scarlet-coated infantrymen marching from somewhere to somewhere else. She smiled, recalling Mr. Daviot's quizzing her about the effect of smart uniforms on the feminine sex. Lord Snell seemed disinclined for conversation so she held her tongue.

Approaching the southern end of the park, they slowed to a trot again to negotiate the sharp turn. But then Lord Snell whipped up the team into a gallop. Miranda grabbed the side of the curricle with one hand, her bonnet with the other as they whirled around the bend by the Serpentine.

Reining in sharply, he swerved into the right turn to the Ring at a mere canter, then held the horses back to a trot to complete the circuit around the grove in the centre. Miranda breathed again.

"Showy slugs," he disparaged the team. "The curricle corners well, however. I have a mind to purchase it, but I shall take it round again before I decide."

"I can see you drive to an inch, my lord," Miranda gasped, "but pray set me down first."

He turned to her. "I beg your pardon, Miss Carmichael,"

he said stiffly. "It was remiss in me not to enquire whether you would dislike my springing the horses."

"I should very likely have said no, sir." She could not help a sneaking suspicion that had she been an eligible, blue-blooded damsel he would not have been so remiss. "Alas, I find I am chicken-hearted."

Lord Snell smiled faintly and shook his head. "That I refuse to credit, but I shall drive at a more sedate pace this time."

"Speed is quite exhilarating on the straight. It was the corners which alarmed me."

"Don't tell my aunt, if you please. I would not wish to alarm her, too. She is fond of you, I believe."

"I am certainly very fond of Lady Wiston. She has been all that is kind to me."

"Ah." Looking thoughtful, he turned north on the main drive. Not until they reached the Cumberland Gate and headed south once more did he speak again. "My aunt Wiston's conduct is distinctly odd at times, even bizarre. Does it not disturb you, Miss Carmichael?"

"Not at all, sir," Miranda assured him tranquilly, gratified by his concern for her peace of mind. "It is not my place to judge her ladyship, and if it were, I should still find nothing amiss. To be sure, Lady Wiston has some original notions, but how dull the world would be if everyone marched in step!"

"I daresay. You find nothing to complain of, then?"

"Only Mudge!" She laughed. "I am truly quite content, my lord. Since I must work for my living, I cannot imagine a pleasanter situation."

"I see." Lord Snell fell silent as they approached the tricky corner and rounded it.

This time he took the bend by the Serpentine at a reasonable pace, allowing Miranda to enjoy the sight of the swans and ducks paddling about on the water. Even bribery rarely persuaded Mudge to walk so far.

"How delightful it is to drive in an open carriage on such a lovely day!" Miranda exclaimed.

He smiled at her enthusiasm. "It is still more enjoyable in the country."

"Oh yes. Lady Wiston sometimes takes a drive out to Richmond in the landau. The countryside is very pretty."

"You have always resided in Town?"

"My father did not care for the country." It had bored him to distraction. "And my two previous positions were with ladies living year round in London."

"This is your third?"

"It is usually elderly ladies, often invalids, who require companions."

"Your first two employers both . . . er . . . went to their reward?"

"Yes." And tyrannical as they had been in life, Miranda sometimes wondered what sort of reward they had met in death. "I fear it is a hazard of my profession."

"No doubt. Miss Carmichael, be assured that if anything should happen to Lady Wiston, I shall make it my business to ensure your future welfare."

"You are very kind, sir, but I hope and believe it will be many years before her ladyship succumbs to the weight of years. She is not so very aged, and her health is excellent."

"One can never tell what may happen," Lord Snell pointed out gravely. "Just remember that in case of need your comfort will be my concern."

"Thank you, my lord."

Miranda fell silent, somewhat puzzled. What precisely did he mean? Perhaps only that if Lady Wiston dropped dead he would give her a good character. Perhaps that if her ladyship lived many years and Miranda stayed with her, he would provide her with a pension should his aunt fail to do so.

Or could he possibly want to marry her yet hesitate to deprive Lady Wiston of her services? But if such were the case, surely he would not be willing to wait many years. He was of an age to wish to take a wife and set up his nursery.

Maybe he had not quite made up his mind. It would be

natural in him to hesitate before the irreversible step of lowering himself to wed a hired companion. In that case, his promise of concern for her comfort was intended to reassure her, to remove one possible source of anxiety from her life.

He must love her greatly even to consider making her an offer. She would never have guessed from his demeanour. How sensitive of him to avoid raising hopes which he might find himself unable to satisfy!

Did she love him? Miranda asked herself. She was forced to answer in the negative.

She admired him, held him in high esteem. But her notion of love included a lack of reserve, a free exchange of ideas, which she presently found impossible with his lordship. She was not at her ease with him.

Yet Samuel Richardson had written that no young lady was justified in giving her heart until convinced she had engaged the affections of the gentleman in question. If Lord Snell made it plain he loved Miranda, she was very sure she would quickly come to return his sentiments. Then she would be comfortable with him and able to laugh and tease as she did with Mr. Daviot.

It was a shame Mr. Daviot did not appreciate Lord Snell's many qualities. His unwarranted animosity must stem from envy, Miranda thought. It only threw into higher relief his lordship's amiability with regard to the Explorers' Club.

She glanced at him. His frown had returned, making his face rather forbidding. Could he regret his openness, perhaps afraid she read more into his words than he had intended? The silence between them had gone on long enough, Miranda decided, and she seized the first subject that came to mind.

"Did Mr. Daviot join the Explorers' Club this morning, sir?"

"He was offered a temporary membership, and I left him at their premises."

"Lady Wiston will be pleased."

"He seems to have won her devotion with remarkable ease."

"I assure you, sir, he had no need. Her ladyship recognized him the moment he stepped through the door and was filled with joy to see him again. He has always been something of a favourite, I collect."

"Lucky for him. It is not every vagabond wastrel who can count on a doting aunt to preserve him from debtors' prison."

Miranda wondered why he had vouched for Mr. Daviot to his friends if he considered him a vagabond wastrel. Doubtless the phrase sprang from a natural disgruntlement at knowing the Prodigal Nephew was his aunt's favourite. She ought not to have mentioned it.

"He is working very diligently at his book," she offered.

"With your generous assistance." Lord Snell drove the curricle out of the park and turned down Oxford Street. "Daviot has the gift of ingratiating himself. Do not let him take advantage of you as he does of Lady Wiston."

"I have been on my guard since first we met." That first meeting was engraved on her memory. Lord Snell would not have assaulted her so disgracefully. Lord Snell would not have been sleeping in the gardens in the first place. "But it is only sensible to assist Mr. Daviot in his efforts to break free of the need for Lady Wiston's support. And should he begin to neglect his writing, I am in the best possible position to know it at once."

"Very true, Miss Carmichael." The baron smiled at her. "I am glad to discover his specious charm has not succeeded in hoodwinking *you*."

As yet Mr. Daviot showed no sign of neglecting his work, though he did not come in to luncheon that day. What with walking Mudge and accompanying Lady Wiston on various visits, Miranda was not free to go to the study until late in the afternoon. He had left, but she found a new batch of papers to be transcribed.

At dinner he was lively, making his aunt, Miranda, and
Mr. Bassett laugh with his description of the Explorers'
Club and the gentlemen-travellers he had met there. Lord
Snell sat silent, unamused, and Mr. Daviot made no
acknowledgement of his lordship's part in obtaining his
membership.

Even as she laughed at his irrepressible drollery, Miranda
was dismayed by his indifference to common politeness.
However much he disliked Lord Snell, he ought to admit
to being beholden.

After dinner, Mr. Daviot and Mr. Bassett went out, being
engaged to make up a party with several acquaintances to
attend the Little Theatre, which remained open for the
summer. Miranda, busy all day, had not yet written her
regular letter to her brother. She sat down to the task at
the small writing desk in the sitting room, while Lady
Wiston challenged Lord Snell to a game at piquet.

Miranda hoped her ladyship would not cheat. She feared
his lordship would not be amused.

Lord Snell won several hands, by large scores. At last
Lady Wiston announced her intention of retiring for the
night and Miranda went out with her.

As they parted in the passage, Lady Wiston whispered
with a mischievous look, "I saw your face and guessed
precisely what you were thinking. I did not *quite* dare.
Godfrey is a sadly sober young man. It is a pity he will not
learn from Peter to be a little more lighthearted."

"And Mr. Daviot from his lordship to be a little more
serious!" Miranda retorted.

"Hmm," said Lady Wiston enigmatically, and bade her
good night.

On Miranda's dressing table a note awaited her, propped
where she was certain to see it, with her name on it in Mr.
Daviot's familiar scrawl. What did he have to say that could
not wait until the morning?

Nothing, as it turned out. "I must speak to you urgently,"
she read. "Try to come to the study before breakfast."

So, wild with curiosity, next morning after taking Mudge

out Miranda went to the study. Mr. Daviot was there before her, rising from his writing table as she entered. He looked as serious as she could wish—even grim.

"Why before breakfast?" she asked, closing the door behind her.

He went to the door, opened it, and glanced down the hall. "I want to be sure we shan't be interrupted. Please, do sit down, Miss Carmichael."

She sank into an easy chair. "What is the matter? Do you mean to castigate me for some dreadful error in your manuscript? The original has not been thrown away, so it cannot be difficult to repair."

"No, no, nothing like that." Perching on the edge of the table, he gazed down at her for a moment, then slipped down and took a hasty turn about the small room. "Damn . . . dash it, I don't know how to tell you."

"Begin at the beginning," she suggested prosaically.

With a lopsided grin, quickly fading, he plumped into the seat opposite her. "I'll try." He leaned forward and spoke with emphatic earnestness. "You won't like what I have to say, but I beg you will hear me out. You must be aware that Snell does not regard Aunt Artemis's foibles in quite the same indulgent light as do you and I."

"I know her conduct makes him concerned lest she run into difficulties. I did my best to reassure him, and he has made no attempt to persuade her to change her ways."

"He has no desire for her to change her ways!"

"Then what troubles you?"

"Miss Carmichael, yesterday when we were walking together, Lord Snell made me the most infamous proposal. He tried to convince me that my aunt is showing signs of lunacy. . . ."

"I cannot believe it!" Miranda cried, aghast.

"And he offered to bribe me—with her money, once he has control of it—to support his application for committal."

"I cannot believe it. You misunderstood. Lord Snell is

an honourable gentleman, he would never propose such a cruel, underhanded scheme.''

"He did," Mr. Daviot insisted. "I know you too well to credit for a moment that you would fall in with the scheme, but I had to warn you to beware. What I want your advice on is whether to inform Aunt Artemis."

"Certainly not! Why distress her to no purpose? This cannot conceivably be anything but a ridiculous mistake, a simple misunderstanding."

"Snell was most explicit," he said quietly. "I did not, *could* not misunderstand."

"Then you must be making it up," Miranda accused him, angry and agitated. "You have disliked him from the first. You hope to blacken him in my eyes."

Mr. Daviot glared at her. "Why the devil should I wish to try anything so baconbrained?" Jumping to his feet, he towered over her. "How like a totty-headed female! The only conceivable motive for denigrating him to you would be jealousy. I promise you that is an emotion with which I am wholly unacquainted! I don't give a tinker's damn if you go ahead and marry the prating hypocrite!"

And with that Parthian shot, he flung from the room.

Chapter 11

Miranda was furious. How dare the wretch insinuate that she fancied him jealous of Lord Snell! That would mean she supposed Mr. Daviot to be in love with her, and the notion had never crossed her mind. She was no vain, frivolous, *totty-headed* schoolroom miss, imagining every man she met must admire her.

Totty-headed, indeed! If that was what he thought of her, why did he ask her advice and entrust her with his precious manuscript?

As for suggesting she had set her cap at Lord Snell, it was the outside of enough. She could hardly help treating his lordship with a trifle more than ordinary courtesy when he was a relative of her employer and a guest in the house. If Peter Daviot were not in the same position, she would not so much as pass the time of day with the odious man!

Wiping away an angry tear, Miranda stalked over to the writing table and scowled down at the burgeoning book. She owed it to Lady Wiston to go on assisting him with the transcription, but she would take care to do her share of the work in his absence in future. Let him go elsewhere for advice. It was no business of hers to rein in his embellishment of the facts. Let him cross the line into sheer fantasy!

He had a vivid imagination. Could he have imagined Lord Snell's infamous plot? But despite her earlier doubts, she had never seen any sign that he might be unable to distinguish fact from fiction. Nor had he ever made a real attempt to mislead her or his aunt. On the contrary, he had always been perfectly frank and open, even about his own shortcomings.

So he must have misinterpreted whatever Lord Snell had proposed to him. Miranda racked her brains, trying to conceive what his lordship might have said which could be misunderstood in just that fashion.

"You there, miss?" Alfred stuck his head around the door. " 'Er lidyship says are you comin' acos she's got. . . ."

"No!" came a pained cry from the passage. Twitchell appeared behind the new footman. "Start again, boy."

Alfred opened the door wide and drew himself up. He was already beginning to fill out his livery as prophesied. Miranda gave him an encouraging smile.

"If you please, miss, *h*er l*a*dyship wants. . . ." He glanced back over his shoulder. Twitchell's lips moved. "Her ladyship would like to know," Alfred continued, "wevver you will join *h*er at breakfas' being as *h*ow there's stuff . . . there are matters she wants to gab about . . . no, wishes to discuss!" he ended in a triumphant burst.

"Well done," said Miranda. "I can see you are going to be an excellent footman. Yes, I shall come directly."

All three gentlemen were at the breakfast table with Lady Wiston. Her ladyship, Lord Snell, and Mr. Bassett all greeted Miranda with "Good morning," and a smile. Mr. Daviot grunted. He did not even glance at her, so she did not have to avoid his eyes.

The infuriating thing was that she found it difficult to meet Lord Snell's gaze, too. She managed it, and smiled at him, but she was quite glad to take a seat next to Lady Wiston and opposite Mr. Bassett, who was positively beaming.

"Miss Carmichael," he said eagerly, "I do hope you'll like my notion. It's the perfect day, with the sun shining and no wind. The water will be flat as a duck pond, I vouch for it."

Miranda laughed. "I am quite prepared to believe you, sir, but may I ask which water? And why we should be concerned for its calmness?"

"The Thames, dear," said Lady Wiston. "Mr. Bassett proposes to hire a wherry to carry us all down to Deptford to take a look at the *Adder.*"

"She's out of dry dock," Mr. Bassett told Miranda, his face alight with enthusiasm, "and moored in the river."

"Is your command confirmed then, sir? Have you heard from the Admiralty already this morning?"

"No," he admitted, slightly crestfallen, "but I was told yesterday I shall more than likely get her. Once I have my orders, I may have to leave in a hurry. And the weather might not be so good, either. Do you not care for the outing, ma'am?"

"It sounds like great fun." But not with both Mr. Daviot and Lord Snell aboard, Miranda thought. "Do you wish to go, Lady Wiston?"

"Yes indeed, dear. It will make a delightful change. Sometimes I think we are getting very set in our ways," Lady Wiston said to Miranda's startled amusement. "Besides," she continued, "when dear Mr. Bassett is gone, it will be pleasant to have a picture in our minds of the very ship he sails on."

"If I get her, ma'am."

"I am sure you will," said Miranda, sorry she had voiced a doubt, "but just in case, we must carefully note all the *Adder*'s faults. Should something go amiss, we may abuse her to our hearts' content, though if you become her captain we shall, of course, entirely forget every little blemish."

Mr. Bassett grinned. "If I become her captain, I'll *see* no blemish," he assured her. Turning to Lady Wiston, he asked, "What time suits you best, ma'am? High tide is mid morning."

"What difference does the tide make?" she enquired.

"An ebb tide going and a flood tide returning makes easier work for the oarsmen."

"But at high tide," Lord Snell put in, "the mud flats are covered, which makes for a more agreeable journey."

"They stink," Mr. Bassett admitted, "and they're not pretty."

"Then by all means let us go as soon as we can," said Lady Wiston. "I shall add a tip for the watermen for their hard work. Does this morning suit you, Godfrey?"

"Excellently."

"Peter?"

"I shan't go, Aunt Artemis. I must get on with my writing."

"Do come, Daviot," cried Mr. Bassett. "I particularly want you to see the *Adder.*"

"Yes, do, dear boy. An extra gentleman is always to be desired on such an expedition, do you not agree, Miranda?"

Miranda could hardly contradict her outright. Hesitantly she said, "If Mr. Daviot is otherwise engaged, ma'am, surely Lord Snell and Mr. Bassett will suffice to take care of us?"

"Upon my oath we will," said Lord Snell.

Mr. Daviot cast a sidelong glance full of suspicion at the baron. "You are right, Aunt," he said. "Your consequence demands a superfluous gentleman in your escort. I shall come."

"Silly boy," she said fondly.

"Splendid!" Mr. Bassett rose to his feet. "Pray excuse me, ma'am. I'll be off to Surrey Stairs to make arrangements."

"We shall meet you there as soon as possible, Mr. Bassett," said her ladyship, and he hurried off. "Miranda," she continued, "when you have finished your breakfast, pray send to tell Mr. Sagaranathu not to come this morning. Ask him to come later this afternoon, and to stay to dinner, and if he cannot, assure him I shall pay him for my lesson anyway.''

"Yes, ma'am.''

"Oh, I have a charming notion! Tell Cook to pack up a hamper, cold meat, bread and butter, fruit, whatever is to hand, and we shall go on to Greenwich for a picnic. Now is not that a delightful notion?"

"Delightful,'' Miranda echoed with what enthusiasm she could muster. At least an extra two hours of Mr. Daviot ignoring or glowering at both her and Lord Snell, she reckoned.

"You had best bring a shawl, dear, or a cloak. I daresay it may be chilly on the water, especially if a breeze should spring up. I shall change. Trousers are undoubtedly more practical for boating, but alas I have not the temerity to wear them in public. Peter dear, pray order the carriage.'' She bustled out, followed by Mr. Daviot.

Lord Snell smiled at Miranda. "Lady Wiston takes a childish pleasure in this expedition," he said.

"Child*like*,'' Miranda murmured, not quite audibly. An educated man like the baron ought to know the difference, she thought uneasily. "I am looking forward to it, too," she said aloud. "Excuse me, my lord, I must go and speak to Cook at once."

Leaving half her muffin uneaten, she went down to the kitchen to order the picnic, telling Cook to do her best at such short notice. Alfred went off with the message to Mr. Sagaranathu, and Miranda dashed up to her bedchamber.

When she descended a few minutes later, wearing her bonnet and spencer, carrying gloves, reticule and a shawl, she turned towards the back stairs to go and check on Cook's progress. Lord Snell was just coming out of the study.

"Miss Carmichael, a word with you, if you please," he requested politely.

Miranda felt an apprehensive tightness in her chest. Did he want to discuss Lady Wiston's mental faculties? The seed of doubt sowed by Mr. Daviot had sprouted.

Reluctantly she approached. "My lord?"

"I have neglected to bring with me my cousins' directions, and I am hoping you will be able to supply the deficiency."

"Certainly, sir." Relieved, she led the way into the study and crossed to the shelves by the roll-top desk. "Lady Wiston writes to them quite often."

"You see, in general we correspond regularly, and if they don't receive the expected letters, they may wonder what has become of me. I looked in the bureau for a memorandum book but could not find one."

Miranda frowned. Even a peer ought not to rummage in his aunt's desk without permission. She took down a large volume. "Here it is. As you see, it is too big to fit in the bureau. Lady Wiston has a great many acquaintances. I shall copy down the directions for you."

"If you would be so good as to read them aloud, I shall write to your dictation." He sat down at Mr. Daviot's writing table, pushed aside Mr. Daviot's manuscript, took a sheet of Mr. Daviot's paper, and dipped one of Mr. Daviot's pens in Mr. Daviot's ink.

Mr. Daviot would not be pleased, but then, Miranda had no intention of telling him.

" 'Frederick Fenimore, Solicitor,' " she read, " 'Queen Street, Ipswich, Suffolk,' or I have Mr. Fenimore's direction at home if you prefer."

"This will do very well."

She turned to the Js. " 'The Reverend Edward Jeffries, Cathedral Close, Winchester, Hampshire.' " On to the Rs. "And 'James Redpath, Esquire, Redpath Manor, near Brighton.' "

They were all very simple addresses. Miranda could have recited them without looking them up had she not feared Lord Snell might mistrust her memory. She was surprised he could not recall them since he corresponded regularly. But perhaps he had a secretary who directed his letters, or perhaps he simply had too many important things on his mind to clutter it with extraneous detail.

In any case, it was gracious in him to preserve a close
relationship with his family connexions in less exalted
spheres of life. Of the admiral's sisters, only Lord Snell's
mother had married into the aristocracy, and many in such
a position would have severed all ties.

The cousins must be very close indeed for three of them
to wonder at not hearing from the fourth for a few weeks.
Miranda's own brother did not expect to receive a letter
more than once a month, she thought as she hurried down
to the kitchen.

At the head of the Surrey Steps, Mr. Bassett awaited the
rest of the party. Handing first Lady Wiston and then
Miranda down from the high landau, he exclaimed in
delight over the picnic basket. His pleasure redoubled
when Lady Wiston insisted the fare from Deptford to
Greenwich was her treat.

"A famous notion, ma'am!" he exclaimed. "I have got
us a good boat with two men at the oars, none of your
single scullers for us."

The wherry bobbed below on the swift slate-grey stream,
one waterman holding fast to a chain fixed to the stone
steps while the other came up to carry down the hamper.
Two cushioned benches at the stern would hold six passengers; another in the bows had room for two more.

"Allow me to support you, ma'am," Lord Snell said to
Lady Wiston. "The steps are awkwardly steep and bound
to be slippery. Pray take my arm."

"I'll go down first, Aunt Artemis," said Mr. Daviot, "to
catch you should you miss your footing." He gave Lord
Snell a hard look, as if he half suspected him of intending
to push her ladyship down the steps.

Lady Wiston reached the bottom unscathed. She seated
herself on the rearmost bench, and Lord Snell sat down
beside her. Mr. Daviot promptly took a place on the opposite seat, facing the pair. Miranda decided he was afraid

the baron was going to toss his aunt overboard. He really was making a cake of himself.

With a smile she accepted Mr. Bassett's arm and they took the seat in the bows, facing backward. He helped her arrange her shawl about her shoulders as the boatmen pushed off. Ripples sparkled in the sun, while overhead seagulls wheeled and cried.

As the wherry moved out into the river, Miranda saw the terrace and magnificent south façade of Somerset House, home of the Royal Academy of the Arts. Just beyond, the new Waterloo Bridge was under construction. Mr. Bassett, who was unfamiliar with London, asked her about the bridge and the palace.

Telling him what she knew, she watched the others. Both Lord Snell and Mr. Daviot addressed all their remarks to Lady Wiston, none to each other. Miranda was glad to be separated from their childish feud by the two burly oarsmen.

They rowed on downstream. Miranda pointed out the sights, the Temple Gardens and various church spires. Ahead, as they looked over their shoulders, the great dome of St. Paul's loomed over all, matched—if far from equalled—on the southern bank by the church of St. Saviour, Southwark. The river was busy with barges and luggers, the banks for the most part lined with wharves and warehouses.

Under the wide, round arches of Blackfriars Bridge they passed in swirl of water. That was when Miranda recalled tales of the violent turbulence beneath the narrow arches of London Bridge, not much more than half a mile downstream.

There, if anywhere, Lady Wiston would be in danger, when the wherry tossed on the rapids and Mr. Daviot was distracted by the spectacle.

Could she somehow crawl past the boatmen and warn him? No, she was being as caperwitted as he was. He had imagined the whole business of Lord Snell being a threat to Lady Wiston. And even if he had not, a committal for lunacy was a far cry from a murder by drowning in the River Thames.

Of course he had imagined it! All the same, Miranda watched the three in the stern with painful intensity as London Bridge neared.

The roar of rushing water drowned every other sound. Suddenly the boat shot forward into the shadows between massive piers. The rowers made one last stroke and rested their oars as the fragile little craft skipped amid clouds of spray. Miranda clutched the seat, her gaze fixed on Lady Wiston.

For a moment they seemed to fly through the air, then they were out in sunshine again. The boatmen bent to their oars.

Lady Wiston laughed. "Heavens, that was quite exciting!" she exclaimed.

Sagging with relief, Miranda realized Mr. Bassett had his arm about her waist.

"Are you all right, Miss Carmichael?" he asked anxiously, removing his arm with evident reluctance as she sat up straight. "I didn't know the passage under the bridge was so rough or I'd have arranged to take to the river below it."

"No, no, I am quite all right, sir. I was a little concerned about Lady Wiston, but see, she has come through in fine spirits. As she says, it was quite exciting. Look, there is the Monument, commemorating the Great Fire."

The wherry skimmed downstream, past the Tower of London, among ships of every size from every corner of the world, a forest of a thousand masts. Mr. Bassett chatted knowledgeably about the vessels and the nations represented by their flags, happily oblivious of undercurrents—at least of the human kind.

Miranda tried to give him the attention he deserved. What a goosecap she was to fear even for an instant that Lord Snell had wicked designs upon Lady Wiston! Why should he? He was a wealthy man with no reason to covet her fortune.

But some people were never satisfied, whispered a little voice in her head.

Finding H.M.S. *Adder* moored at the Royal Dock Yard quay, they rowed slowly along her length. Lady Wiston, with her naval background, was the only one able to ask Mr. Bassett intelligent questions. She wanted to know the sloop's beam and tonnage, the size and number of her guns, how close she could sail to the wind and other details whose significance completely escaped Miranda.

No one could possibly consider her mad after such a display of practical erudition.

They went on to Greenwich and picnicked on a grassy slope overlooking the Royal Hospital. Lady Wiston monopolized Mr. Bassett with further discussion of his hoped-for command, and Mr. Daviot stuck close to them, so Miranda was left to Lord Snell.

Though, courteous as ever, he kept her supplied with food from the excellent spread Cook had so quickly put together, he had little conversation. Indeed, he was distinctly *distrait*.

Had Mr. Daviot treated Miranda so—before their quarrel—she would have accused him of wool-gathering and teased him to tell what occupied his thoughts to the exclusion of his companion. Such banter was out of the question with his lordship. She wondered if Mr. Daviot's unwarranted hostility was enough to bring the frown to his forehead.

In fact, Mr. Daviot was altogether to blame for ruining what might otherwise have been a delightful outing.

By the time the boatmen rowed back under London Bridge, the tide had ebbed far enough to decrease the turbulence. On either side of the river, narrow mud flats now lay exposed, crossed by channels dredged to the various wharves and steps. An occasional whiff of a foul effluvium drifted across the water, making the wherry's passengers wrinkle their noses.

They passed beneath Blackfriars Bridge. The exposed flats were wider now. Here and there solitary figures trudged slowly along, gazing down, occasionally stooping to pick something out of the foul muck.

Most were ragged men, walking with a shambling gait, but below the Temple Gardens, Miranda, in the bows with Lord Snell, spotted a whole family. At the waterline a tattered, emaciated woman carried a baby on her hip, and near the bank the man had a toddler on his shoulders. Between them, three children not much older plodded along with bent heads.

The eldest of the children suddenly bent down, then ran to his father to show what he had found. The motion caught Lady Wiston's eye.

"What are those people doing?" she asked the nearest oarsman.

"They'm mudlarks, y'lidyship, lookin' fer scraps o' rope or iron, rags, wood even, anyfink as'll fetch a meg. Most on 'em's boozin' coves past carin' fer owt but the next pot o' blue ruin."

"Scavengers," translated Mr. Bassett at her side. "Drunkards hoping to sell what they find for a ha'penny to buy gin."

"Not that family, surely?" said Lady Wiston.

"No'm." The man shook his head sadly. "That there's poor Jeb Tuttle as was a waterman. Bust 'is arm and can't row no more."

"Did you hear, Miranda?" called her ladyship. "Those poor people trying to make an honest living in such a horrid fashion! I am certain it must be dreadfully unhealthy."

"Shall I walk back when we get ashore, ma'am, and speak to them?"

"Yes, dear, if you please. Tell the woman to come to Portchester Square. Women are generally so much more sensible than men."

"Can you not dissuade her?" Lord Snell said to Miranda in a low voice. "It is sheer folly to waste money on such wretches. The fellow will spend it on gin and his family be not one whit the better for it."

"Lady Wiston will not simply give them money," Miranda explained. "She says to give a man a fish is to feed him for a day, to teach him to fish is to feed him for a lifetime. I expect she will set them up in some business he can manage with his crippled arm."

Lord Snell's lips pursed. "The only trade he knows is rowing."

"He will learn." About to cite the example of Daylight Danny, Miranda paused. His lordship would not approve of his aunt's friendship with Mr. and Mrs. Potts.

The day after tomorrow was Lady Wiston's at-home day. Suddenly Miranda was dreadfully afraid that not only would Lord Snell not care for her ladyship's guests, he might consider them evidence of madness.

If he was looking for evidence, which of course he was not . . . was he?

Chapter 12

Perched on the end of Miranda's bed, Lady Wiston tucked her nightgown around her toes and readjusted her shawl about her shoulders.

"How fortunate the sunshine lasted until we reached home," she said. "I should not have cared to be out on the river in this wind and rain. Would you like a fire in here, dear?"

"In August? Heavens, no! What shocking extravagance that would be." Miranda pulled her own shawl closer. Though she was not really chilly, the raindrops beating against the windowpanes sounded cold. "We *were* lucky with the weather today."

"Yes indeed. I should have enjoyed our voyage excessively if it were not for. . . . Miranda, I greatly fear Godfrey and Peter have come to cuffs. They scare exchanged a word all day, and then Peter going off to dine at his club. . . . Do you know what they have quarrelled about?"

"I think you had better ask them, Lady Wiston."

"Oh no, I could not do that. Gentlemen are so *odd* about such things." She sighed. "Has Godfrey mentioned to you how long he means to stay?"

"He said a few days originally. But I am sure when his business in Town is done he will tell you, not me."

"But you get on very well with him, do you not?"

"Well enough, ma'am. He has been most kind and courteous."

"He admires you, I am certain of it. Though it was not quite gallant of him, I vow, to refuse when I asked him to walk with you down to the Temple Gardens to speak to those poor people."

"I assure you, ma'am, I took it as a mark of his distaste for my errand—which is only natural in a gentleman of his rank—not as a lack of politeness towards me. Mr. Bassett was an excellent escort, and in sympathy with my goal."

"Dear Mr. Bassett, we shall miss him sadly when he is gone. But I believe you wrong Godfrey, Miranda. I was telling him about Daylight Danny's success as a pie-vendor and he was most interested. He is looking forward to meeting him. In fact, he asked permission to invite two of his own acquaintances to the next at-home."

Miranda stared. "Lord Snell? Acquaintances of *his* can scarcely be the kind of people we shall be entertaining. Does he properly understand?"

"I explained most carefully. It seems they are medical men, not gentlemen of fashion." Lady Wiston lowered her voice. "I believe Godfrey came up to Town to consult them, but he would not tell me what ails him. I fear it must be what Sir Bernard used to call Venus's Revenge. Sometimes quite half his crew would be incapacitated with it."

"Indeed, ma'am, but Lord Snell . . . !"

"Young, unmarried gentlemen do frequent those unfortunate women, alas. Of course all that sort of thing will stop once dear Godfrey is married." She patted Miranda's knee. "Well, I am off to bed, dear. Sleep well, and let us hope Godfrey and Peter soon come to a better understanding for it is most uncomfortable when the dear boys are at odds."

She slipped down from the bed and trotted off through

the connecting dressing room to her own chamber, leaving Miranda with much food for thought.

Medical men! The notion of the toplofty baron with the pox brought an irrepressible giggle to Miranda's lips. Yet whether he suffered from "Venus's Revenge" or some less unmentionable disease, why on earth would Lord Snell wish to extend his aunt's hospitality to his physicians?

It was far more likely that he wanted them to observe her. From the very first, Miranda recalled, he had expressed concern over Lady Wiston's lack of rationality, as he perceived it. Since then, he had uttered many an anxious comment on her antics.

Miranda tried to reassure him, but she was young, and female, and in other ways unqualified to voice an opinion he would take seriously. To desire a professional diagnosis was not unreasonable, nor did it mean he hoped for a negative diagnosis, as Mr. Daviot assumed.

If Lord Snell had actually consulted Mr. Daviot about his beloved Aunt Artemis's sanity, Mr. Daviot had no doubt waxed so indignant as to be incapable of listening properly. Small wonder they had quarrelled. Much ado about nothing!

Snuffing her candle, Miranda snuggled down under the covers. The rain battered the window and the wind howled dementedly. Against her will, memories returned.

She and Lady Wiston had once visited the Bethlem Hospital for the Insane—once only. Her ladyship, who faced with scarcely ruffled equanimity the horrors of squalid tenements, hospitals, and even Newgate prison, had vowed never to return. The fettered creatures shrieking in their darkened cells were bad enough. Far worse were the treatments described in answer to Lady Wiston's queries: isolation, strait waistcoats and shackles, blisters and purges, cold plunges, forced feeding, cauterizing, and the deliberate inculcation of fear.

The idea of Lady Wiston undergoing those tortures made Miranda feel sick. Lord Snell could not possibly contemplate subjecting his aunt to such horrors only because she liked to stand on her head.

Mr. Daviot *must* have misunderstood—but suppose he had not? If Mr. Daviot was right, Lord Snell had asked for his support, which suggested he needed support for his application. He would not get it from any of her servants or friends. On the contrary, dozens of people would be more than willing to stand up in court and swear to her sanity and goodness.

So she was safe. On that reassuring thought, Miranda at last fell asleep.

Nevertheless, she passed a disturbed night. At one point she dreamed Lord Snell was driving her in a curricle at a terrifying pace through the corridors of Bethlem. He kept assuring her that it was for her own good, to cure her of madness.

Waking, she recalled his promise to take care of her should anything happen to her employer. How she had fretted over whether he was hinting that he loved her! Now she saw a new and sinister significance to his words. Had he been attempting to bribe her not to stand up for Lady Wiston?

Miranda slept late the next morning. Washing and dressing in haste, she hurried downstairs.

"Oh dear," she said to Alfred in the hall, "Mudge must be desperate to get out. Where is he?"

"Her ladyship took 'im out, miss, after I tried and 'e bit me. I went along wiv her ladyship's humberolly acos o' the rain. Her ladyship said as you wasn't to be disturbed."

"Oh *dear!* You did wash the bite, didn't you? Let me see. Not too bad, luckily, but I shall put some basilicum on it. Come along to the study, Alfred."

The first thing she noticed as she entered the study was the absence of Mr. Daviot's manuscript. The table in the window was clear, no paper, pens or inkstand. A horrid sinking feeling invaded the pit of her stomach.

"The house is very quiet," she said as casually as she could, opening her medicine chest. "Where is everyone?"

"Her ladyship's gorn to see summun about them mudlarks, miss, the Tuttles. She'll be back for Mr. Sagaranathu. 'Is lordship's gorn out on business. Mr. Daviot's at 'is club, and Mr. Bassett's at the Admiralty."

At his club! Miranda closed her eyes in brief thankfulness. For a moment she had feared Mr. Daviot's quarrels with both herself and Lord Snell might have driven him to go off adventuring again.

"But what about his book?"

" 'Is book, miss?"

"Mr. Daviot's papers. They are gone."

" 'E took 'em wiv 'im, miss. Told her ladyship 'e'd get more done at 'is club."

He did not want to work with her any more. Miranda fiercely blinked back a sudden rush of tears and concentrated on applying the basilicum to Alfred's wound.

"Ta, miss. I'll bring your breakfas' to the dining room right away."

"Thank you, Alfred. All I want is a cup of tea."

"Her ladyship said you was to eat proper," Alfred said disapprovingly. "Tell you what, miss, Mrs. Lowenstein got some plums this morning. If you don't fancy muffin and eggs, I'll bring you some o' them."

Over tea and greengages, Miranda tried without success to give her attention to *The Times*. Last night's fears now seemed nonsensical, as midnight terrors so often do in the light of morning. What distracted her from the daily news was the hurt of Mr. Daviot's defection.

She felt abandoned, which was ridiculous. After all, she had helped him, not the reverse, and only because Lady Wiston had desired it.

And because she enjoyed his company more than that of anyone else she had ever met, said the traitorous little voice in her head.

To her relief, she heard Lady Wiston in the hall, asking after her. Draining the last drop of tea, she went out.

The club's page boy materialized at Peter's elbow with a cat-soft tread uncanny to one accustomed to Alfred's cheerful racket. "Mr. Bassett to see you, sir," he murmured discreetly, unheard by the other denizens of the hushed reading room.

Peter dropped his pen on the inkstand. He started to straighten his papers but gave up with a silent groan of despair. Who would have thought they could get so muddled in only a day and a half without Miss Carmichael's care? Leaving them scattered, he went down to the lobby.

Bassett's beaming face told all.

"You have your command," said Peter with a smile.

"Yes, the *Adder*'s mine! I'm to go aboard this day sennight and take her down to Gravesend to await orders."

"Congratulations, my dear fellow. I'm devilish glad for you. This calls for a toast. Come into the coffee room and we'll drink to H.M.S. *Adder* and all who sail in her."

"Just a quick glass, old chap." Bassett followed Peter into the front room, nearly empty at this hour. "I can't wait to tell Miss . . . the ladies. I say, Daviot, d'you mind if I ask your advice?"

"By all means," Peter assented cautiously. They sat down at the table in the window and he ordered a bottle of claret before he went on, "What's on your mind?"

"The trouble is," Bassett burst out, "now the moment's come there isn't time, what with getting kitted out with a new uniform and all. I want to do it up all right and tight, no havey-cavey business, which means telling my parents and asking her brother's permission. But they're in Devon and he's in Lincolnshire and in just a week. . . ."

"Whoa! Her brother's permission?" Between his pique at Miss Carmichael's misplaced regard for Lord Snell and his aunt's plot to marry off the pair, Peter had overlooked Bassett's admiration for that infuriating female. "Never say you mean to pop the question?'' he asked as the waiter arrived with a bottle and two glasses.

"I mean to ask her to marry me. Do you think I have a chance?''

"But it's only a fortnight since you told me you cannot support a wife.''

"Nearer a month, and I'm not a half-pay lieutenant any more. Though we'd still have to wait, at least until after my first voyage.''

"I don't believe in long betrothals,'' Peter said firmly, filling their glasses. One way or another he had to put a stop to this nonsense. A woman who succumbed so easily to a title and a handsome face was not worthy of his friend. "It wouldn't be fair to tie her down when she might meet someone else in your absence.''

"I suppose not.'' Bassett looked disconsolate. "But if she doesn't know I care for her, she might accept an offer from someone she doesn't like half so much. I do think she likes me, at least a little, don't you?''

"I'm certain she regards you as a very good friend, old chap, but I'm afraid her head's been turned by that damned snake Snell. I'll tell you what, why don't you ask her if you may write to her? She will realize you have serious intentions, and if she agrees, you will have hope for the future, without a binding promise either of you might come to regret.''

"I daresay that will be for the best.'' The young officer sighed, but to Peter's relief he did not appear heartbroken. "I'd hoped to go aboard an engaged man. Still, I'll have plenty to keep me busy. A ship of my own at last!''

Peter raised his glass. "The *Adder*, her new captain, and all who sail in her!''

The joyful grin restored to his face, Bassett joined in the toast.

"I'm off,'' he said then. "She'll be glad for me, anyway, and so will Lady Wiston. I'll see you at the at-home.''

"Oh, I shan't be there. I really must get on with the great work, you know. Time and tide wait for no man.''

Bassett laughed. "That's a fine thing to tell a sailor. But you have to eat. I'll see you at dinner."

Peter nodded. Though he had not intended to go home for dinner, either—he hadn't yesterday—an excuse to satisfy his aunt would be hard to find. He could not tell her that the less he saw of Miss Carmichael flirting with Snell, the happier he was.

No, that was not it! He did not give a damn if she set her cap at a nobleman, though he'd have expected her to have better taste. It was the sight of Snell himself Peter could not stand. The sneaksby had wormed his way into his aunt's favour like a maggot into an apple, and the devil of it was, Miss Carmichael was right about not warning Aunt Artemis.

To disillusion her would only distress her for nothing, not because Snell had no evil designs but because he was at point non plus when it came to carrying them out. He had failed to suborn Peter, and there would be scores of others to swear to the soundness of her mind.

Returning to his writing, Peter reflected on how much less complicated life had been among the Iroquois.

Miranda was glad to see Mr. Bassett go off happily to order the proper gold braiding put to his cocked hat. His face had fallen when she composedly told him she and Lady Wiston would always be delighted to receive news of his travels. He was a dear fellow, but a private correspondence was more of a mark of intimacy than she was prepared to grant.

Eustace and Alfred came in to clear away the tea things. Lady Wiston was looking unwontedly fatigued. With all the arrangements to be made for the Tuttles' future, she had scarcely sat down all day.

"Do go and lie down, ma'am," Miranda urged.

"I believe I shall, dear. Pray tell Cook Godfrey's friends will stay to dinner."

"They will?" Miranda was dismayed. She did not like

the looks of the two physicians who now stood by the window talking to Lord Snell. Why had he chosen to consult such unprepossessing characters?

One was a bulky man with a triple chin underpinning his red, greasy, sycophantic face, and a habit of rubbing his hands together. The other, small and angular, had a sly, foxy expression which reminded Miranda of the pickpocket Lady Wiston had hit with her umbrella. Both wore black with a rusty cast, suggesting their practices were neither extensive nor lucrative.

From that point of view, they fitted in well with the rest of the guests, but they had not mingled with the others. Instead they had lurked near Lady Wiston, eavesdropping on her conversations and whispering solemnly together as they now did with his lordship.

They reminded Miranda of carrion crows. "You mean you have invited both those doctors to dine?" she asked doubtfully.

"Yes, dear. Or rather, Godfrey asked me if he might invite them. I must say they seem rather odd people, do they not?" Such words from Lady Wiston amounted almost to outright condemnation. "Not at all the sort whose company one might expect Godfrey to frequent." She gave Miranda an anxious glance. "You know, dear, Godfrey never stayed in the house before, even when the admiral was alive, and I begin to think perhaps I did not know him very well."

"I daresay Lord Snell has his reasons for issuing the invitation." How she wished she could be certain of those reasons.

Ought she to warn Lady Wiston of her fears? If only Mr. Daviot were there to be consulted, but of course he was missing just when he was needed. In any case, he had made it plain he wanted nothing further to do with her. She would not lower herself to chase after him, even to tell him about the carrion crows.

"It is a pity they will be here tonight," said Lady Wiston with a sigh. "I fear they will cast a damper on our celebration for dear Mr. Bassett. You spoke to Twitchell about the champagne?''

"Yes, ma'am."

"Excellent. I shall go up now and lie down until it is time for my exercises."

The less the doctors saw of *yoga* the better! Accompanying her ladyship out into the hall, Miranda said hopefully, "You are tired, Lady Wiston. Surely you may omit your practising just this once?"

"Oh no, dear. It does not tire me. Indeed, it quite renews my energy. I have something new to show you this evening."

Miranda smiled at her. "I am going to take Mudge out now before it starts raining again," she said, "but I shall be back in plenty of time to watch." And to endeavour to keep the crows away, she added silently.

She was too late. It was a windy day and Mudge took exception to a scrap of paper blowing across their path in Hyde Park. He yanked the lead out of Miranda's hand. Chasing him, she broke a bootlace. When at last she hobbled home, Eustace informed her that her ladyship and the two medical men were all above stairs in the green sitting room.

Miranda hurried up to her chamber, threw off her bonnet, kicked off the wretched boots, and scarcely pausing to don slippers, sped along the passage.

In the centre of the room, Lady Wiston sat cross-legged in her green and beige Cossack trousers, neatly matching the carpet. Her eyes were closed and in a tranquil voice she intoned, over and over again, a string of incomprehensible syllables: *"Om mani padme hum. Om mani padme hum."*

By the window, the black-clad physicians stared and gravely shook their heads. Lady Wiston appeared serenely oblivious of their presence. Miranda was not.

Crossing to them, she said softly but with all the courteous firmness at her command, "Do come down to the drawing room, gentlemen, and take a glass of Madeira."

The fat man licked his lips. "That's very kind of you,

miss," he said in an unctuous undertone. "However his lordship's already promised us a glass and he asked us to wait *here* while he dresses for dinner."

The skinny one, his gaze still fixed on Lady Wiston, nudged his fellow in the ribs with a sharp elbow. "Look!" he gasped.

Miranda realized the chant had ceased. Turning, she saw her ladyship's legs rise slowly and smoothly into the air and stabilize in a perfect, wobble-free Candle.

"Lady Wiston is wonderfully limber for her age, is she not?" Miranda said quickly.

The doctors glanced at each other and exchanged portentous nods.

"The daily exercises are doing wonders for her health," she gabbled on. "So very *sensible* of her to take steps to avoid the ills which so often undermine the constitution of the elderly. I am half inclined to adopt the same regimen."

Though they neither interrupted nor contradicted her, the two men paid little attention to Miranda's lecture on the benefits of *yoga*. In fact they looked right past her, eyes alight with avid curiosity absorbing every detail of Lady Wiston's contortions.

Miranda gave up in despair. They had made up their minds about Lady Wiston. All that remained was to cram as many of her friends as possible into the court when the time came for the committal hearing.

If Mr. Daviot was right about Lord Snell's intentions. But he must be wrong!

Chapter 13

When Miranda went down to the drawing room after changing for dinner, only Lady Wiston, Lord Snell, and Mr. Bassett were there. Lord Snell came towards her.

"I must apologize, Miss Carmichael," he said. "I fear my guests have disrupted your domestic arrangements. A patient in whose treatment they are both involved took a turn for the worse and a messenger arrived to fetch them."

Miranda simply could not force herself to say she was sorry. She was not even sure she believed in the declining patient, or that his lordship had ever intended to sit down to dinner with the carrion crows. The invitation could have been a ruse to explain their staying on after the at-home to see the *yoga*.

"Does Twitchell know?" she asked.

"Yes, yes, I informed him myself."

"Thank you, my lord." Did she dare request an explanation of their visit? He would have every right to take snuff at being interrogated by his aunt's companion. While she was summoning up the nerve, he changed the subject.

"I regret that we have had no opportunity these last few days to drive in the park again. The weather appears to be improving. If it is fine tomorrow afternoon, will you honour me with your company? I promise not to spring the horses," he added with a smile.

Perhaps he wanted a chance to explain to her in private. "If Lady Wiston can spare me, sir, I shall be delighted."

"Splendid." His smile suddenly vanished. Looking over Miranda's shoulder he gave a chilly nod.

She glanced around. Mr. Daviot had just entered. Not having seen him for two days, Miranda was struck by his tall, elegant slenderness in evening clothes, black coat, buff breeches, and spotless white linen. In contrast, Lord Snell seemed lamentably thickset, even beginning to run to fat about the middle.

Thank heaven he had come, Miranda thought. She must talk to him, find out more exactly what Lord Snell had said to him, tell him about the crows.

He bowed to her coldly and went on to join his aunt and Mr. Bassett. Miranda wondered if he had heard her express delight at the prospect of driving out with Lord Snell. He had vigorously and convincingly denied any possibility of jealousy—not that she had suspected him of it for a moment, she thought wistfully—so he must suppose she had gone over to the enemy. Did he trust her so little?

The impulse to consult him shrivelled and died.

Though one of the company was not on speaking terms with two others, under the influence of champagne dinner was almost a convivial occasion. Mr. Bassett's high spirits bubbled like the wine, and Lady Wiston, less oblivious of discord, remained steadfastly cheerful. Following her example, Miranda did her best to hide her chagrin at Mr. Daviot's disapproval and her wariness of Lord Snell.

Mr. Bassett was loud in his thanks to Lord Snell and Lady Wiston for their recommending him to the Admiralty.

"What is influence for if not to be wielded?" said his lordship with a condescending complacency which set Miranda's teeth on edge.

In contrast, Lady Wiston beamed at the young officer and said, "I should be glad to think I had a hand in helping a friend, but I am persuaded your promotion is entirely due to your merits, dear boy. What a pity it means you must go away so soon.''

''Jove, yes,'' said Mr. Daviot. ''You'll be sorely missed, Bassett. I trust you won't forget us when you return loaded with honours.''

''You must promise to come straight here next time you are in London,'' Lady Wiston affirmed.

''And I shall write a book about your adventures when I'm finished with mine!''

As he spoke, Mr. Daviot did not so much as spare Miranda a glance. His lack of acknowledgement told her her part in his work was over. Their friendship was over.

She wanted to cry, but instead she said brightly, ''Don't forget, Mr. Bassett, you have already promised a letter from every port.''

For some reason this simple statement earned her a glare from Mr. Daviot. She could not decide whether his inexplicable anger or his indifference was the more apt to throw her into the dismals.

Unable to consult Mr. Daviot, Miranda was the more determined to attempt to extract the truth from Lord Snell. At home, even supposing she succeeded in cornering him, the risk of being interrupted was too great, so she was relieved when a fine day permitted their drive in Hyde Park.

To her dismay, after joining her in the curricle he told his groom to get up behind. Still, if they spoke quietly the sound of wheels and hooves on gravel would cover their words. She decided to go ahead anyway.

The trouble was, every time she began to turn the conversation towards Lady Wiston, Lord Snell deftly returned it to commonplaces. They talked of the weather; the latest exhibition at Somerset House; the rumours that *Waverley* and *Guy Mannering* were written by the poet Walter Scott; Napoleon's being exiled to St. Helena and the restoration of the monarchy in France. When they left the park after a leisurely circuit and trotted along Oxford Street, his lordship was holding forth upon the folly of republicanism.

At last, in desperation as they approached Portchester Square, Miranda broke in. "Sir, pray excuse me, but I must ask: What are your intentions towards Lady Wiston?"

"Why, simply to see that she is properly cared for." He flashed her a smile. "Your loyal concern does you credit, Miss Carmichael, but there is no need for you to trouble yourself. Lady Wiston's welfare is the responsibility of her family, and the duty will not be shirked, I assure you. Ah, here we are. You will forgive my not getting down, but I am looked for elsewhere."

Handed down by the groom, Miranda stood on the pavement watching the curricle circle the garden and turn south again. For all her boldness, she was none the wiser.

Despite the smile, the commendation of her loyalty, she felt she had been put firmly, if politely, in her place. She was not to trouble herself—Lady Wiston's future was none of Miranda's business. After such a set-down, she doubted she would ever have the courage to question him again.

But if he thought so little of her, why had he taken her driving in his new curricle? He must hope to buy her off with a few crumbs of gallantry to add to his promise to ensure her welfare if anything happened to Lady Wiston.

And that wretch Peter Daviot thought she had succumbed to his lordship's flattery!

Yet if Lord Snell wished to lull her into compliance with his nefarious aims, surely he would not risk giving her a set-down. She was not to trouble herself—perhaps he simply wanted to relieve her from anxiety, to assure her that broader shoulders were ready to carry the burden.

Which might mean he was genuinely attracted to her.

Everything he had said was open to interpretation. Taking care of Lady Wiston could mean seeing to her comfort. Or it could mean subjecting her to dreadful tortures in the name of treatment for her presumed madness.

Slowly Miranda mounted the steps and entered the

house. One thing was certain, there was no point attempting to broach the subject again. If Lord Snell meant well by his aunt, her enquiries were sheer impertinence. If not, he was obviously not going to reveal his plans to her as he had to Mr. Daviot.

According to Mr. Daviot—and she had called Mr. Daviot a liar. She knew very well he was not, however fantastical his imagination. She could not blame him for refusing to speak to her, but oh, how it hurt!

"What a pity, it is beginning to rain," said Lady Wiston, glancing out of the study window. "No drive in the park for you today, my dear."

"I am not so spoilt as to expect it, ma'am! There, that letter is finished. Have you the list for me?"

"Here it is. I have crossed off Miss Mellings, you will see. It was very honest of her to tell me she has taken another lover, but it simply will not do to continue to invite her. Actresses are lamentably exposed to temptation, I fear." She sighed, but then brightened. "I have added the Tuttles. Such a delightful family, the children so well-behaved. Ah, I hear the door-knocker. That will be Mr. Sagaranathu."

She went off to her lesson, leaving Miranda to address the cards of invitation for next week's at-home.

Finishing the last, Miranda rang the bell. The butler stumped in. "Yes, miss?"

"I need one of the footmen, Twitchell, to deliver these cards."

"They're both out, miss," he said apologetically. "Eustace went with Mrs. Lowenstein to market, and his lordship sent Alfred on some errand."

"He did? That goes to show how well you have trained Alfred already. I shall never forget their first meeting. Well, send me whichever returns first, if you please. I have one or two more letters to write for her ladyship."

It was not long before Alfred came in. His livery now fit

quite well and his speech and bearing were much improved. An impassive face was more than he could contrive, though. He grinned at Miranda.

"Mr. Twitchell said you wanted me, miss? Sorry you 'ad to wite . . . wait. I weren't loafing, honest. His lordship 'ad me running all over, Limmer's 'Otel wiv a note for Mr. Redpath, and the Crown and Anchor for Mr. Fenimore, and Ibbetson's for the Rev. Jeffries. Blimey, miss, that place is full of parsons as a brewhouse is of barrels."

"Fenimore, Redpath, and Jeffries?" Miranda asked in surprise. "Are you sure of those names?"

"Dead sure, miss. I don't read 'andwriting that good yet—leastways, yourn is clear as a bell, miss, but 'is lordship's ain't—so I arst 'im to read 'em over to me and I memorized 'em."

She frowned. All the admiral's nephews were in Town, three of them without making their presence known to his widow, though in contact with the fourth who was staying in her house. Miranda recalled Lord Snell requesting their directions. She had thought it odd at the time.

" 'As I done summat wrong, miss?" the footman asked anxiously.

"No, Alfred, on the contrary. I am very glad you told me about his lordship's errands. In fact, I am going to ask you to inform me if he sends you again to those gentlemen. And please tell Eustace to do the same, but don't let anyone else know. Will you do that?"

Alfred's eyes sparkled with excitement. "Cor, miss, course I will. You know who them gents is? The names sounded kind of like I might've 'eard 'em afore."

"I believe they must be Sir Bernard's nephews. The names are the same."

"That's it, miss! When 'is lordship first come, they was talking about 'em, all four, in the kitchen. But what I 'eard is, 'is lordship's too 'igh and mighty to give 'is cousins the time o' day, and the rest can't stand the sight of each uvver. That's what Mr. Twitchell said."

"O*ther*," Miranda corrected absently. "Did he, indeed!" Yet Lord Snell had said he corresponded regularly with his cousins.

Servants' gossip, she reminded herself. But as soon as Alfred had gone off with the at-home cards, she started to draw up another list.

Mrs. Fry would testify to Lady Wiston's sanity. So would the governors of the Foundling Hospital and St. Bartholomew's, and the doctors, and the directors and matrons of several other orphanages, all highly respectable people. The servants all adored her, but if they were questioned in court they might inadvertently let slip something to damage her case.

Miranda herself, though, must surely be reckoned to know her employer as well as anybody. Her testimony ought to count for a great deal. So would Mr. Daviot's. His quarrel with Miranda would not be allowed to stand in the way of protecting his aunt.

She knew she could count on him for that, and the knowledge was a great comfort.

Taking down the memorandum book, she set about writing explanatory letters to everyone on her list. When the summons to court came, they would be ready to send out. Surely enough of Lady Wiston's friends and admirers would respond to counteract anything Lord Snell, his cousins, and his paltry, bribed doctors might say.

The days past and nothing happened. At first Miranda felt the tension within her growing, but busy as ever, she had little time to brood. She began to think the whole business was a storm in a teacup. All the little things which seemed to confirm Mr. Daviot's story could be quite easily explained away.

He continued to spend every day at his club and most evenings out with Mr. Bassett. After believing he was too angry with her to spend time in her company, Miranda started to wonder if he was now too ashamed of having slandered Lord Snell to face her.

The day of Mr. Bassett's departure arrived. Torn between regret at leaving his new friends and excitement at his new command, he went off laden with preserves and fruitcakes and a fine ham from Lady Wiston's kitchen.

An hour after he left, when Lady Wiston was at her lesson above stairs, Alfred came to find Miranda in the study.

"It's 'appened, miss," he announced portentously, waving three sealed letters at her. "Fenimore, Jeffries, and Redpath, just like afore."

"Let me see!" Taking them, she stared at the names on the front, the seals on the back—not stamped with his lordship's signet, she noted. She was wild to know what they said. She had to know! "Turn your back, Alfred," she said, reaching for a pen-knife.

"You wants to 'eat it up a bit, miss," Alfred advised as obediently he turned.

Miranda lit a candle and held the knife blade in the flame for a few moments. Gingerly she slid it under the seal of the Reverend Edward Jeffries' note, hoping a clergyman was less likely to suspect anything amiss. She unfolded the sheet.

"Crown & Anchor coffee room, half past noon," she read, written in Lord Snell's sprawling, arrogant hand, signed only with an S. That, the lack of signet impression, and the conciseness bespoke nefarious business. Feeling slightly sick, she quickly resealed the note.

"Whassit say, miss?" Alfred begged.

"Do you know the Crown and Anchor coffee room?" she asked as he swung round. "Would it be possible to overhear a conversation there without obviously eavesdropping?"

"I 'spec so, miss. Coffee rooms in the City mostly has boxes, like, leastways round the sides. Jus' say the word and I'll give it a try."

"I could not ask you to go. I must do it myself."

"Not bloody likely, miss, 'scuse the Billingsgate. 'Is lord-ship sets 'is glims on you 'e'll know right orf there's summat havey-cavey. Now me, 'e don't notice me face, only her ladyship's livery. All I gotta do's take orf me coat and wig and 'e won't know me from a hole in the wall."

Miranda had to agree, yet there were other considera-tions. If he was seen leaving the house without his livery, explanations would have to be made. She could not be sure he would understand or accurately report what, if anything, he heard.

"No, I must do it myself," she repeated firmly. "Where is the Crown and Anchor?"

"Just south o' the Strand, miss, by St. Clement's."

Near the law courts, where Mr. Fenimore would feel at home—and where a petition for committal to a lunatic asylum would be heard.

She gave him Lord Snell's notes. "Go and deliver these, Alfred, and then come straight home. You may be needed here."

"Quick as lightning, miss."

He dashed off, and Miranda hurried up to her chamber. She changed into an old gown of dark brown cambric, from pre-Lady Wiston days. Lord Snell had only seen her in pretty, coloured dresses. She put on her plainest bonnet, but its narrow brim left her face exposed. Mrs. Lowenstein wore poke bonnets. Miranda sped down to the housekeep-er's room.

In view of Lady Wiston's large acquaintance in the nether parts of London, neither Mrs. Lowenstein nor Twitchell considered Miranda's desire to be inconspicuous worthy of remark. Twitchell was only distressed at the lack of hackneys in the square at this season. Leaving a message for her ladyship that she would be late for luncheon, Miranda set off for Oxford Street, where the shops ensured an abundance of hackneys all year round.

She reached the Crown and Anchor at twenty minutes past noon. Though not crowded, the coffee room was quite busy, with several tables occupied by barristers in old-fashioned wigs, engaged in vociferous argument. There were few women present but those looked like respectable travellers. The Crown and Anchor, while not one of the great coaching inns, ran a few stages into Kent and East Anglia.

Miranda stood reading the bill of fare, chalked up on a slate. Covert glances about the room showed no sign of Lord Snell, though it was hard to be sure. As Alfred had said, the seats around the sides of the room were high-backed settles, forming a sort of box around each table. The advantage was, if she could obtain a seat at the table next to her quarry, she would be invisible to them.

She stopped a scurrying waiter and enquired whether Mr. Fenimore was present. "He is staying here, I believe," she explained.

"Over there, madam." Without looking at her, the waiter gestured and bustled on.

Miranda saw two men sitting at a table against the wall. She did not dare study them closely lest they observe her interest, but they both looked to be between thirty and forty. One had a pale, indoor face suited to a lawyer. The other was a large, ruddy man in a green coat who must be Squire Redpath.

Miraculously the next table was empty. She made her way to it and sat down with her back to her quarry.

A moment later, Redpath and Fenimore were joined by the Reverend Edward Jeffries. Exchanging greetings, they sounded tense and edgy, and not at all as if they were on terms of intimate friendship. Miranda forced herself not to snatch a peek at the clergyman.

What followed she missed as a different waiter came up to take her order. She asked for coffee and bread-and-butter. As he left, she heard Lord Snell's hushed, complacent voice. She had to strain her ears to make out the words, and bursts of laughter from a nearby table kept interrupting her eavesdropping.

". . . all settled. I have the order here in my pocket, signed and sealed."

"Let me see."

"Yes, let Fenimore check that everything is properly done. In my position, I cannot afford to. . . ."

Coffee and bread-and-butter arrived. Miranda paid for them on the spot in case she had to leave in haste.

". . . testimony of four anxious relatives and. . . ."

". . . the money?"

"Patience! It will be a few days. I have to make that fool Bradshaw understand the position, and. . . . In any case, the first thing is to. . . ."

"When . . . ?"

"This afternoon. No sense in delaying any longer, now the sailor is gone."

"What about Daviot?"

". . . chance of trouble from him . . . spends all his time at that club of his. He. . . ."

"But the. . . ."

"Everything is under control, I tell you, all arrangements. . . . As a matter of fact I have hired. . . ." Lord Snell's voice dropped so low, it was indistinguishable from the general buzz of conversation in the coffee room.

Icy chills running up and down her spine, Miranda decided she had heard enough. Mr. Daviot had not misunderstood, had not exaggerated, had not even plumbed the depths of Lord Snell's villainy. In secrecy his lordship had pushed through his application for committal, with no opportunity for Lady Wiston's friends to defend her.

She must be warned, at once! Miranda abandoned her untouched coffee and buttered bread. Keeping her face turned away from the four greedy, stony-hearted cousins, she hurried out.

Chapter 14

There was no shortage of hackneys in the Strand. The first one Miranda waved at stopped for her. Telling the jarvey to drive to Portchester Square as fast as his horse could trot, she sprang into the aged carriage.

Agitation, not awareness of the dirty seat, made her perch on the edge, hanging onto the strap. She must think, but her mind returned again and again to what she had just overheard.

The judge's order for committal was theirs, and some-one—Mr. Redpath?—was impatient to lay his hands on his share of the loot. Lord Snell had reminded him of something to be done first, presumably the actual spiriting away of his victim. *This afternoon.*

Whether because of the law's delay or deliberately, he had waited until Mr. Bassett was gone. The reason for his help in obtaining H.M.S *Adder* for the young officer was now obvious. Mr. Bassett would never have allowed him to carry off Lady Wiston.

Nor would Peter Daviot. Hence the introduction to the Explorers' Club.

Ought Miranda to fetch Mr. Daviot before she went

home? She did not know where the club was. The jarvey might know, but it was a small, obscure club, not like White's or Brooks's in St. James's Street, familiar to all and sundry. Though she longed for the comfort of his presence, she dared not waste time hunting for him. Better to go home, warn the household, then send for him.

This afternoon. How soon? She had left before Lord Snell, but his curricle was much faster than this wretched hackney. No use trying to persuade a London jarvey to whip up his horse, not without a larger bribe than she carried in her purse. He was as likely to take offence and slow down.

Sinking back on the seat, her hands clenched in her lap, Miranda fought back threatening tears.

Portchester Square at last. The hackney stopped at Number Nine and Miranda jumped down. "The butler will pay you," she cried to the driver and ran up the steps into the house. "Eustace, pay the jarvey and come back quickly. Where is her ladyship?"

"In the dining room, miss." The well-trained footman contrived not to look more than faintly startled by her urgency, but he permitted himself a question. "Whatever's the matter, miss?"

"I shall tell you. Bring Twitchell and Alfred," she threw over her shoulder, already half way to the dining-room door.

"Yes, miss. At once, miss."

Lady Wiston was placidly demolishing a slice of damson tart. "Oh there you are, dear," she said as Miranda burst into the room. "Have you taken luncheon already? Do try a piece of this tart. Cook's pastry gets better every day, I vow."

"I have no time to eat, ma'am. Listen! I have just discovered that Lord Snell is going to have you committed to . . . to an asylum." She had to force the word past the lump in her throat, and she could not bear to look at Lady Wiston's face. "I believe he means to come this very afternoon and take you away, or perhaps he will send those dreadful doctors, I cannot be certain.''

"Miranda, sit down. My dear child, you are shaking like a leaf. Here, drink this." Lady Wiston, unnaturally calm, pressed a glass of wine into Miranda's hand. "Are you quite sure of your information?"

"Yes, oh yes! I heard him myself, discussing it with his cousins. And Mr. Daviot warned me, an age ago. I did not believe him," she said in bitter self-condemnation. "We must send for him at once."

"Yes, at once. Ah, Twitchell, pray send the carriage at once to fetch Mr. Daviot."

"No, wait!" Miranda took a gulp of wine and tried to collect her thoughts. "Harnessing up the carriage will take too long. Oh, why did I not ask the jarvey to wait! Twitchell, Eustace, Alfred, there is a plot to abduct her ladyship. We have to protect her."

The butler's weatherbeaten face was horrified, and behind him the two footmen gaped. Mudge, who had followed them in, danced around Lady Wiston's chair, begging for comfits.

"We need Mr. Daviot," Twitchell said grimly, "and Mr. Potts!"

"Oh yes, Daylight Danny," Miranda agreed.

"I knows where to find 'im, miss," cried Alfred, "and I can run faster nor any 'ackney. I'm off." Without waiting for orders or permission, he dashed out, an excited pug snapping at his heels.

Twitchell made no attempt to call him back and rebuke his lapse from footmanly propriety. "We'll lock all the doors," the butler proposed. "Surely they won't bash them down in daylight, miss?"

"Godfrey has a key," said Lady Wiston. She was beginning to sound a bit shaky.

"Lord Snell!" Eustace gasped incredulously as the front door slammed behind Alfred. With a disappointed yelp, Mudge trotted back.

"Lord Snell is behind it," Miranda confirmed. "Eustace,

you must go for. . . ." Her voice trailed off as she realized
he was now the only able-bodied man in the house. "No,
you had best stay here. All of you, if they come, try to delay
them. I shall go for Mr. Daviot. Twitchell, where is the
Explorers' Club?"

"Not far, miss. Twenty-nine, North Audley Street, just
the other side of Oxford Street."

"Stay with me, Miranda," Lady Wiston entreated. Her
hand went automatically to her pocket for a comfit for the
begging dog.

Miranda had already jumped up. "I cannot," she said,
hugging the old lady. "We must have Mr. Daviot here but
I cannot leave you without Eustace to protect you. To
explain to a maid would take too long, and then the club
porter might not take her request to see Mr. Daviot seriously. I must go."

Hurrying down Orchard Street, Miranda kept breaking
into a trot. She crossed Oxford Street at a run, skirts lifted,
dodging between a lumbering dray and a stage-coach. In
North Audley Street, she eagerly scanned the house numbers. 19, cross North Row, 20, 21 . . . 27 on the corner of
Green Street, cross over, 28, 29—beside the green front
door gleamed a brass plate: The Explorers' Club.

She seized the lion's-head knocker and beat a tattoo.

The door swung open. The hall-porter frowned down
at her. "Yes, madam?"

"Please, tell Mr. Daviot it is Miss Carmichael," she
panted. Tell him he must come at once. The case is desperate."

"Mr. Daviot? He's above stairs. I can't let you in to wait,
madam. No ladies allowed."

"I shall wait here. Hurry, oh pray hurry."

The door closed. As she stood on the doorstep, painfully
regaining her breath, Miranda was struck by her own ago-
nizing stupidity. She should have told Twitchell to send
one of the maids for the coachman and groom, both able-
bodied and loyal.

Still more addlepated, why try to protect Lady Wiston

at home when all she need do to be perfectly, if temporarily, safe was to leave the house?

Peter gazed gloomily through the window at the house opposite. He was going to miss Bassett damnably. Almost as badly as he already missed the easy comradeship of Miss Miranda Carmichael.

He could not let that estrangement continue, even if she had called him a liar. Even if it meant apologizing for what he had said of Lord Snell. It seemed he was wrong there anyway, or perhaps his refusal to cooperate had forced Snell to give up his detestable scheme. At any rate, nothing had come of it.

The loss of Miranda's friendship left a great hole in his life. True his manuscript was in a mighty mess, but Aunt Artemis would not quibble at hiring some penniless clerk to sort things out for him. Miranda need never pore over his scribbles again if she chose not to, if only she would discuss the book with him, laugh at his tales, quiz him about his wild fancies.

Sighing, he dipped his pen and reached for a fresh sheet.

"Mr. Daviot, sir!"

Two or three heads turned to glare at the page boy. He scuttled over to Peter, who dropped his pen and demanded, "What is it?"

"There's summun downstairs for you, sir," said the boy in an urgent whisper. "A dowdy sort o' female, upper servant, likely, 'cording to Porter. She says Miss Carmichael's in desperate case and you're to come at once."

"Oh God!" Peter sprang to his feet, overturning his chair. Miranda ill, hurt, maybe dying? He raced down the stairs. A dowdy female—Baxter or Mrs. Lowenstein? Both footmen out, sent running for physicians, surgeons, apothecaries?

No one but the porter in the hall.

"Where is she?"

"Out on the step, sir. No ladies. . . ."

Brushing the man aside, Peter flung open the door. "Miranda! Ye gods, what's wrong?"

Beneath a hideous bonnet, her face was very pale. "Come." Her voice quavered. "Come quickly."

He reached for her arm. They were half way across Green Street by the time the hall porter called after them, "Your hat, sir! Your gloves!"

Peter scarcely heard him. "Miss Carmichael, what is it? I understood you were in desperate. . . . Is it Aunt Artemis?"

"You were right," she said wretchedly. "I should have known. Lord Snell has obtained an order to commit Lady Wiston to a lunatic asylum."

Explanations could wait. "He's at the house now?"

"Not when I left, but any minute he may arrive."

"Then I must run. Forgive me for leaving you."

"Go, go! It's all my fault."

He turned to face her, clasping both her hands in one of his and raising her chin with the other, forcing her to look up at him. Her brown eyes swam with tears and her lips were pressed together in an unsuccessful effort to stop them trembling.

"It is not your fault," he said decidedly. "If anyone is to blame, I am. I knew and did nothing."

"But. . . ."

He touched the trembling lips and forced a smile. "Not now. We'll argue the case when Aunt Artemis is safe. I'm off."

A third of a mile, half at most. No distance to stroll homeward on a pleasant evening. No distance to run six months ago, when he was accustomed to loping along tortuous forest trails with the Iroquois braves—in moccasins, not fashionable Hessians. Now it seemed endless.

How long had it taken Miranda to walk it? How long had it taken the porter to send the page boy after Peter at the behest of a dowdy, unimportant-looking female? Surely not long enough for Snell or his minions to present the order and persuade the servants to let him carry off their mistress?

At Oxford Street Peter was delayed by an unruly herd of bullocks on their way to Smithfield Market. He circled the rear of the herd, in his haste almost falling over one of the drover's dogs. Saving himself he twisted his ankle. The pain was acute, but after hobbling a few steps he decided it was only a crick and would wear off. He ran on.

He would smuggle Aunt Artemis out the back way, he decided; take her to an inn where Snell could not find her, and consult a lawyer about rescinding the committal order.

At last he reached the square. His heels pounding the pavement were the only sound in the summer-midday quiet—the only sound except for a dog's mournful plaint. From half way down the side of the square, Peter could see his aunt's house. The front door stood ajar. On the threshold sat Mudge, his short neck outstretched, his mouth open wide in a howl of despair.

Peter lengthened his stride, but he already knew he was too late.

Automatically dodging Mudge's automatic nip, he pushed open the door. Chaos met his eyes.

Twitchell sat on a chair, staring down at his splintered peg-leg. A stream of naval profanity issued from lips that had not pronounced an unbutlerian word in a decade. Seeing Peter, he said helplessly, "Shattered it with one kick, he did, sir. A bloody great bruiser none of us could stand up to. We did our best, but they took her ladyship."

Peter laid a consolatory hand on the butler's shoulder and took in the rest of the scene. In the middle of the hall, Eustace lay flat on his back, unconscious. The little housemaid, Dilly, knelt beside him waving a vinaigrette under his nose. The other two housemaids huddled together farther back, at the foot of the stairs. On the stairs sat Mrs. Lowenstein, her apron over her head, rocking and wailing. Baxter, the abigail, with tears pouring down her dour face, stood beside the housekeeper patting her shoulder.

Along the passage from the back stairs, Cook lumbered

forward waving a cleaver with reckless abandon, the scullery maid clinging to her skirts. "If they'd've just told me sooner, sir," she lamented, "if they'd've just called me right away, I'd've split their skulls for 'em like a pig's head."

The domestic disarray daunted Peter. He would quite frankly rather have faced a charging bull moose in the rutting season with nothing but a bow and arrow in his hands. To his relief Miranda arrived.

"He has taken her?" she asked breathlessly, then cast a glance around the hall and took charge. "Cook, stop flourishing that knife about before you hurt someone, and go and make tea for everyone. Baxter, my medicine chest from the study if you please. Mrs. Lowenstein!" Marching across to the stairs, she shook the woman. "Hysterics are quite fruitless. Ask Mr. Twitchell for his keys and bring some port and brandy. Dilly, pray help Mr. Daviot carry poor Eustace to a sofa in the drawing room."

Peter jumped to her implied command as fast as any of the servants. He and Dilly deposited the footman on an elegant blue-and-white satin sofa, while Miranda threw off her bonnet and supported Twitchell as he hopped after them.

Baxter arrived with the medicine chest. Miranda sent her for linen and Dilly for cold water for a compress for Eustace's swelling jaw. "Comfrey and arnica," she said, kneeling beside the prostrate victim and feeling his head. "There is a bump on the back, too." She unlocked the chest.

Eustace groaned and opened his eyes. "What's them, miss?" he asked with muzzy apprehension.

"Just herbs to soothe the bruising. How do you feel?"

"Sore!"

"Mr. Daviot, will you help him to sit up? I must know if he is dizzy."

Eustace was not dizzy, so Miranda allowed him a glass of the port Mrs. Lowenstein brought in. Peter poured it, and also took a glass to Twitchell, who looked alarmingly old and shaky.

"Tell us what happened," he said to the butler.

"Truth to tell, sir, it all went so fast I hardly know. Just after Miss Carmichael left to fetch you, his lordship came in with a fellow as might have been Mr. Daylight Danny Potts's twin."

"Bigger," said Eustace. "I tried to stop him, sir, but he floored me with a wisty castor and that was the last I knowed of it."

"He bust my leg," mourned Twitchell.

"You shall have a new one," Miranda promised.

"They came upstairs," said Baxter, by now helping Miranda to bandage the footman's head. "Her ladyship had come up to her chamber not a moment before. Marched right in they did, his lordship spouting a lot of rubbish about medical certificates and what-not. He soon stopped when Mudge bit him."

"Mudge bit him?" Miranda crowed. "Oh, splendid! At least our side got in one blow."

Peter took a biscuit from the tea-tray which Cook herself had carried up, and fed it to the pug. He sniffed it with disdain—no aniseed flavouring—but accepted it.

"It didn't help, miss," Baxter pointed out sorrowfully, tears beginning to flow again. "The pugilist simply brushed me aside. He slung her ladyship over his shoulder as if she weighed no more than a feather bolster, and off they went."

"They had two carriages, miss," Dilly put in. She was distributing cups of tea to all and sundry as Mrs. Lowenstein poured. "I seen 'em. His lordship druv that new curricle o' hisn, and there were a trav'lin' carriage wi' closed blinds and bars across what the bruiser bundled her la'ship into like she was a parcel. Not but what she were hittin' him over the lugs hard as she could, but he di'n't even seem to feel it."

"Did you see which way they went, Dilly?" Peter asked sharply.

"I di'n't watch, sir," said the maid, dismayed. "There

were Eustace lyin' on the floor senseless, and I thought
for sure they'd be goin' to St. Luke's or the New Bethlem.''

"The New Bethlem?" Daylight Danny charged into the
drawing room, Alfred panting at his heels. "They've
tooken m'lady to Bethlem?" he roared. "Don't fret, miss.
Never fear, sir. Daylight Danny'll bust down them doors
be they never so stout and get your auntie out again.''

Chapter 15

Miranda held out both hands to Daylight Danny and he engulfed them in his huge paws. "Don't you fret, miss," he repeated. "I'm on me way, and Old Nick hisself won't stop me."

"Daniel Potts!" said a breathless voice severely. "You mind your tongue." Mrs. Potts appeared on the threshold. "Beg pardon for intruding, miss, only I thought I better come too and see is there anything I can do to help."

"They've took her, Mary," said Danny, "but I'm off to the 'sylum to fetch her back." He took a step towards the door as his wife nodded approval.

"Wait!" Mr. Daviot beat Miranda by a fraction of a second. Grateful as she was for Danny's resolute enthusiasm, an outright attack on the New Bethlem or St. Luke's Hospital was more likely to lead to trouble for him than release for Lady Wiston. "Don't go off half-cocked, Danny," Mr. Daviot went on. "It's not so simple. I rather doubt my aunt has been taken to an asylum."

"What?" Miranda turned to him. "But it was you who said Lord Snell wanted to commit her as a lunatic."

"He did. He does. He has. But he swore to me she would

be cared for privately. That could mean a private hospital. However, the blackguard would have less control over her fate and her fortune than if he keeps her confined in his own house."

"He or one of his cousins," said Miranda.

"His cousins?" Mr. Daviot asked in surprise. "What have they to do with this?"

Miranda realized she had had no chance to explain how she found out about Lord Snell's plot. She did not want to waste time on it now, when every minute might be carrying Lady Wiston farther away from her friends. "They all came up to Town to give evidence against her," she said briefly. "I believe you are right, though. Lord Snell would prefer to have her under his own thumb."

"We can't count on it. She might be with any of them. Let's see, Brighton, Winchester, Ipswich, none more than a day's journey from London. Where is Snell's country seat?"

"Derbyshire, near Chesterfield."

"The best part of three days, sir," Baxter volunteered, "taking it comfortably. We stayed at Northwaite Hall two or three times in the old baron's day, when the Admiral was alive, God rest his soul."

"The others are more likely, then."

"Lord Snell would not trust any of them." Miranda was convinced that Lady Wiston was on her involuntary way into Derbyshire. "Besides, I doubt a country lawyer or a clergyman would have a large enough house for convenience, nor isolated enough to conceal her from neighbours."

"A good point. What about Redpath Manor?" Mr. Daviot asked Baxter. "Do you know it?"

"It's a great sprawling manor, sir, a mile from the nearest village. Mr. Redpath could keep her ladyship hid all right."

"And it's closest to London. I'll go there first."

"I am sure Lord Snell is taking her to Northwaite Hall," Miranda insisted. "Trying Brighton first will just lengthen her suffering."

"Far more time will be wasted in going to Derbyshire if she is in Brighton," he pointed out.

Helpless in the face of this logic, Miranda said, "Very well, we shall go to Redpath Manor first, but. . . ."

"We! I shall travel much faster alone on horseback."

"And what will you do when you find her? You will need Danny, at least, to help rescue her."

Mr. Daviot turned to Danny, who shook his head lugubriously. "Can't ride, sir."

"Alfred, go and order the carriage."

"On my way, sir!" Alfred vanished.

"I am going too," Miranda said. "Baxter, pray pack me up a change of linen, quickly, and a nightgown, too, and the same for her ladyship."

"At once, miss." The abigail hurried out.

"Victuals!" Cook exclaimed, and followed.

"Be reasonable, Miss Carmichael," Mr. Daviot pleaded. *"They* won't stop on the way—too much risk of Aunt Artemis creating a to-do. If she is not at Redpath Manor, if I have to go all the way to Derbyshire, I shall want to travel day and night. . . ."

"Beg pardon, sir," Mrs. Potts interrupted, "but if you was to ask me, miss is in the right of it. Her ladyship'll want a woman's support when you find her. 'Sides, if so be she's in anyways hurt, miss is good as a 'pothecary any day."

Her hulking husband gave her an admiring look. " 'Sright, sir. My Mary's allus right," he rumbled. "We best take Miss Carmichael."

"Perhaps," Mr. Daviot conceded, then ruefully smiled at Miranda. "Oh, very well. Can you be ready to leave when the carriage gets here?"

"Of course. I shall not hold you up, I promise, neither now nor on the way. I must just explain to Mrs. Lowenstein how to care for Eustace."

"He won't be able to travel for a while, I daresay?"

"Course I will, sir, if you need me!" said Eustace stoutly.

"Certainly not. You wanted to take him with us?"

"No, I was thinking of sending him and Alfred by the Mail to Ipswich and Winchester to investigate Fenimore and Jeffries, to save time if we draw a blank with the other two. The groom will have to go instead, and I'll take turns with Ted Coachman on the box."

"Danny can drive," Mrs. Potts told him proudly. "He used to drive a haywain at harvest-time when he was naught but a boy."

"Excellent."

"Begging your pardon, sir," said Twitchell, "but a seat on the Mail costs a pretty penny, and changing a team of horses is downright ruinous. It's not my place to ask, sir, but have you got the blunt?"

Mr. Daviot groaned and clutched his head. "Nowhere near enough."

"I have several pounds," Miranda said, "and the key to Lady Wiston's cashbox. I shall not scruple to use what is there for her own sake, but it is not a great deal."

"I've got a bit put by," Twitchell said gruffly. "Far as I'm concerned, her ladyship can have the lot and welcome."

With a shaky hand, Eustace pulled a few shillings from his pocket. "Here, sir."

Mrs. Lowenstein had a few pounds squirreled away. Baxter, returning with a neat parcel of clean linen for Miranda and a second for Mr. Daviot ("You'll excuse the liberty, sir," she said primly), produced another twenty-two guineas. Alfred reappeared and willingly handed over two bright, shiny half-crowns, his tip from Lord Snell for running errands to the cousins, as he announced with a grin. Dilly gave a threepenny bit, two pennies, and a ha'penny. Miranda saw Mr. Daviot open his mouth as these carefully hoarded coins appeared. She shook her head at him. The little maid would be heartbroken to have her offering refused.

The door-knocker sounded. The landau awaited.

Cook's hastily filled hamper was tied on behind, the medicine chest and other packages stowed under the seats. Meanwhile Mr. Daviot dashed up to his chamber to throw off his morning clothes and don something more suitable for driving in the country. He left Miranda to give Alfred and the groom their instructions for spying on Mr. Fenimore and the Reverend Mr. Jeffries.

At last all was ready. The whole household, even one-legged Twitchell and ashen-faced Eustace, came out to wish the rescuers God-speed.

"We'll have her ladyship home in no time," said Mr. Daviot heartily, and turned to assist Miranda up into the high carriage.

Mudge scampered between them and scrabbled up the steps. As he made a final spring to the floor of the landau, Miranda grabbed for his collar. She missed.

Fortunately his sideways slash also missed. He crossed to the far side and turned, teeth bared in a snarl.

"We cannot take Mudge!" Miranda exclaimed.

"Too bad," Mr. Daviot sighed, "but let's not waste time over him. With a bit of luck we'll contrive to lose him on the way. Up you go, Miss Carmichael."

Careful to keep her ankles out of the pug's way, she settled on the forward-facing seat, shaded by the raised rear hood. Mr. Daviot sat beside her. The carriage rocked as Daylight Danny clambered up and subsided on the opposite seat. Ted Coachman raised the steps, closed the door, and mounted to the box.

Just as the carriage began to move, Dilly flung in the dog's leash and a twist of paper. Her aim was excellent. The leash landed on the floor, the paper on Miranda's lap. The paper split and a shower of aniseed comfits slid to the floor.

No one disputed ownership with Mudge. He gobbled up a dozen bonbons and promptly fell asleep, his head on Miranda's foot, snoring.

Peter leant down to pick up the few remaining comfits. "Here, better save these for future need," he said, handing them to Miss Carmichael.

Nodding, she dropped them into her reticule. From it she took a small memorandum-book and a pencil, and, consulting Peter, wrote down the exact amount each servant had donated for the cause.

She put the note-book away. Now that the need for decisions and action was over, she was wan and listless. Leaning her head, still in that hideous bonnet, back against the blue velvet squabs, she closed her eyes. Yet her hands in their darned cotton gloves were tightly clasped in her lap, every line of her body revealed by the dowdy dress was tense, and two white teeth chewed on her rosy lower lip.

Hastily dragging his mind from that delectable body, those enchanting lips, Peter assumed she was brooding over her supposed responsibility for his aunt's abduction. He must put a stop to that.

"Miss Carmichael, you haven't yet told me how you discovered Snell's villainy," he said.

She turned her head to give him a fragile smile, as if she guessed he was trying to distract her from unpleasant thoughts. "I didn't credit what you told me," she admitted, "but it made me notice little things, start wondering, questioning his sincerity. Then the carrion crows. . . ."

"The *what*?"

"Those dreadful doctors he called in . . . Oh, you never saw them, did you?" She shuddered. "They were like vultures circling about an animal in its death throes. But it was their shabbiness which really aroused my suspicions. They were not at all the sort of well-respected physicians one would expect a nobleman to consult. I believe they would say anything for a large enough bribe. They would have certified Lady Wiston as mad however normally she had behaved."

"But of course she gave them plenty of ammunition."

"*Yoga*, the usual *un*usual guests." She threw an apologetic glance at Daylight Danny, who returned a grave nod. "Little enough, yet quite enough. I should have acted then, but I was sure there would be an opportunity for her friends to testify in her favour. I even wrote letters to everyone I could think of, but I did not send them. I was waiting for notification of a court appearance."

"So was I," Peter said in bitter self-accusation. "I should have known the sneaksby would set the whole thing up behind my back."

"No, how could you?" Miranda cried. "You are too open and above board to imagine such underhanded conniving!"

Though glad of her praise, Peter shook his head. "He had revealed himself to me as a wolf in sheep's clothing. At least I ought to have kept an eye on him instead of retiring to the club to lick my wounds."

"Which were my doing, not his," she said remorsefully. "I ought to have had enough faith in you at least to listen properly. I thought Lord Snell was the one to be relied upon, when all the time it was you."

The glow in her beautiful eyes caught and held Peter for a long moment.

Daylight Danny coughed. "If you was to ask me," he put in, "I reckon, his lordship being a lord and all, he'd've been and gone and done it somehow no matter what. It's no good crying over spilt milk, like my Mary allus says. What we got to do is mop it up."

"Very true, Danny." Peter reached over and squeezed Miranda's hand. "We have had the argument I promised you. Now tell me how you found out matters had come to a head."

As she explained, the carriage sped down Whitehall, deserted in high summer and peacetime, and across Westminster Bridge. The river, shining in the sun, reminded Peter of Bassett's outing and how irritated he had been by Miranda's pleasure in the officer's company on the way to Greenwich. Mere irritation was not what he felt when she passed the picnic and the return journey at Snell's side. He had been infuriated, blue-devilled, and, he had to admit, downright jealous.

Snell had been most particular in his attentions, the dastard! No wonder the poor girl's hopes had flourished.

The only question was whether he had also aroused her affections.

"I'm more sorry than I can say that Snell has disappointed you," Peter lied when she finished her tale.

"Me? I blush to think I ever supposed him partial! But whatever his faults toward me, it is his aunt he has most grossly deceived, and she alone is suffering for it."

With that he had to be satisfied, especially as Mudge chose the moment to raise his head and utter a heartrending howl.

"It's like he understood you, miss," said Daylight Danny.

"Perhaps he did," Miranda agreed. "He knows his mistress is in difficulties, and I believe he knows we are going to the rescue. Why else should he insist on coming, when usually he refuses to go near the carriage?"

"Sheer perversity," suggested Peter, happy to see her lips twitch.

Mudge keened again.

"Perhaps, but how sad he sounds. He is quite devoted to her."

"Cupboard love. Or rather, pocket-love."

At that Miranda laughed. "Well, yes, but comfits have never earned *me* his devotion."

"You only hand them out when you want to distract him, or bribe him. Aunt Artemis is Lady Bountiful."

"That she is," Danny affirmed, his battered face doleful. "There's many and many'd lay down their life for her la'ship, give 'em half a chance."

"Let us hope it won't come to raising a private army!" said Peter. "We must make plans for when we reach Redpath Manor. Before taking Aunt Artemis there they had first to make preparations to confine her, which cannot have been kept secret. I wish I knew the place."

"Ted Coachman must be familiar with it," Miranda pointed out. "He used to drive Lady Wiston and the Admiral there."

"True. We're nearly at Croydon—I saw a milestone a hundred yards back. When we stop to change teams, Ted shall join us and you take over the driving for the next stage, Danny. Take it easy at first. I'd wager a high-perch landau handles rather differently from a haywain, and carriage horses from carthorses.''

"Reckon they does!" said Danny, grinning. Then he sobered. "I won't be overturning you, miss, don't you fret. Not when it'd hold us up, and her la'ship in the hands o' them rum custermers. Her own nevvies turning agin her! What she's going through, it don't bear thinking on.''

Miranda was desperately trying not to think about it. She did her best to take an interest in the flowers in the hedgerows and the traffic they met.

The Brighton road was busy, for the Prince Regent's oriental Pavilion attracted many members of the fashionable world to the seaside town every summer. One result was that the innkeepers along the way kept a good supply of post-horses available. The change at Croydon was quickly accomplished. Danny cautiously tooled his team down the village street with Ted kneeling on the seat to provide anxious instruction.

Miranda hung onto the strap as the carriage swayed around a corner. Mudge yipped a protest.

"I hope it will not prove a mistake to trust Danny with the reins,'' said Mr. Daviot with a grimace.

"He'll do." There was more hope than certainty in Ted's voice but he turned and sat down. "Now just what was it you was wanting to know, sir?''

"How we are to find out whether Lady Wiston is at Redpath Manor without throwing the household into a commotion if she is not.''

Ted scratched his stubbled chin. "Well, sir, 'tisn't likely they c'd hold her ladyship there wi'out the servants catching wind o' summat, were it nobbut Cook wi' an extry mouth to feed. And so happens me and Cook was used to be thick as thieves back when the admiral and her ladyship goes a-visiting down there often. Ah, 'twould break the admiral's heart to see what his nevvies is up to!''

"No doubt he's turning in his grave. So if we can get

you into the house, you'll be able to find out what's going on?''

"Sure as eggs is eggs, sir. Proper sweet on me, Cook were, and no cause for hard feelings being as it weren't my fault we didn't go to the Hall no more after Mr. Redpath up and tied the knot.''

"Then we must think of a way to smuggle you into the kitchen,'' Mr. Daviot said thoughtfully.

"Why?'' Miranda was too impatient to find Lady Wiston to put up with subtle methods. "Why not just drive up to the front door and ask if she is there? Should they deny it, surely we will be able to tell whether they are lying.''

"We might, unless we only saw the butler. All butlers are practised at convincing callers that the residents are not at home whether they are or not.''

"Then we must contrive to gain admittance and speak to the family. Besides, if we are in the house, Ted has every excuse to go round to the stables and drop into the kitchen, so even if we discover nothing he will have his chance with Cook.''

"You have a point there, but how do you propose to persuade the butler to let us in? If Aunt Artemis is there, he may well have instructions to look out for us and keep us out.''

Miranda frowned. "So if he does admit us, there is a good chance she is not there.''

"Provided we have a story to tell him which one might normally expect to induce a country squire to receive two absolute strangers in his house!''

"Oh.'' Downcast, Miranda reflected on the irritating tendency of even the most imaginative of gentlemen to value logic above feelings. She still had a strong feeling they were wasting their time driving into Sussex. Lord Snell would not give Lady Wiston into the hands of a man he disliked and despised. He would want to keep her under his own control, under treatment by doctors he controlled.

She must not think about that or she would break down and be unable to help when the moment for action came.

On enemy ground, Lady Wiston had no one to count on but her nephew, her companion. . . .

"But we are not absolute strangers!" she exclaimed. "At least, we may not know the Redpaths personally, but you are Mr. Redpath's uncle's wife's nephew and I am Lady Wiston's companion, as Mrs. Redpath once was. There must be a way to take advantage of what connections we have!"

Mr. Daviot gave her an approving look. "A good point. As a matter of fact, I did meet Redpath more than once at the admiral's, before I went to America. Wait a minute, I have an idea."

His abstracted expression was so familiar to her she could see it with her eyes closed. For the first time in hours Miranda allowed herself to relax a little. She had perfect confidence in Peter Daviot's ability to come up with a credible, effective story once he set his mind to it.

How could she ever have doubted him?

Chapter 16

The sunset was fading over the South Downs as the high-perch landau rolled up the avenue of oaks. Though the raised leather hoods protected against the stiff breeze blowing off the Channel, Miranda was glad of the cloak Baxter had provided.

"You know your parts?" Mr. Daviot asked.

"No one won't never b'lieve I'm your vally," said Daylight Danny for at least the tenth time, gazing down at the frieze coat, moleskin waistcoat, and baggy-kneed unmentionables that covered his massive person.

For the tenth time, Mr. Daviot patiently reassured him. "The Redpaths are all too aware of my aunt's unusual choice of servants. They will think she hired you for me. As my valet you should be entertained by the upper servants rather than in the kitchen, giving us another string to our bow."

Danny sighed. "Right, sir. I got the rest by heart."

"Miss Carmichael?"

"Yes. It is so clever it cannot fail. It *must* not fail!" Miranda cried.

Mr. Daviot took one of her clenched fists in a warm,

comforting clasp. "It even explains why you are in such a tweak," he teased.

She attempted mock indignation. "To have Lady Wiston prefer Baxter's company to mine!"

"No one in his right mind would," he said laughing. "It's a weak point in the story, I admit. We'll gloss over it."

"No need." Miranda's effort to summon up an answering smile failed dismally. "You forget, they don't believe she is in her right mind."

The carriage pulled up before a sprawling brick manor-house with lights shining in several windows. Though sizable, the building had nothing grandiose about it, no pillars, porches, or pediments. It looked like a one-time farmhouse converted and extended into the comfortable home of an unpretentious country squire.

Danny opened the carriage door and let down the steps, while Miranda put on her bonnet. She expended an aniseed comfit in order to avoid being bitten as she clipped Mudge's leash to his collar.

"Drive straight round to the stables, Ted," Mr. Daviot reminded the coachman as Miranda followed Danny to the front door. "Don't wait to see if they let us in. Go on into the kitchen right away, leaving the horses harnessed, remember. Whichever way things turn out we'll want to get away without delay."

"Aye, sir. Good job it'll be a moonlit night. I'll do my bit, never fear."

Horses' hooves crunched on gravel. Danny lifted the brass door-knocker, a fox's mask, and beat a resounding tattoo.

Mr. Daviot joined them on the step. The door swung open, and he strode forward as if perfectly certain of his welcome.

"Here we are at last!" he said, handing the disconcerted footman his hat and pulling off his gloves. "I'm Daviot, and this is Miss Carmichael, of course. And my man, Potts."

"Yes, sir. But, sir. . . . That is, what . . . ?" stammered the bewildered man. "I mean. . . . Oh, Mr. Wick." He turned with relief to the approaching butler. "Mr. Daviot and Miss Carmichael. Were we expecting . . . ?"

"I'm afraid there is some mistake, sir," said Wick, puzzled but not visibly dismayed—but for a flicker as his gaze passed across Danny's admittedly distressing face and figure. He seemed to be more of a countrified old family retainer than a starchy town butler.

"What, is my aunt not yet arrived?" Peter Daviot glanced at Miranda, laughing. "And she so eager to get on she would not wait for the carriage to be repaired! The postilion must have lost his way."

"I hope she has not met with an accident," Miranda said forebodingly.

"Surely not, or we'd have come across them. No, the poor old dear is wandering about the lanes somewhere nearby, I wager."

"Your aunt, sir?" queried the butler.

"Lady Wiston." As Mr. Daviot spoke the name, he and Miranda and Danny all scrutinized the faces of Wick and the footman. Miranda, for one, saw no sign of perturbation. If Lady Wiston was here, they did not know it.

"The late admiral's widow, sir? On her way here?"

Miranda stepped forward. "I am her ladyship's companion. Do I understand Mrs. Redpath is not expecting us? Mr. Redpath is not yet come home?"

"No, madam, the master's in London."

"Oh dear, I knew all was bound to go awry with such hasty arrangements!"

If James Redpath had left London when Lady Wiston was abducted, to accompany her hither, he had a good hour's start on them. He should be home by now.

"You'd best speak to the mistress," Wick decided.

Two minutes later, Miranda and Mr. Daviot, with Mudge trotting behind, were shown into a small sitting-room decorated in charming flowered chintzes. A pretty young woman set down her embroidery hoop and rose to greet them. At least, she would have been pretty but for her peevish expression. A stout middle-aged matron continued to sit by the fire, her needle poised over her stitchery as she examined the visitors.

"Wick, close the door," Mrs. Redpath said fretfully. "It is windy tonight. You know the draught always gives me nervous spasms."

Miranda avoided exchanging a glance of triumph with Mr. Daviot. How clever of him to recall correctly that Marjory Redpath was the ex-companion his aunt had described as a hypochondriac!

"Lady Wiston is not here, ma'am?" he said with cheerful insouciance.

"Certainly not, Mr. Daviot," she snapped. "I cannot imagine why you should suppose she might be."

"Why, because she set out from the inn well ahead of us. You see, the carriage wheel started to wobble, so we stopped to have it mended. Aunt Artemis was wild to get here—well, stands to reason, she hasn't seen you in quite a while, I gather—and she chose to go on in a post-chaise with her maid. I stayed behind to supervise the repairs. Didn't take long. We were soon on the road again, Miss Carmichael and I. . . ."

"Indeed!" Mrs. Redpath, momentarily distracted, glanced from him to Miranda and back in a way that made Miranda squirm.

"Yes, quite soon, but we were sure my aunt would arrive before us."

"You mistake me, sir. I care not why you expected Lady Wiston to precede you. What I fail to understand is why she was travelling to Redpath Manor in the first place."

"By Jove, doesn't seem very odd to me, ma'am." Mr. Daviot's tone carried the merest hint of sarcasm. "She is your husband's aunt-by-marriage, after all, and she was your . . . ahem, you resided with her for some time, did you not?"

Mrs. Redpath flushed. "Lady Wiston rarely leaves London," she said defensively.

"But that's just it. In Town at this time of year there is a good deal of putrid fever about. Aunt Artemis. . . ."

"Putrid fever!" She backed away, her handkerchief pressed to her mouth.

"Typhus. Gaol fever."

"I knew it! Gaols, hospitals, back-slums, I knew she would catch some dreadful infection sooner or later."

"Oh no, ma'am," said Mr. Daviot, shocked. "She has not actually come down with the fever yet or she could not travel. It is to avoid it that Mr. Redpath suggested removing hither for a few weeks. Such a healthy situation, here on the Downs close to the sea, is it not?"

"Putrid fever! She will bring it with her. She cannot come here. I will not have her in the house! What can James have been thinking of to invite her? You must go away, quickly. Find her. Stop her coming any closer. Go away!" She flapped her hands at them as if driving geese.

Mudge took exception to the gesture and started to bark, tugging on the leash.

Mrs. Redpath had not previously noticed him. "Take it away!" she cried, tugging hysterically on the bell-pull. "That dreadful dirty creature. Animals carry disease. I do not permit dogs in my house! Wick, show these people out at once, and if Lady Wiston arrives do not let her set foot over the threshold! James must have run mad!"

The carriage rolled northwards through the night. Moonlight silvered fields and trees, leaving inky shadows which might conceal lurking highwaymen—or simply ditches.

Considering the latter the greater hazard, Ted refused to hand over the reins to either of the amateurs. Slumped on the rear-facing seat, Daylight Danny snored, as did Mudge on the floor. Mr. Daviot lounged back in his corner, his long legs stretched out before him. Miranda could not tell whether he was asleep.

She took off her bonnet for comfort though she was

sure she could not possibly sleep. The time they had wasted in going to Redpath Manor made her want to scream. From the first she had known Lady Wiston was not there, certain that Lord Snell had whisked her away to his lair in the north.

Mr. Daviot had dismissed Miranda's arguments and over-ruled her. Every extra instant of suffering endured by his aunt was his fault.

The bubble of tension within her threatened to burst out in a storm of reproaches. Somehow she succeeded in holding her tongue. The damage done by her last outburst was all too fresh in her mind. If she had not driven him to spend his days at the Explorers' Club, he would have contrived to put a spoke in Lord Snell's wheel.

How could she have been such a ninnyhammer as to fancy for so much as a moment that the baron had any interest in her beyond winning her support against Lady Wiston? Why had she ever *wished* for his regard? She had never felt comfortable with him. She did not even like him. Like the veriest servile toad-eater, she had let his title blind her to his manifest faults.

Between the two of them, she and Peter Daviot had made a dreadful mull of everything—and Lady Wiston was paying the price.

Fighting to banish memories of the visit to Bethlem, Miranda concentrated on the sounds of the night. Horse-shoes thudded on packed earth, clinked now and then on stone; the harness jingled and wheels creaked; an owl hooted in the distance, answered by another not far off; somewhere a dog barked, or perhaps a fox. Danny and Mudge snored on. Restlessly Miranda dozed.

She roused to lantern light outside, low, hurried voices and hooves clopping on cobbles. Another stage past.

The warm, heavy weight on her shoulder was Mr. Daviot's head. "What . . . ?" he muttered, half-waking. "Post-house? Sorry!" The weight vanished as he settled back in his corner. Miranda felt bereft.

With fresh horses hitched up, the landau rolled on.

At the next inn, Miranda found her head resting against Mr. Daviot's shoulder. He made no protest and it was too much effort to move, so she did not. When the carriage halted in Portchester Square in the small hours of the morning, her arm was numb and her neck painfully cricked.

"We leave at daybreak," Mr. Daviot announced. "An hour or so."

To Miranda, heavy-eyed, he sounded insufferably alert. She trudged into the house and up to her room. Flat on her bed, she still felt the sway of the landau. She lay there, hearing the sounds of the household coming to life. Dilly brought a can of hot water; Baxter appeared to help Miranda change her dress and tidy her hair.

"You're burned to the socket, miss," the abigail said, shaking out an old grey cambric more suitable for travelling than the new coloured muslins. "I could take your place."

Miranda shook her head. "No, I shall go on. What I need most in the world is a cup of tea."

"Cook's making breakfast, miss, and she's already prepared a heap of food to refill the hamper. Mrs. Potts's notion it was. She stayed, and for all she's a common body, I'll say this for her, she's a grand organizer. She's already got ahold of a new leg for Mr. Twitchell."

"Splendid! How is Eustace?"

"Better, miss, though still a bit wobbly."

"No word from Alfred or the groom, I suppose? No, it's much too soon. But in any case, I am convinced Lady Wiston is on her way to Derbyshire. We must go!"

"It's still pitch dark, miss. You've half an hour for a bite and a sup."

The new gas street lamps still lit the sleeping streets when Mr. Daviot took the reins and turned his team towards the Great North Road. Inside the carriage, Miranda shared her seat with Danny, while Ted sprawled in exhausted slumber on the other. The moonlight he prophesied had shone all the way from Brighton to London, but now gathering clouds hid the first gleam of light in the eastern sky. A brief flurry of raindrops dashed against the window.

Mudge was still curled up on the floor, still snoring. He had not stirred when they stopped in Portchester Square, and Miranda had forgotten about him.

"Otherwise I should have left him at home," she said to Danny in a low voice.

He grinned. "Maybe, miss, but he's one as gets his own way more often'n not."

"At least, if I had remembered him, I could have replenished my supply of comfits. I have only two left."

The pug needed no bribe to persuade him to descend at the end of the third stage, which they reached at about the hour of the morning when Miranda usually took him out. The hour when she had fallen over Mr. Daviot, she recalled; the hour when he had kissed her.

In retrospect her anger at the time seemed petty. What was a stolen kiss in comparison with Lord Snell's crime? In retrospect it had been a delightfully intriguing experience—and one she would not in the least mind repeating. Would Peter Daviot ever kiss her again?

After driving three stages, he looked almost as tired as she felt. Hanging on to the leash as she climbed down after Mudge at the Bull's Head Inn at Baldock, she said, "Is it not time Danny took over?"

"Yes, he should be safe enough now, at least as long as the rain holds off. We are beyond the worst of the market-wagon traffic going into Town. Gad, I'm stiff!" He stretched and yawned and turned to speak to Danny.

Mudge found a patch of grass and relieved himself physically. He then relieved his feelings by attempting to chase the stable cat. Miranda dragged him back to the landau by the leash, but it took a comfit to entice him back up the steps. One left.

The pug then decided he wanted to sit on the seat for a change. Standing on his back legs with his front paws on the blue velvet, he glared at Miranda. She told him to get down. He made a pass at her knee. Wearily she lifted him up. He trampled across her to where he could, by craning his neck, see out of the window.

No sign of the cat. He trampled back just as Mr. Daviot climbed in, stripping off his heavy York tan driving gloves.

"Ouch! Devil take the beast! I've a good mind to toss him out and abandon him."

"Nothing would please me more," Miranda said regretfully, "but it is for your aunt to make that decision. I am not prepared to swear she has absolutely no fondness for him. Let me look. Heavens, he really caught you this time! Where is my medicine box?"

As Danny drove out of the inn yard, Mr. Daviot extracted the chest from under the seat. Tending his bleeding hand, Miranda thought back to the first time she had done so. She had known no more of him then than that he was a self-confessed adventurer with a great deal of quizzical charm and absolutely no sense of decorum.

No, she had already known he was kind and considerate: he had offered to restrain Mudge while she rescued the cat he thought hers, and he had slept outside rather than rouse his sleeping aunt.

And his quick reaction had saved Lady Wiston from a nasty tumble down the stairs. What if he did rely upon her generosity to support him? Was that not what families were for? Should Miranda ever find herself destitute, she knew she could always claim a temporary home with her brother—heaven forfend!

It might come to that, if they failed to rescue Lady Wiston. After interfering with Lord Snell's plans, Miranda could not expect him to keep his promise to provide for her, if, indeed, he had ever meant it. She would have to look for a new position, and she would never find one half so comfortable. Instead of a busy, useful life with a lively old lady she held in great affection, she would turn back into a mouse scurrying about with shawls and smelling salts. Worse, for the rest of her life she would carry the guilt of her responsibility for Lady Wiston's confinement. Worst of all, she would never see Peter Daviot again.

Her hands trembled as she bound a strip of linen around his wound.

She forced her voice to remain steady. "There, that will keep it clean. Be careful not to dislodge it when you put your gloves back on."

"Uh." His hand flopped as she let go of it. Looking up, she saw that his chin was sunk on his chest, his eyes closed. He slumped back in the corner of the seat, dislodging the indignant pug.

While she tormented herself with a thousand dire possibilities, the wretch had fallen asleep!

Chapter 17

Long before they reached St. Neots and the end of
another stage, rain was pelting down, drumming on the
landau's double hood and running down the sides with a
gurgling swish. On the box, with no top-coat, Danny must
be soaked through.

He seemed to be coping admirably, despite Mr. Daviot's
doubts of his competence in bad conditions. Miranda left
the other two to their repose.

In the circumstances, she marvelled at their capacity for
peaceful slumber. Though her lids were weighted with
lead, her eyes dry and scratchy with fatigue, a fitful doze
was the most she contrived to snatch. This was partly due
to Mudge, who had appropriated her corner so that she
could not lean back in comparative comfort.

Last night she had made use of Mr. Daviot's shoulder,
but to do so deliberately in broad daylight was far too
unseemly to be considered. She doubted she could sleep
properly anyway. A sense of urgency gnawed at her.

However well Danny drove, or even if Ted Coachman
took the reins again, rain and mud were bound to delay
them. Lady Wiston and her captors, twelve hours or more

ahead, were probably unaffected as yet by the foul weather blowing in from the south-west. Indeed they had very likely arrived at Northwaite Hall some time since.

Lady Wiston must be sunk in the depths of despair, if not yet subjected to torturous remedies. Her oblivious nephew slept on.

He and Ted both woke when the landau pulled up at the Cross Keys in the marketplace at St. Neots.

"Danny Potts driving?" said Ted. "Well, he ain't overset us yet, but he don't know nowt about horses. I'll just hop down and see they give us a decent team, and get 'em harnessed up right."

"Don't tweak Danny's nose," advised Mr. Daviot.

The coachman grinned. "I'm not dicked in the nob, sir. I'll tell him I need to stretch me legs, the which I do."

Through the open door, Miranda saw Danny, his sodden clothes plastered to his skin. She called to him.

"You will take a chill," she said anxiously.

"Lor' bless you, miss, not I. 'Tis August, arter all, not Janu'ry, and there be a mortal sight o' me to keep meself warm. Don't 'ee fret."

"Are you good for another stage, Danny?" Mr. Daviot asked.

"Why, surely, sir. Dunno why I never thought to take up for a coachman, saving I wouldn't want to leave my Mary home alone. Here, now, the rain's a-blowing in. You'll be wet as I be ifn I don't close the door."

"Get yourself something to eat from the hamper. No, wait, better bring it here. I'm peckish myself, and you must be ravenous, Miss Carmichael. You scarcely swallowed a bite last night or at breakfast."

Miranda was touched that he had noticed her lack of appetite. Though she still was not really hungry, when he cut the cold chicken from the bone for her, shelled an egg, buttered a roll, quartered and cored a pear, she could not refuse to eat.

"That's better," he said approvingly. "You must keep your strength up, you know, for Aunt Artemis's sake. Lemonade or wine? No, I withdraw the choice. A drop of wine will warm you since tea is, I fear, impossible.''

"How can I complain? Cook has done us proud. Stop, stop! That may be a small tankard, but if you fill it more than half full I shall be tipsy in no time.''

"What happens when you're foxed?'' Mr. Daviot enquired with interest. "Will you serenade us, or do you grow belligerent, or am . . . amusing?''

He had been going to say "amorous,'' Miranda was sure. She had heard of wine having such an effect. What would he do if she became amorous? Would he be pleased, or disgusted?

"I do not choose to find out,'' she said primly, taking the half-full tankard.

She sipped slowly, warmed more by her thoughts and his teasing solicitude than by the wine. Mr. Daviot crunched a crisp pear, while Ted munched stolidly on his fourth or fifth ham-filled roll. Suddenly a loud belch resounded.

Mr. Daviot looked down at the floor, but not in embarrassment. "Mudge,'' he accused. "How can so small a beast produce so mighty a wind?''

"He'll be doing it t'other end soon,'' grunted Ted, "begging your pardon, miss. He's ate every scrap o' that slice o' ham Mr. Daviot dropped.''

"Good gracious,'' Miranda said in dismay, "it was huge. I think I had best take him out, just for a minute or two, if you will tell Danny to stop.''

"No need for you to get wet,'' said Mr. Daviot. "I'll take him.''

"I shall be glad of a chance to move about a little.'' Every limb was cramped, every joint ached, but she was not going to tell him so after his fears that she would hold him back. "I ought to have got down at the last inn.''

"You would have been soaked in a moment. At least the downpour seems to have turned to a mere drizzle now. Ted, tell Danny to pull up, and then take what more you want from the hamper. We might as well get it out of our way.''

Mudge, although in obvious need of relief, had to be bribed with the last comfit to jump down from the carriage.

"You should not have spoken in his hearing of abandoning him," Miranda said to Mr. Daviot, and he laughed.

He and Ted stowed away the hamper. Mudge scrambled anxiously back up the steps and curled up on the floor. Miranda left his leash on. She repossessed her corner, the men climbed in, and once again they set off.

Slowly, so slowly the miles slipped behind. The wine sent Miranda into an uneasy sleep. She dreamed she was in Peter's arms. A rare serious look in his bright blue eyes, he asked if she was feeling amorous—then he kissed her. Lord Snell appeared and dragged her away. He forced her into a curricle which somehow had barred windows. This he drove at a terrifying speed around a twisting circuit which yet carried her farther and farther away from Peter.

The carriage stopped, and she was vaguely aware that the landau had really come to a halt. Peter climbed out and Danny climbed in, a huge, dripping mass. Then Miranda drifted off again. This time in her dreams shackled madmen gabbled, gibbered, screeched, then shrieked in pain as a pair of huge, yellow-eyed carrion crows pecked viciously at their helpless bodies.

"Kill or cure," cawed one. "Kill or cure."

"Drive the devils out," the other croaked.

The nearest human figure took on Lady Wiston's features, and Miranda knew she was Prometheus being punished for her gifts to mankind.

Miranda awoke as the landau again pulled up. She felt not at all rested, wearier and stiffer than ever in fact. Her head ached, and the horror of her dreams loomed over her like menacing storm clouds.

Outside, though the rain had stopped, a funeral pall of sloe-black clouds hung low across the sky, shutting out the evening light. Inside the carriage dusk had already come and lamps shone in the windows of the Haycock Inn.

Ted opened the door and clambered down. Miranda heard him say, " 'Twill be dark soon, sir. There's a nasty hill in Stamford, seven mile on, wi' a tricky spot at the top and then a fork where we turn off the Great North Road t'ward Oakham, easy to miss in the dark. 'Tis time I earned me keep, methinks."

Opposite Miranda, Danny stretched and yawned enormously. "Have a good sleep, miss?" he asked.

"Well. . . ."

He grinned. "I reckon you'd give your eye-teeth, same as me, for a floor as don't joggle and sway about, and a nice feather bed."

Miranda tried to smile. "I don't know about my eye-teeth, but I should give a good deal."

"Never fear, miss, Ted says we'm past half way."

"Half way! Is that all?" she cried to Mr. Daviot, who climbed in and sank wearily to the seat beside her.

"Past half way," he said soothingly as the carriage began to move, "and that's half the journey from London to Northwaite Hall, remember. Before we started out this morning we had travelled over a hundred miles already. We have not near so far still to go."

"But the night will be utterly black. Even Ted will not be able to drive faster than a snail's pace. Oh, I wish we had not gone first to Redpath Manor!"

"It's a pity, I agree, but I still believe it was the sensible thing to do. Though of course I'm sorry Aunt Artemis will be confined for a few extra hours, in the end it will not make much difference. I daresay she will sleep it away. The worst must have been the first shock of Snell's betrayal and her abduction."

"If only that were the worst! Do you know how physicians try to cure madness?"

"No, but. . . ."

"They told us, Lady Wiston and me, when we visited the New Bethlem Hospital." The horror of her dreams swept over Miranda again. "First they isolate the lunatic from all friends. Then they beat him to make him afraid, so that he will be obedient. If he protests, he is immobilized in a strait waistcoat and shackles, and they burn his scalp with hot irons and. . . ."

"My dear girl, listen!" Mr. Daviot took her by the shoulders and gave her a little shake. "I'm sure all sorts of horrors go on in the public hospitals, but Aunt Artemis is in private care."

Miranda felt tears pouring down her face. "They did all those dreadful things to poor King George," she said flatly. "Right there in Windsor Castle, his own home. They told us."

"Well, I am very sorry for the unhappy King, but the case is quite different. His doctors were desperate to restore his sanity. Snell does not wish to cure Aunt Artemis; indeed, quite the contrary. If she were judged rational, he would lose at a stroke his control of her funds, which I am convinced is the sole motive for the whole affair. The last thing he'll do is pay for treatment."

"Makes sense, miss," said Danny.

It did make a sort of sense, but Miranda was too tired to be consoled by mere reason. At that moment Mudge, who had been trying in vain to draw her attention to his desire to join her upon the seat, lost his minimal patience and bit her knee. That was the last straw. The sobs she had so far restrained burst forth.

Peter Daviot gathered her into his arms and held her close, her cheek pressed to his already damp lapel as he stroked her hair. "My poor girl," he murmured, "you are quite burned to the socket."

"I did not mean to behave like a watering-pot," she wept. She ought to pull away, but the warm strength of his embrace was so comforting she clung to him. "I'm sorry."

"Balderdash! You have every excuse. I've been admiring your composure, and it's the more to be wondered at if you have been imagining such horrors."

"She has been like a mother to me. I cannot bear to think . . ."

"Hush, Miranda. Hush, love." He rocked her gently,

like a small, unhappy child. "Don't think about it. It will not happen. The villain is rapacious and callous, but we have no cause to suppose him to be deliberately cruel, and he has no reason to desire a cure. Trust me."

"If only I had trusted you in the first place, instead of him!"

"Well, of course, you should have guessed at once that when I described myself as an adventurer I meant it as a synonym for knight errant."

She looked up to smile at him, grateful for his effort to cheer her. In the gloom their gazes locked. Miranda could not stir; her breath caught in her throat; a flood of heat washed through her as he bent his head. His lips touched hers.

Mudge yelped and made another attempt to clamber onto the seat. Miranda was suddenly conscious of Danny, tactfully snoring scarce three feet away. She jerked back.

Mr. Daviot let her go. Unlike the first time he had kissed her, he made no apology—but this time she had not slapped his face.

Lifting Mudge onto the seat between them, he glanced at Danny with a rueful grimace. His eyes on Mudge he said in a casual tone, "The beast bit you, did he not? We shall stop at the next inn for you to treat the wound and . . ."

"Oh no, it is nothing."

"Show me."

"Certainly not!"

"Then give me leave to doubt, and to insist that you— what was it you told me?—do it right in the first place to avert the need to amputate! And, as I was going to say, we shall stay for a few hours rest."

"Unless you mean to make me drive a stage, which I cannot advise, I can rest perfectly well as we go along," Miranda protested.

"That's a taradiddle if ever I heard one. One may fall asleep in the carriage but one does not awake rested. I'm not speaking only of you. We are all exhausted. Besides, however warm the day, the night will grow chilly. Ted and I are damp, and Danny is sodden. I should not dare to return him to Mrs. Potts with an inflammation of the lungs."

"No fear o' that, sir," said Danny, confirming that his snores had been a matter of tact.

Mr. Daviot frowned at him. "But we shall be better able to tackle Snell and his bruiser if we are well rested. Also, the clouds may clear in a few hours, which would allow us to travel faster and with less danger of coming to grief. Tell Ted to stop at the next respectable inn, if you please."

He made it impossible for Miranda to argue. In any case, she had not sufficient energy for dispute. Leaning back in her corner with her eyes closed, she had scarce sufficient energy to ponder the kiss which still burned on her lips, the "love" which had issued from his lips.

A slip of the tongue, the latter, she decided sadly. As for the kiss, she could not place any importance on an embrace no different from the one he had once bestowed on her without so much as knowing her name.

Adventurer or knight errant, he distributed his caresses with a freedom which robbed them of all significance.

Black night had fallen when the landau turned into the cobbled yard of the Bull and Swan at Stamford. Ostlers with lanterns converged upon the horses, and a waiter in a short, striped coat with a napkin over his arm hurried up.

"Ye'll dine, sir?" he asked as Mr. Daviot opened the door, "and stay the night? Fine food and fine accommodations ye'll find at the Bull and Swan."

"We shall stay a few hours," said Mr. Daviot, descending and turning to help Miranda down.

Mudge sprang down ahead of her. With the loop of his leash in her hand, she stumbled on the steps. Mr. Daviot caught her. For just a moment he held her much closer than was strictly necessary. She found her feet and he let go.

Danny at their heels, they followed the waiter into the inn by the side door.

They entered a foyer with a low, black-beamed ceiling. Off it opened a coffee room and a noisy taproom, a wide passage to the front door, and an oak staircase to the upper stories. The landlord, a short, round man with a round, ruddy face, eyed them with somewhat startled curiosity: a well-dressed gentleman with a decidedly drab female on his arm and the battered visage of Daylight Danny towering over them, obviously in attendance.

"What can I do for you, sir?"

"We shall rest here for a few hours," Mr. Daviot informed him, "but we must go on before morning, at one o'clock, say. So we shall require horses then, and a meal at half past eleven, and in the meantime tea for the lady and chambers for the three of us and my coachman."

"One chamber for the coachman and your manservant, sir, and one for yourself and your good lady?"

"My good lady? Oh, Miss Carmichael is not my wife."

"Indeed!" The innkeeper looked as if he felt they might at least have had the decency to pretend.

Miranda flinched. She had not thought how her travelling without a chaperon would appear to strangers.

"She is my cousin," Mr. Daviot said swiftly. "And Mr. Potts is my friend, not my servant. We shall need four. . . ."

"Begging your pardon, sir," said Danny, "but I'll gladly share wi' Ted. What's more, 'twouldn't hurt none if you was to take the bed, and him and me to have a pair o' pallets on the floor." He leaned forward and muttered in Mr. Daviot's ear, "It being low tide with us as you might say, sir."

Straining her ears to hear this sensible comment, Miranda was half aware that Mudge had caught the scent of either food or a cat. Head raised, he snuffed the air intently with his flat nose, then leaned down and sniffed at the floor, casting about like a foxhound. He looked around, nostrils aquiver. All at once he yelped, yanked the leash from Miranda's hand, and galloped up the stairs.

"Oh dear!" She picked up her skirts and raced after him.

As she reached the top of the stairs, he stopped at a door half way along a dimly lit corridor. Scrabbling at it, he started to howl.

"Mudge, be quiet! Come here at once, you horrid dog!"

He paid her not the least attention, as usual. Miranda hurried after him to quiet him before the landlord decided to turn them all out.

The door opened. Silhouetted against the candlelight within, a huge, burly figure stood foursquare on the threshold. With a joyful yip, Mudge darted between his treetrunk legs and into the room.

"I'm so sorry," Miranda stammered. "My dog. . . ."

The colossus did not budge an inch. From behind him came a familiar voice.

"Mudge! Good gracious, where did you spring from? Yes, yes, dear boy, you shall have a comfit."

"Lady Wiston!" Turning back towards the stairs, Miranda called, "Mr. Daviot! Danny! Come quick, oh, do hurry! Lady Wiston is here."

Faster on his feet than Danny, Mr. Daviot reached Miranda while the bulky bruiser was still pounding up the stairs. Seeing the stranger, much of a height but twice his bulk, Mr. Daviot slowed to a halt and started to speak. Before he could utter a word, the giant stuck out an apparently casual fist and socked him on the jaw.

Mr. Daviot flew backwards across the passage, hit the opposite wall, sagged, and slumped to the floor.

Chapter 18

Peter lay still. He was not senseless, but the fireworks in his head made him wish he was. Rockets blazed a path of agony from chin to crown and back; squibs exploded in his ears; Catherine wheels spun dizzily against his closed eyelids.

Then a cool hand touched his forehead, a gentle voice said anxiously, "Peter ... Mr. Daviot, can you hear me? Speak to me, please! Open your eyes!"

He no longer wished he was senseless. With a pitiful groan, he opened his eyes and looked up into a dear, anxious face. Reaching up, he ran his fingertips down her cheek.

"I shall live," he croaked. The movement of his jaw sent fresh showers of sparks along every nerve. He closed his eyes again.

From beyond Miranda came Danny's severe voice. "Better put them fives down afore you does any more damage. Well, if it ain't Chopper Charlie! And what might you be a-doing of here?"

"Pertecting my lady," said Chopper Charlie truculently.

"Pertecting! All my eye and Betty Martin, that is. Don't

tell me it weren't you as run off wi' her la'ship in the first place."

"Anybody c'n make a mistake." The brute sounded distinctly abashed.

"Danny!" That was Aunt Artemis. "What a delightful surprise. Miranda, my dear, is poor Peter in sore straits? I fear Charlie did not realize in time that friends had arrived."

"Oh ma'am!" Miranda hiccuped on a dry sob.

Peter opened his eyes to see his beloved embrace his beaming aunt. Very touching. He recalled their attention with a heartrending moan.

"Sore," said Miranda, "but not, I think, in desperate straits. Danny, pray fetch my chest from the carriage. You— are you a chambermaid here? I shall need cold water and linen, if you please, and ice if you have any. The rest of you, ladies and gentlemen, I am very sorry you were disturbed, but there is nothing for you to see now, so pray go away."

Peter loved to hear her taking charge. Practical, yet sensitive; straightforward, yet tolerant of other's foibles; easily moved to both amusement and sympathy; that was the girl he wanted.

Too bad he had nothing to offer her.

"Mr . . . er . . . Charlie, pray carry Mr. Daviot into the room. Careful, now. He is Lady Wiston's nephew, you know. It was lamentably ill done of you to attack him without warning, and without waiting to find out who he was or what he wanted."

"I knows it, miss," said the huge bruiser guiltily. "Many's the time I been in a heap o' trouble acos I fergits to think afore I acts."

"I'll walk," Peter mumbled. The thunder and lightning in his head had subsided to a mere double throb.

Charlie offered a hand like a slab of raw beefsteak, and with its help Peter rose unsteadily to his feet.

"No hard feelings, sir?" Charlie begged. " 'Twas for your auntie's sake I grassed you."

"No hard feelings," Peter consented, adding austerely, "but try to remember that bribery is always to be preferred to violence."

Miranda smiled at him, and he recalled saying the same to her with regard to Mudge and comfits, shortly after their first meeting. Shortly after their first kiss. She had not slapped him the second time he kissed her. Either she had forgiven him for the first time—or she had forgotten it.

Mudge had been responsible for the unfortunate circumstances of their first meeting. He had not improved upon acquaintance. As Peter, supported by Charlie's oaken arm, stumbled after Miranda into his aunt's private parlour, the pug decided Charlie was an intruder. Snarling, he darted at the big man's ankles.

"Not now, you wretched creature," cried Aunt Artemis, fumbling in the pocket of her Cossacks for comfits. "Where were you yesterday when I needed you? He is a friend now, not an enemy."

Mudge ignored her. Charlie tripped and staggered forward. Peter lost his balance. Miranda, swinging around to reach for the dog's leash, caught him as he toppled.

Once more he had her in his arms, but he was in no case to appreciate the situation. A bass drum boomed in his head. It was all he could do not to shoot the cat on the spot.

"His face has gone green!" Miranda said sharply. "Quick, a basin."

A fine figure he cut! Definitely not hero material, Peter thought sadly as she sat him on a sofa, made him lean forward, and held his forehead. Aunt Artemis shoved a basin under his nose, but the nausea passed off. At least he had not utterly disgraced himself.

The chambermaid reappeared with napkins and a jug of cold water. Aunt Artemis at last succeeded in extracting a handful of comfits from her pocket and enticed Mudge away from Chopper Charlie's boots. Danny thudded in, panting, with the medicine chest, followed by Ted Coachman.

Miranda set about making up cold compresses with comfrey and pungent arnica. As she worked, she addressed the maid, "Pray tell the landlord we shall all stay the entire night. Have you dined, Lady Wiston?"

"No, dear, not yet. My friends will join me," she told the girl.

"Mr. Daviot will require gruel and a strengthening broth," Miranda added.

Peter was already too much recovered to let that pass. "Here, I say . . ." he began to protest, but the pain in his jaw changed instantly from a throb to a stabbing agony, cutting him short.

"And a bottle of claret," Miranda ordered, giving him a quizzical smile. "You would find chewing excessively uncomfortable, I fear. Here, hold this." She gently placed a chilly, dripping, aromatic cloth against his aching face. "The back of your head is sore too, is it not? I shall make another compress."

"You're an angel," he said through scarcely moving lips. Already the pain was ebbing, but he needed something to distract him from her closeness. "Will you ask Aunt Artemis to tell us her story?" he mumbled. "Though I am not in the least surprised that she has made a friend and defender of her captor, I should like to know how it came about."

She laughed. "Nor am I, and so should I. Lady Wiston, will you not enlighten us? How come you to be here in Stamford when we assumed you must be confined at Northwaite Hall by now? We cannot wait to hear."

"A mighty fidget we bin in," Danny confirmed.

"You must be patient, my dears," said Aunt Artemis. "I have just twenty minutes to do my *yoga* before dinner. I missed yesterday, what with one thing and another." She looked around the room to find a suitable spot.

"*Yoga?*" asked Charlie with interest.

"I daresay your chamber is the best place," Miranda hastened to advise. "The inn servants will be in and out of this room, setting a table and bringing chairs."

"I expect you are right, dear," Aunt Artemis agreed

meekly, but the glance she shot her companion was full of mischief. Her horrid experience did not appear to have cowed her in the least.

Mr. Daviot insisted on joining the rest of the company at table. Miranda surveyed his face, noted that his cheeks were no longer quite as white as the encircling bandage which held the cold compresses, and conceded.

"If you promise to say at once should you feel the least bit dizzy or sick."

"I promise." He still mumbled from the corner of his mouth.

"Dinner is served, madam," announced a waiter.

A table had been moved from its place against the wall to the centre of the small parlour. Set with a white cloth, blue-and-white china, and gleaming Sheffield-ware, it looked most inviting, especially as it was not rocking to the motion of a carriage. A steaming tureen stood at one end, a leg of mutton at the other, with a raised pie in the middle, a large loaf, and various other dishes crowded around. The excessive size and probable matching appetites of two of the diners seemed to have been taken into account.

Another waiter came in with a covered bowl. "The gentleman's gruel, ma'am."

"I refuse to carve the mutton if I'm not to eat of it," said Mr. Daviot.

"Sit where you will. Danny, will you be so kind as to carve? I shall fetch Lady Wiston." Miranda went to the inner door and knocked.

"Miranda? Come in, dear. I am a little more fatigued than I thought. I do think Godfrey might have hired a better sprung carriage!" That was the nearest she had yet come to voicing any criticism of her husband's wicked nephew. "Pray lend me your hand to rise."

Helping her up from her crosslegged position, Miranda

gave her a quick hug. "I was so frightened for you," she whispered.

Lady Wiston kissed her cheek. "I was a little frightened at first," she confessed, "but I *breathed,* as Mr. Sagaranathu taught me, and soon felt quite composed. And then, of course, I discovered that Charlie is really a most good-natured person, in spite of his shocking conduct. Oh dear, I have not asked after Eustace and the rest."

"We left them all well, though deeply distressed by your fate. Every penny they possessed they gave to help pay for our rescue mission."

"They shall have every penny back, and more besides."

"I knew you would wish to recompense them, so I made a note of the amounts."

"I should have been surprised if you had not," said Lady Wiston, laughing, as they went through to the parlour.

Mr. Daviot looked round, smiled, winced, and stopped smiling. He and Miranda sat each side of Lady Wiston at the head of the table, while Danny proudly took the foot. Chopper Charlie and Ted Coachman flanked him, both abashed, unsure of the propriety of dining with the gentry though Miranda had assured them her ladyship included them among her friends.

Miranda ladled out the oxtail soup. "Sop some bread in it," she suggested to Mr. Daviot as he looked gloomily from his bowl of soup to his bowl of gruel. "That should be easy to eat and it will help allay the pangs of starvation."

"I'm that sorry, sir!" said Charlie. Eager to make amends, he cut a thick slice from the loaf, trimmed off the crusts, diced the soft part, and scooped the bits into Mr. Daviot's soup. Lady Wiston was right, he was an amiable ox unless one chanced to be in his way.

"Tell us what happened, ma'am," Miranda urged.

"Well, you will have heard how I was carried off from home, so I need not describe that." Lady Wiston smiled at Charlie, who blushed and concentrated on his soup. "I was shut up in a travelling carriage with the doors locked and the blinds closed, and bars across the windows. By the light of a lantern hung from the ceiling, I saw Charlie on the opposite seat—I did not know his name then, of course."

"No more I didn't know yourn, my lady. His lordship showed me them false papers what said you was mad, but he never told me 'twas a ladyship he wanted me to grab, nor yet as she was his own auntie."

"Did you arst?" Danny demanded. "You've fell into bad comp'ny, me lad, if you goes a-grabbing of folks wi'out so much as knowing who they be. Dunno what my Mary'll say when she hears a cove what'd do such a thing was once a pal o' mine."

"I never done it afore," Charlie said humbly, "and I ain't never going to do it agin."

"Mind you don't!"

Miranda decided it was time to intervene. "Lord Snell did not travel with you, ma'am? Dilly thought not, but I could scarce believe it. He confined you in the coach with a . . . with Charlie?"

"Oh no, dear, not just the two of us. You must allow Godfrey credit for more sense of delicacy than that."

"Delicacy!" Miranda exclaimed, and Mr. Daviot snorted.

"Decorum, then," said Lady Wiston. "At least, he provided a female attendant, in the shape of a hatchet-faced gaoler by the name of Quin. She claimed to be a nurse, but the very sight of her would be enough to curdle an invalid's stomach. Fortunately, she proved to be addicted to gin."

Charlie nodded. "Four penn'orth o' Blue Ruin and th'owd squeeze-crab wouldn't know Paul's steeple from Tyburn tree."

"However, we did not discover that until later. I was a trifle flustered at first, so I lay down and practised my deep breathing exercises until I was calm."

Mr. Daviot's lips twitched, but he had learned better than to try to smile. Miranda observed him as he dribbled another spoonful of soup and sops into his mouth. His colour was much improved, and he no longer held his head stiffly as if the slightest motion was agony. Though no doubt he had a prodigious headache, nothing was seriously amiss. With luck, her remedies had averted the worst of the swelling and bruises.

He caught her eye. Something in his rueful look made her wonder if he felt he had made a cake of himself, or that Charlie had made a cake of him.

But Charlie was twice his size, and had given him no chance to defend himself. With time to think, time to speak, time to plan, Peter Daviot would outmanoeuvre Chopper Charlie with the utmost ease.

Miranda was about to tell him so when she realized she had not heard a word of Lady Wiston's tale for several minutes. Something about piquet?

Piquet?

"Lord knows I ain't clever," said Charlie, "but I ain't thick as two planks, neither, and I plays a fair hand at piquet, I does. Don't I, Danny?"

Danny's sour grunt suggested he had found out the hard way.

"Beat me handily, she did," his erstwhile friend informed him. "That was when I knowed for sure she weren't mad."

Miranda regarded her employer with deep suspicion.

"I confessed to cheating," Lady Wiston assured her, "but he just seemed to think that was even cleverer."

"Strewth, who ever heard o' such a thing?" Charlie demanded admiringly. "It takes a downy cove to Greek the cards wivout getting nabbed and here's a gentry mort as gulled me like any flat. The rig she run, well, you can't tell me she's out o' her senses!"

Though Miranda was not so sure it was a rational act to cheat—let alone admit to cheating—a prize-fighter with whom one was confined in a small space, she did not dispute his conclusion. She glanced at Mr. Daviot. He raised his eyes to heaven, so she assumed he agreed.

Lady Wiston caught his look. "Whatever you think of the state of my senses," she said tartly, "Mrs. Quin was by then bereft of hers. I cannot approve encouraging overin-dulgence in spirits, but in the circumstances I found it possible to reconcile my conscience. Charlie abstracted the key to the carriage doors from her pocket. At the next post-house, we descended and locked her in."

"What about the coachman?" Miranda asked.

"We had no coachman, just postilions hired at each stage who cared not a groat who their passengers were."

"Where was Snell?" Mr. Daviot croaked.

"Oh, Godfrey drove on ahead right from the start, to arrange for my reception. He must have been at North-waite, or nearly, by that time. Charlie simply paid off the last postilion, hired another, and sent the carriage and Mrs. Quin on their way, while we hired a post-chaise and turned back to Stamford."

"So at the next stop," said Miranda, "the man would obtain no response from within the carriage. The doors were locked, so it must have taken some time to discover the only passenger was insensible."

"I'd've gave a monkey," Charlie said wistfully, "to see his face when he found out he weren't going to get paid."

"I cannot let the poor man be left out of pocket," said Lady Wiston, "nor the innkeeper who supplied the horses. Miranda, pray make a note to reimburse them."

"That is surely Snell's responsibility," said Mr. Daviot, "but no doubt he would leave them to whistle for it—as he was left whistling for you, Aunt Artemis. The coach would go no farther with neither pay nor orders, so he was left quite in the dark as to what had become of you."

"Yes, dear," Lady Wiston said anxiously, "and I trust he will not decide until the morning to search for me. Perhaps we should have gone farther, but I was rather fatigued by the time we reached this inn. We stopped to rest and eat. Do you think we should go on towards London immedi-ately?"

Her nephew reflected for a moment. "No, I think not. You may be a little rested but we are not, and you are safer by far on the road with an entourage than at home without.''

"Oh Peter dear, I am so glad you found me. I was not at all certain what to do for the best.''

"It was not Mr. Daviot who found you, ma'am,'' Miranda pointed out with a smile. "We should have passed like ships in the night if it were not for Mudge.''

"Yes, the dear creature. I daresay I leave a trail of aniseed wherever I go, apparent only to a dog's nose. How very fortunate that I happened to have just renewed the supply of comfits in my pocket.''

Mr. Daviot sighed. "If he is the hero of the hour, I suppose we shall have to take him home with us after all. But not until the morning. You requested chambers for us, Miss Carmichael, but if you have no objection, I believe we ought to stay together. You and my aunt may share the chamber, and the rest of us shall sleep here in the parlour. Do you not agree?''

"Undoubtedly.'' She was pleased to be consulted, still more pleased to note that he now spoke without great difficulty. Yet his return to formality struck a chill to her heart. Not so long since, he had held her in his arms and called her Miranda, "my dear girl,'' even "love.''

With no sign that he recalled their brief moment of intimacy, he said jauntily, "Good, that's settled then. As for what is to be done about dear Godfrey and his plots, I for one shall be able to counter-plot much better after a proper night's sleep.''

"Miranda dear,'' said Lady Wiston, "you have not taken a bite for the past five minutes. You are more in need of rest than nourishment, I vow. Off to bed with you. I shall join you shortly. Heavens, I shall have to beg a bed-gown from the innkeeper's wife. Did you bring one?''

"Yes, ma'am, and Baxter packed one for you.''

Miranda was more than willing to retire. She wanted to talk to Lady Wiston about Peter, but not until the morning. After a proper night's sleep, she would be able to think clearly about him—she hoped.

Chapter 19

Broad daylight showed through the blue dimity curtains when a brisk knocking on the chamber door dragged Miranda up through foggy layers of sleep. She could have sworn her head had only just touched the pillow.

"Time to wake up, ladies," came Peter Daviot's unbearably cheerful voice. "Hot water in five minutes."

On the other side of the feather bolster, her bed-fellow stirred.

"Are you awake, ma'am?" Miranda whispered.

"Yes, dear, more or less. Good morning, Peter," Lady Wiston called. "A dish of tea would be more than welcome."

"Your wish is my command, Aunt."

"Dear boy," she murmured fondly.

Dear boy? Last night's quandary flooded back to the forefront of Miranda's mind. How was she to ask Lady Wiston's advice about her beloved nephew without offending her, distressing her, or setting her at odds with him?

Fortunately, she was not at all easy to offend. Miranda lay trying to think of a way to avoid the other two undesirable alternatives. For the first time in years she wished she had a mother to consult, a sister, someone whose first loyalty was to her, or at least an impartial friend.

Perhaps she ought to keep her perplexity to herself. Yet she burned to disburden her troubled mind, and she was quite sure Lady Wiston had her welfare at heart.

She was gathering her courage when a chambermaid came in carrying a tray laden with tea-things and two cans of hot water for washing. To Miranda's overstretched nerves, it seemed that the girl regarded her with out of the ordinary curiosity. All too clearly she recalled the landlord's look of shocked disapproval when Mr. Daviot announced she was not his wife.

The maid left. Miranda poured tea for Lady Wiston and took the first turn at the washstand. Her back safely to her ladyship, she rushed into speech.

"Ma'am, Mr. Daviot and I travelled together for a whole day and night."

"Yes, dear, and I am excessively grateful to both of you."

"Oh no, I did not mean . . . that is, I don't expect particular thanks, truly. How could I not do all in my power to save you from such a fate? Though indeed I don't believe my presence was useful. I fear I was simply incapable of sitting at home waiting for news."

"I quite understand, dear, but I assure you your presence is the greatest comfort to me. Though gentlemen are all very well in their way, there are times when one feels sorely in need of female companionship."

"That is just what I wanted to talk to you about." Hesitating, Miranda reached for a towel and dried her face.

"Yes, dear?"

"You see, when I left London with Mr. Daviot, we were in such a hurry I did not stop to consider the impropriety of travelling with a gentleman without a chaperon. Mrs. Redpath looked very oddly when. . . ."

"Mrs. Redpath?" Lady Wiston asked in astonishment. "Marjory? What has she to say to anything?"

"Heavens, we have heard your story, but you have not

heard ours. The reason we were so slow to catch up with you is that we were not perfectly certain where you had been taken. Mr. Daviot thought it best to check whether you were at Redpath Manor before we embarked upon a long journey to the north."

"But why should Godfrey take me to Redpath Manor?"

Miranda hated to disillusion her, but she had to know none of the admiral's nephews was to be relied upon. "Lord Snell was the instigator, ma'am, but they were all in it together, all four cousins. Surely I mentioned overhearing him plotting with them?"

"Perhaps," Lady Wiston said sadly, climbing out of bed and taking Miranda's place at the washstand. "I daresay I was in too much of a pucker to listen properly. How very shocking. What can I have done, Miranda, to make them betray me?"

"Nothing at all! They care naught for what you do, only for what you possess. Their only interest is your money. Lord Snell offered to support Mr. Daviot for life if he stood aside, and I am persuaded he made similar promises to the others for their cooperation. Of course, Mr. Daviot refused."

"Dear Peter!"

Miranda pulled on her clean chemise and poured herself a cup of tea before she spoke again. "Mr. Daviot is all that is honourable, but I fear he has little respect for propriety. Indeed, I doubt he is even aware that my reputation might be compromised by our journey together. He cannot be counted upon to do the gentlemanly thing."

"To offer for your hand? My dear, do you wish it?"

Put into words, it all sounded horridly calculating. What a mull she was making of it, Miranda thought, hastily demurring. "Not in the least! I should not accept if he did make an offer." At least, not if he proposed marriage solely from a sense of obligation.

"But you are concerned about your reputation? Pray help me with these hooks, dear. I am glad I was abducted in trousers, so much more comfortable for travelling, though the landlord was rather taken aback."

"You would not care for that. But *such* a look as he gave me when Mr. Daviot told him we were not married! And did you not notice how the maids and waiters gaped at me?"

"At all of us, what with my costume and Mudge, not to mention Danny and Charlie, who are striking figures, you know!"

"Mudge!" Miranda exclaimed, fastening the last of her ladyship's hooks and turning to the small looking-glass to pin up her hair. "I never took him out after dinner. I must hurry."

"No need. Charlie offered to take him out last night and this morning. I gave him—Charlie—a few comfits, though he vowed he is not afraid of being bitten. The dear fellow is prodigious eager to be of service. He is sadly mortified by his recent mistakes."

"I am excessively glad he has seen the error of his ways. A pitched battle between him and Danny would have been too frightful to behold, when I consider the damage he did to Mr. Daviot with a single blow."

"You kept your composure admirably, dear, and I believe your ministrations saved poor Peter from a much more uncomfortable time." Lady Wiston gave Miranda a thoughtful look. "As for your reputation, it cannot be regarded as besmirched since you had both Danny and Mudge to play chaperon."

Miranda could not help smiling a little. Mudge had, after all, put a stop to Mr. Daviot's kiss, and he was not going to tell any tales. Danny might inform his Mary of the embrace he had witnessed, but Mrs. Potts was no gossip and Miranda doubted he would reveal her shocking conduct to anyone else.

"*I* do not consider you compromised," Lady Wiston continued firmly, "and, though I do not wish to appear immodest, my opinion is surely the only one that matters. The inn people are irrelevant. In any case we have provided them with more interesting and far more unusual subjects of conversation."

At that, Miranda had to laugh, but she said, "What about Mrs. Redpath?"

"James would be a chucklehead to permit Marjory to breathe a word about anything so closely connected with his own perfidious conduct! Oh dear, I do hope Peter has thought of a way to prevent Godfrey from carrying me off again."

"I'm sure he has, my dear ma'am. Mr. Daviot is not at all wanting in sense or resolution, still less in imagination, only in. . . ." She bit her lip.

"In gallantry," said Lady Wiston, patting her hand with a more perceptive sympathy than Miranda quite liked. "Well, I am ready for my breakfast. Let us go and see whether Peter has come up with a sensible, resolute, imaginative counterplot."

As they went through to the parlour, Mudge scuttled up to Lady Wiston, planted himself in front of her, and glared at her with beady eyes, slavering. The hero of the hour was an unattractive sight. Provided with a comfit, he permitted the ladies to advance into the room.

The men were already seated at the table. Mr. Daviot, Daylight Danny, and Ted Coachman rose to say good morning; so did Charlie after Danny elbowed him in the ribs. They had started on their breakfasts. The smell of bacon and new bread reminded Miranda she had been too tired to eat much dinner and too anxious for the preceding four-and-twenty hours to have much appetite.

Mr. Daviot had made considerable inroads into a large beefsteak, Miranda observed. The only sign of the damage to his face was a slight discoloration.

"Your jaw is less painful, I take it?" she said. Somehow it was impossible to feel embarrassed when she was with him, in spite of the emotions aroused by talking of him with Lady Wiston.

"Almost as good as new, thanks to your care." He smiled at her, holding a chair for his aunt while Danny did the same for Miranda. "Your pardon, ladies, for beginning without you, but, though I don't want to rush you, the sooner we depart the better. I took the liberty of ordering eggs, bacon and muffins for you, and chocolate and fresh tea." He removed the covers from a pair of dishes.

"Thank you, dear. I own I shall feel safer once we are on the road."

"My stratagem is more complex than that, Aunt Artemis. I don't want you to return to London yet."

"Lady Wiston cannot remain here, meekly waiting for Lord Snell to find her," Miranda said heatedly. "Not even with Danny and Charlie on guard. He may bring a cohort of minions with him."

Mr. Daviot took the wind out of her sails. "Exactly. And we cannot tell how soon he set out from Northwaite Hall. He may be searching the road south already."

Lady Wiston paled, and she set down her cup of chocolate with a clink as her hand shook.

The old lady was much more frightened by her abominable adventure than she had let anyone see, Miranda realized. With a minatory glance at Mr. Daviot, she pressed Lady Wiston's hand and said, "We shall not let him take you again, you may be quite certain of that."

"That we won't!" Danny confirmed fiercely. "My Mary'd skin me was I to let any harm come to my lady."

"I'll be damned if a soul lays a finger on your la'ship," swore Charlie, earning another elbow in the ribs from Danny. "Begging your pardon, m'lady, I'm sure."

"If so be it do come to a dust-up, I'm wi' you," said Ted with a worried look, "but it'd be best not to get catched and the landau's mighty easy to spot, being that diff'rent."

"Snell shan't find it on the road to London," said Mr. Daviot, "because it will not be there. You must go somewhere else, Aunt Artemis, anywhere else, while I go on to Town and sort things out."

"Oh yes!" Lady Wiston clapped her hands. "Miranda assured me you were bound to come up with a clever plan."

"It is a good notion," Miranda said, "but I fear we have too little ready money to go far or stay away for long."

"I have plenty, dear. Godfrey paid Charlie *very* well and I won every penny. Of course, having cheated, I shall reimburse him to the last farthing, but we agreed that I should keep it for the present to pay our way." She smiled at Charlie, who grinned and nodded. "Miranda, do you recall the name of the asylum Mrs. Fry told us about, near York?"

"The York Retreat, ma'am? Founded by a Quaker for the humane treatment of the insane? Tuke was the name, William Tuke, and now his grandson Samuel, I believe."

"That is it. We shall go there. If it is as humanely run as Mrs. Fry claims, I shall make a large donation. I have a personal interest in the subject now! And what is more, my dear friend Amelia, Lady Garston, lives not far from York. She has been begging me to visit this age, but I have always been too busy. We shall stay with Lady Garston, and so stretch our funds. How long do you suppose it will take you, Peter dear, to arrange matters in London?"

Mr. Daviot frowned. "I am not sure where to begin."

"With those letters I wrote," Miranda said eagerly. "You remember I told you I wrote to every influential person I could think of who might testify for Lady Wiston? The letters are all in the bureau in the admiral's study."

"That gives me an excellent start!" he said with a smile which warmed her from head to toe. "What next, Miss Carmichael?"

"Once you have their promises of support, go to Mr. Bradshaw."

"Aunt Artemis's solicitor?"

"Yes. It was his report that gave Lord Snell the idea for his scheme, I fear, but I have no reason to suppose he had any hand in it. He is the other trustee, so you will need to consult him at least. If he is unhelpful, time enough to find another lawyer."

"Mr. Bradshaw has always been most obliging," said Lady Wiston, "though he does not always quite approve of how I choose to spend my money. He cannot have been aware of Godfrey's treachery."

"Mr. Bradshaw it is." Mr. Daviot pushed back his chair and stood up. "Time we were on the road. Ted, go and have a team harnessed to the carriage, and choose a decent hack for me. I shall ride beside the landau until you are safely past the turn to Oakham and Chesterfield. Snell will never look for you on the road to the North."

"Aye, sir." The coachman hurried off.

Mr. Daviot turned to the two bruisers. "Gentlemen, I fancy you are both ready and willing to go with her ladyship and guard her. Am I right?"

"Right enough, sir," said Charlie. " 'Tis the least I c'n do."

"I wouldn't dare go home wi'out her, sir," Danny avowed. "My Mary sent me to take care o' her, di'n't she?"

"Then, if you will just write down Lady Garston's direction for me, Miss Carmichael, let us be off!"

Miranda wrote the requisite information in her notebook and tore out the page. "Pray keep us apprised of your progress, sir," she said as she gave it to Mr. Daviot.

"Thank you. I shall write if it seems likely to take more than a few days. Otherwise assume all goes well, and you shall hear from me the moment it is safe to return. I wish. . . ." He hesitated, and seemed to change his mind about what he was going to say. "I'll do my best, Miss Carmichael," he finished.

"I know you will."

Ten minutes later, the landau stood in the passage leading beneath the inn from the yard to the street. Mr. Daviot had gone to ride through the town to check that Lord Snell had not by some evil chance arrived at just the wrong moment. Miranda, her head stuck out of the window in the most vulgar fashion, saw him reappear and wave to Ted.

Once more bits jingled, hooves clopped on flagstones, wheels rumbled; the carriage emerged from the tunnel and turned down the hill between façades of pale grey stone. Danny was playing footman, up behind. Inside the landau, both hoods raised despite the fine day, Lady Wiston and Charlie prepared to crouch down out of sight at a moment's notice. Should Lord Snell appear, the others would pretend they had no more notion of the whereabouts of the missing pair than he had.

With two rugs to throw over them, Miranda, watching for a signal, had every excuse to keep her gaze fixed on Mr. Daviot as he rode alongside. He made a fine figure on horseback, she thought, upright yet not at all stiff, very much at home in the saddle.

She remembered his stories of learning to ride bareback with the Iroquois, through the tangled primeval forest. When they reached home at last, would he want her help with his book again? she wondered wistfully. Those hours of working together, laughing together, were a very precious memory.

They crossed the bridge at the bottom of the hill and started up the other side. Sharp left, sharp right, across a small square, and there ahead the road branched: Oakham to the left, Grantham and the Great North Road to the right, said the finger-post.

Ted took the right-hand fork. No sign of the dastardly baron—fortunately, as Charlie was not of a size to be rendered inconspicuous by crouching down. Another hundred yards and the road to Oakham and Northwaite Hall was hidden by trees.

Mr. Daviot waved and called goodbye. Turning his mount, he cantered off southward to carry out his plan.

It was a good plan, a sensible plan, Miranda told herself. So why could she not rid herself of the suspicion that Peter Daviot had devised this particular plan because it put two hundred miles between him and Miss Miranda Carmichael?

Chapter 20

"I cannot say, my lady, how deeply I regret any part I may have played, however unwitting, in leading Lord Snell to imagine. . . ." Unable to bring himself to utter the trend of Lord Snell's imaginings, the lawyer pulled out a large white handkerchief and blotted his high, glistening forehead.

The day was excessively hot for early September. The admiral's study, even with the window open to the rose garden, was like a furnace. But Miranda, fanning herself, rather thought the tall, thin solicitor was overcome less by the heat than by emotion. Mr. Daviot said he had almost wept when informed of Lady Wiston's plight.

"There, there," said Lady Wiston soothingly. "My dear Mr. Bradshaw, all is well that ends well. My nephew says your assistance in clearing up the legal situation was invaluable."

"I trust you believe, ma'am, that Lord Snell revealed nothing to me of his plans. When he came to apply to me for access to your funds, he would have found me . . . recalcitrant, yes, that is precisely it, recalcitrant." He nodded to himself, modestly pleased with the word. "Sir Bernard's instructions are quite clear, that in the event of your incapacity I, not his nephews, was to oversee any expenditures on your behalf.''

"I daresay Godfrey failed to make himself thoroughly familiar with the terms of the admiral's trust. Am I correct, Mr. Bradshaw, in thinking my dear Sir Bernard in no way obliged me to leave a penny to his nephews?''

"Not a farthing, ma'am.''

"Well, after their infamous conduct, I no longer feel the least obligation to them simply because of their relationship to him. I wish to change my will.''

"In favour of the Association for the Improvement of the Female Prisoners in Newgate?'' asked the lawyer cautiously.

"I shall not change the provision I have already made for Mrs. Fry's work, but I shall add something for the York Retreat. A splendid place.''

"Indeed, ma'am!''

Her ladyship reflected for a moment. "I am inclined to think, Miranda, that we should attend the Friends' Meeting more often. They are excellent people, if a trifle strait-laced.''

Mr. Bradshaw recalled her to business. "And the other changes to your will, ma'am?''

"I know precisely what I want to do, but I cannot bear to sit indoors any longer. Let us go out to the terrace.''

Mr. Bradshaw's jaw dropped and he cast a rather hunted glance around the comparatively familiar territory of Sir Bernard's study. Would a will composed outdoors be valid, his gaze seemed to ask. Then he squared his narrow, black-clad shoulders. "If you wish, ma'am.''

"There is a table outside for your papers, sir,'' Miranda reassured him. She would not shock him further by revealing she and Lady Wiston and Mr. Daviot had taken breakfast and luncheon on the terrace, and Lady Wiston was determined to sleep there. "Do you want me to come, ma'am?''

"Yes, dear, it is far too hot for you to be poring over

Peter's papers, especially as I sent him off to get some fresh air on horseback.''

Mr. Daviot's manuscript, retrieved from his club, was in a lamentable muddle. He had begged Miranda—literally on bended knee!—to have mercy on him and take it in hand again.

Since their return from York yesterday, he had been his old friendly, joking self. It was exactly what Miranda had prayed for, yet she found herself dissatisfied. She wanted more from him now.

The memory of their brief embrace haunted her. If his hand happened to brush hers, a shock ran through her like the jolt from an electrifying machine. She had to constantly avert her gaze from his mouth, whither it was involuntarily drawn as she recalled the touch of his lips on hers. Sometimes the longing to feel that touch again was so intense she hardly dared meet his eyes.

And when she did, she saw an indefinable difference there, some inexplicable emotion lurking behind the amiable smile, the quizzical, teasing look.

Could he fear that, in spite of his diligence in providing ten days apart for a damper, she might expect him to come up to scratch? It should be obvious by now that she did not mean to press him.

Perhaps he simply felt guilty because he had no intention of offering marriage. In that case, she must do all in her power to prove she had no expectations, to allay his remorse before it poisoned their friendship. Failing his love, she had rather have his friendship than nothing, she decided with a sigh.

If only she could persuade herself she really had no desire whatever to be his wife! It ought to be easy. Despite the myriad lovable qualities she had discovered in him, he was still a happy-go-lucky knight errant, a rolling stone who might decide at any moment to roll on.

Did King Arthur's wandering knights ever settle down with their rescued damsels and raise a family?

"Does that seem reasonable, Miranda?"

"I beg your pardon, Lady Wiston?" She was sitting on the terrace, breathing the fragrance of the summer's last flourish of roses, without any notion of how she had come there. "I fear I was wool-gathering."

Mr. Bradshaw looked flabbergasted. "Can I believe my ears, Miss Carmichael?" he said severely. "We were discussing her ladyship's provision for you."

"For me! But I have no claim on Lady Wiston whatsoever."

"Not of blood, dear, but of affection. I have failed to . . . well, never mind that. It is just as well, as it turns out. But I have strong feelings about little grey mice." Lady Wiston cocked a mischievous eye at the lawyer's bewildered expression. "Though I hope you will choose to stay with me, I wish you to have the choice, and more particularly not to be forced to seek other employment when I am gone."

"Pray don't talk of it, ma'am!" Miranda cried.

"Oh, I expect to be around for a long time yet, provided I keep practising *yoga*, but I should not wish to live forever. Only think how horridly crowded the world would be if everyone lived forever! Mr. Bradshaw, explain what we have arranged, if you please."

As long as Lady Wiston lived, Miranda was to have an income sufficient to live in modest comfort. When her ladyship died, the income from one third of the residuary estate—after servants' pensions and charitable bequests—would be Miranda's.

Lady Wiston cut through the legal complexities. "On terms just like Sir Bernard's for me," she said. "So that if you should happen to marry a husband who makes a habit of outrunning the constable, you will never find yourself at Point Non-Plus. Does that seem reasonable?"

Overwhelmed, tears in her eyes, Miranda could only stammer, "Oh, ma'am, it is too much!"

"Fiddlesticks, my dear." Lady Wiston leaned over and patted her hand. "Peter will get two thirds, and that is plenty for any man, I assure you. But I wish you will not tell him about it, neither his share nor yours.''

"Mr. Daviot is not mercenary!" Miranda flared up.

Lady Wiston's bright eyes gleamed with what might be amusement, though her round face otherwise remained serious. "I know, dear. He has, perhaps, too little regard for money, an endearing trait if not quite practical!''

"Thoroughly impractical," said Mr. Bradshaw austerely, "not to say imprudent. Well, ma'am, if that is all, I shall have your new will properly written up and bring it tomorrow to be signed and witnessed. Good day to you, my lady. Good day, Miss Carmichael.'' He bowed and took himself off.

"Heavens," said Lady Wiston, "I find the legal mind quite exhausting. No, dear, I don't wish to hear any thanks. I believe I shall take a nap, but I cannot bear to go into the house. Will you ask Twitchell to have the chaise-longue carried out?''

"At once, ma'am." Rising, Miranda stooped to drop a kiss on her ladyship's soft pink cheek. "I shall walk Mudge in the park.''

"Be sure to take your parasol, and do not walk so fast as to grow overheated.''

Miranda laughed. "I doubt Mudge will be willing to go faster than a snail's pace—unless, of course, he sees a cat.''

Going into the house, she pondered: if Mudge had not chased that cat, if she had not fallen over Peter Daviot's feet, if he had not then kissed her, would he have ventured to kiss her again in the carriage? And if he had not, would she ever have realized she had fallen hopelessly in love?

Peter left his horse in the mews and walked up through the garden to the house. The fragrance of the roses, distilled by the hot sun, was unbearably romantic, the last thing he needed in his present frame of mind.

On the shaded terrace, his aunt lay asleep. Dropping his hat and gloves on the table, he stood looking down at her. What a small creature she was to be so indomitable! Small, and plump, and innocently rosy-cheeked, yet—for all her grateful thanks to him, to Miranda, to Danny—she had rescued herself. Had Sir Bernard properly appreciated the jewel he had won?

Bright eyes opened. "Peter, did you have a pleasant ride? Miranda has taken Mudge to the park. With luck he will expire of an apoplexy."

"What of her?" he demanded indignantly.

"She is not old and stout, and she has her parasol. Don't glare at me so ferociously, dear boy, I did not send her. It was entirely her own notion. I daresay she felt the need of a breath of air."

"Yes, no doubt." He dropped onto one of the dining-room chairs. "I must talk to you, Aunt Artemis. Have you finished your forty winks?"

"Thirty-nine, and I shall do very well without the last. What is troubling you?"

"Miranda," Peter said bluntly. "Or at least, I feel something is troubling *her*. For the most part she seems just the same as ever, but now and then ... I'm afraid she feels our long journey together in some way compromised her. Ought I to ask her to be my wife?"

"I do not consider her compromised. I have told her Danny and Mudge were perfectly adequate chaperons."

"That's a great relief." His enthusiasm rang hollow in his own ears. Miranda had no need of him even to save her reputation.

"Are you so averse to marrying her?" asked his aunt.

"Averse! Good gad, no. On the contrary, I should be glad to. But you were right," he went on sombrely, "she deserves someone better than a penniless rapscallion. She'd have been better off with Snell than with me."

"Over my dead body!"

"No, of course, now she would not touch dear Godfrey with a pair of tongs."

"And you actually *want* to marry her?" Aunt Artemis persisted. "Why?"

"Well, you have no other nephews left to rescue her."

His aunt gave a snort of disgust. "I do not regard that as a good reason. Nor would she."

Backed into a corner, Peter felt his face turn a fiery red. "As a matter of fact, I love her. That only makes it more impossible to ask her to hitch herself to a sponger with no means to support himself, still less a wife and family."

"But you will soon make your fortune with your book."

"That seems to be a common delusion. I have been talking to some fellows at the club, and one or two booksellers. The odds on making more than a meagre sum are vanishingly small."

"Then you mean to give up?" his aunt demanded disapprovingly.

"I don't want to. I enjoy writing, and Miranda says it's good. In fact I had even thought of going on to write novels of adventure—but I cannot ask her to marry me and starve. Aunt Artemis, do you think she would wait for me if I went to India to make my fortune?"

"Do you want to go?"

Peter sighed. "Not really. Roaming the world is all very well in its way, when one is young and fancy-free, but adventures on paper would more than satisfy me now. All I really care for is to settle down with Miranda and raise a family."

Aunt Artemis beamed. "I cannot imagine anything more delightful. If you are willing, Peter, this is what we shall do."

Miranda stopped in the hall to take off her bonnet. Setting it on the half-moon table, she asked Charlie, "Is Lady Wiston still on the terrace?" In the mirror on the wall above the table, she saw that her face was scarlet from the heat, despite the parasol. Thank heaven the air was cooling now that the sun was on its way down.

"Yes, miss," said her ladyship's bodyguard. "Miss, you knows my lady's going to fig me out all in proper liv'ry?

Well, Mr. Twitchell, he says he'll teach me how to go on like a real footman, so's no one won't know the diff'rence."

"Splendid. So long as you remember not to go running errands. Your place is near her ladyship whether she is at home or out." Miranda tried to tidy her hair, but it clung lankly in dark, damp wisps to her forehead. She gave up. What did it matter if she looked a perfect fright?

"I knows *that,* miss. There's lemonade out there, miss," Charlie added consolingly. "You'll feel better after a nice glass o' lemonade."

She smiled at him. "Thank you. Come on, Mudge."

The pug plodded after her to the back of the house. As she paused on the threshold of the terrace door, he brushed past her. Too exhausted even to approach Lady Wiston to beg for a comfit, he slumped panting on a cool flagstone.

Miranda hesitated. Mr. Daviot was on the terrace, too. *Did* it matter that she looked a perfect fright?

Too late to escape. Hearing Mudge's claws click on the stone, Mr. Daviot and Lady Wiston both glanced round.

"Miranda, my love, you are woefully overheated. Do come and sit down and drink some lemonade. It is very pleasant out here now."

"The park was pleasant, but the streets are still quite hot." As she descended the steps, Mr. Daviot jumped up to fill a glass from the glistening pitcher.

At the same time, Lady Wiston rose from the chaise-longue. "Sit here, dear, at your ease. I believe it is cool enough at last for my exercises." She trotted up the steps and disappeared into the house.

Miranda would much rather not have been left alone with Mr. Daviot, not without his manuscript between them as a subject for conversation. But he was holding out her glass of lemonade. It would be shockingly rude to turn tail and run.

Relieving him of the glass, she sat down. "I fear I have accomplished very little work today on straightening out your *magnum opus*," she said lightly, and took a long draught of lemonade.

"It has been much too hot even to think about it. Will you marry me, Miss Carmichael?"

Miranda choked. As she coughed and spluttered, Mr. Daviot removed the glass from her hand, set it down, and thumped her between the shoulderblades.

Then she was in his arms. The kiss she had dreamt of became an earthshaking reality. She wound her arms around his neck and kissed him back.

"Oh, Peter!"

"You will marry me, Miranda?"

"Not because I was compromised?"

"Aunt Artemis assures me Mudge was all the chaperon we needed." He cast a nervous glance at the pug, but Mudge's eyes were closed. "No, because I adore you."

"Oh, Peter!" Some minutes passed before she was able to say, "And you will not vanish one day in search of adventure?"

"Not I. This rolling stone intends to become a supporting rock. I have taken a position, rather menial but it pays extremely well."

"What position? Will you have time for your book?"

"Bother the book!" He kissed her again.

After a while, Miranda surfaced sufficiently to protest, "You must finish the book. It is *good*, and after all the work I have put into it. . . ."

"I shall have plenty of time to write, but I cannot do it without your help. So you see, the world will lose a great masterpiece unless you marry me."

"Oh, Peter, I want nothing more, but I cannot simply desert Lady Wiston. What position have you taken? Will she be able to go with us?"

He grinned. "Don't fret, my darling. Aunt Artemis shall not be abandoned. You know she has hired Charlie as a permanent bodyguard."

"And Danny to come in on Charlie's time off. But they are no companionship for her, and besides, they are not clever enough to keep her safe against Lord Snell's wicked wiles."

"Precisely, my love, which is why Aunt Artemis has hired me as Overseer of Bodyguards!"

"Overseer of Bodyguards?" Miranda laughed. "Is she not wonderful? How can I possibly resist becoming the Wife of the Overseer of Bodyguards? Particularly as I love him with all my heart."

"Dearest Miranda!"

Mudge suddenly awoke to the disgraceful behaviour taking place not three yards from his nose. He danced around the pair in a paroxysm of rage, shrilly berating them.

Peter and Miranda did not even hear.

Historical note: The Association for the Improvement of the Female Prisoners in Newgate was not founded till 1817 though Elizabeth Fry was already working to that end in 1815. The York Retreat was founded in 1796. Its humane methods gradually had a wide influence on the accepted standards for treatment of the mentally ill.

WATCH FOR THESE REGENCY ROMANCES